What Other

Copper Fire

"The storyline was very engaging and I found the novel to be hard to put down. I read the entire book from start to finish in one day because I could not wait to find out what was going to happen next. Fisher is a very talented historical writer and is really able to draw the reader in and keep them transfixed until the last page is turned. Whether you have read the first novel in the *Copper Star* series or not, I believe that any fan of historical fiction will enjoy *Copper Fire*. I look forward to reading more books by Fisher in the future." - Rebecca's Reads

"A smidgen of romance and a bite-sized portion of suspense rounds *Copper Fire* out nicely, making it a must-read. Congratulations, Ms. Fisher. Another outstanding book." - Title Trakk

"This second novel read very much like a stand-alone novel. There was enough information divulged at the beginning of, and throughout the book, that I had a clear sense of the chain of events that led everyone to where they are now. Throughout *Copper Fire* I really got to know and understand the characters as they are very well-developed. From Elisabeth and her "organizing" to William and his spying, each character has such unique traits and personalities. I don't think there was one major player I did not feel I completely *knew* by the time the novel was finished." - Reader Views

"Fisher is a master at character development, and she's outdone herself with *Copper Fire*." - At Home with Christian Fiction

"Suzanne Woods Fisher has penned a radiant and inspiring novel in *Copper Fire*. Reminiscent of her delightful humor-flecked style in *Copper Star*, the author has painted captivating characters couched in a history-rich setting. A strong and moving novel that causes the reader to feel." - Debora M. Coty, best-selling author of *The Distant Shore* and *Billowing Sails*

Copper Fire
Suzanne Woods Fisher

Vintage Inspirations
An imprint of Vintage Romance Publishing
Ladson, South Carolina
www.vrpublishing.com

ISBN: 978-0-9815592-0-9

PUBLISHED BY VINTAGE INSPIRATIONS, an imprint of Vintage
Romance Publishing

www.vrpublishing.com

Dedicated to my parents,
Joseph and Barbara Woods,
who live their lives with humor and devotion,
based on the principle of "Hangeth Thou in There."
Thanks for your example, Mom and Dad.

Suzanne Woods Fisher

Chapter One

I'll never forget that summer night. Our last vestige of normalcy. One evening we sat down to dinner, and by the time we finished, our lives would never be the same.

It was a beastly hot night in early July, 1945. We were celebrating William's seventh birthday with his favorite dinner: hot dogs and baked beans.

"You're not eating, Louisa. I hope you're not sick," Aunt Martha said, peering at my face to discern an ailment, probably worried it might be contagious. Aunt Martha belonged to my husband, Robert. It was whispered among the church ladies that she hadn't smiled since the Hoover Administration. Just the other day, I overheard one woman asking another if the preacher's aunt had been baptized in pickle juice.

"I'm just not very hungry tonight," I told Aunt Martha.

"That's certainly not like you, Louisa," said Robert, glancing up at me, looking a bit concerned.

It was true. I wasn't one of those women who scarcely ate. I never missed a meal. I brushed Robert's cheek with my hand then deftly changed the subject. "Time to open the presents."

William ripped off the newspaper wrapping of the present I had handed to him. "Junior Spy Kit," he read slowly, in his thick sounding pronunciation, pressing his small finger along the lettering.

"A *spy kit?*" Robert's eyebrows shot up. "Why on earth would you give a spy kit to a boy already blessed with an overabundance of curiosity?"

"Exactly because of that, Robert," I reassured him. "He can practice his reading, his writing, his observation skills, his attention-to-detail. He'll be learning as he plays. I've been reading a book that encourages deaf children to develop their awareness of life around them. It's a good thing for him."

"He'll be spying on everyone in this town!" complained Aunt Martha. "No one will be safe." She pursed her lips in that way I deplored. "You've been telling him stories again about being a resister."

"A Resistance Worker, Aunt Martha," I corrected her, frowning. She had never fully understood the role I played working with the Resistance Movement in Germany. To her, it seemed like child's play. But I took my experience as a Resistance Worker very seriously. Very, very seriously. It was a dangerous but important job.

Well, mostly, I delivered messages to other Resistance Workers. Written messages. In sealed envelopes. While on assignment, I wasn't even permitted to talk. My colleagues seemed to be under the impression that I was too outspoken. Dietrich, my friend and mentor, often remarked that he was sure I would get myself shot if I dared to open my mouth.

So I didn't.

Even still, the Gestapo started following us, tapping our phones. Everywhere I went, an agent watched me, not caring if I saw him or not. Over my objections, Dietrich decided I should leave Germany, at once, and wait out the war in the United States. Before I knew it, Dietrich whisked me off in the dark of night to the Swiss border. After a rushed goodbye, I was in the hands of Resistance Workers, passed like fragile baggage from contact to contact.

One month later, I had arrived in Copper Springs, Arizona, to stay indefinitely at the home of Reverend Robert

Gordon, courtesy of our mutual friend Dietrich Bonhoeffer. The two men had attended the Union Theological Seminary in New York in 1931 and became friends. They had kept in touch over the years. When Dietrich asked if he would sponsor someone for safekeeping, Robert readily agreed, assuming it would be a young man. The surprised look on his face when I stepped off that train will forever make me smile.

Once or twice I have wondered if Robert would still have agreed so readily had he known all that decision would hold for him.

William was studying the bubbles in his root beer bottle. He looked up at Robert. "Mom was brave." Even though William wasn't really my son, the bond between us was as strong as any between a mother and child.

"You're right, William," Robert said. "She *was* brave." He stole a glance at Aunt Martha and noticed she was peering into a pot on the stove. Satisfied she was preoccupied, he leaned over and kissed the violin curve of my neck before getting up to refill his glass of iced tea.

Was I brave? Not really. I never felt very brave. But I never doubted I was doing the right thing. I was a Resistance Worker because I couldn't help myself. The war had to be stopped. Hitler had to be stopped.

Just then, someone knocked on the door. Robert went to open it and found Ernest standing solemnly on the porch. "Come in and join us! We're celebrating William's birthday."

"Thank you, but I'm here on official business, Reverend. I have a telegram for your missus." Ernest handed the telegram to Robert and abruptly left. I looked at Robert, puzzled.

He shrugged. "Open it. It's for you." He held it out to me.

I tore open the envelope, not having any idea about its contents or who might have sent it. But as I pulled the thin yellow paper out of the envelope, our lives irrevocably changed.

* * * *

The next morning, I heard Aunt Martha complaining to Robert in the kitchen by means of a radiator pipe that, if the cap was unscrewed, offered a direct transmission of information sent. Nearly as clear as if I were in the kitchen. I hadn't intended to continue my habit of eavesdropping. I *really* hadn't. Before Robert and I married, it was a useful means, though admittedly shameful, to understand more about the very private Gordon family. Aunt Martha and Robert often had conversations that excluded me. After we were married, I persuaded Robert to move into my room rather than have me move into his room. But it wasn't because I wanted to stay close to my radiator pipe.

It was because of Ruth.

I didn't mind living in the same house where Robert had lived with his wife, Ruth, before she abandoned him and William for another man. After all, I'm a pragmatic woman. I had cooked in her kitchen, showered in her shower, and taken her place in the heart of this family.

But my pragmatism stopped at the bedroom. When I asked Robert if he would be willing to move down the hall into my room, he looked at me for a long moment and then answered, "Of course." I didn't need to explain. He understood.

Unfortunately, that meant I was constantly faced with the temptation to unscrew the top of my radiator pipe and listen in to conversations in the kitchen below. Ordinarily, I could resist. But not this morning. Not about this topic.

"You're going to let her go? And get that child?" I heard Aunt Martha say.

Robert cleared his throat, stalling. "We haven't decided what to do yet, Aunt Martha."

"But you're thinking about it, aren't you? How can you even *think* such a thing? Taking in a child from another country?"

"Aunt Martha, she's Louisa's cousin. She's just been released from a labor camp. She has no one else. No one! How could we ignore that?"

"Well, the Red Cross sent you that telegram. They'll know best how to take care of her. They must have orphanages for her kind."

Then there was silence. I could just imagine Robert's spine stiffening. "What exactly do you mean by her 'kind'?"

Aunt Martha had very brittle requirements about people and an unpleasant tendency to stereotype people into clumps. In this particular situation, she meant Jewish people. I heard the water running in the sink as she started to wash dishes. She wasn't answering his question.

"Louisa is one of that 'kind'," Robert countered.

"She's different."

"You didn't think so when she first arrived. You were quite cold, as I recall. But after getting to know her and understand her, after giving her a chance, now you love her like a daughter."

Like a daughter? Well, that was quite a stretch, but Robert's loyalty turned my heart soft. Many times, I could barely hold my tongue from telling Aunt Martha how I felt about her steady stream of opinions, but he always knew how to gently reason with her. Unlike me, he was often able to change her mind.

"Aunt Martha, what if circumstances were different and that child was William? What if he was left without anyone?" he asked, his words soft and unhurried.

My guilt vanished at once. That was the *very* line of reasoning I had used with Robert last night! I was pleased to hear him repeat it. I wasn't always convinced he listened to me.

"Just how old is this child?"

"Louisa thinks she's about twelve or thirteen."

"Nearly grown, Robert. It just doesn't seem right to take a nearly grown woman out of her homeland."

Now, she's suddenly a woman, I thought, rolling my eyes. I heard dishes clinking in the sink.

"If you ask me, you're both flying blind with the windshield iced over."

I cocked my head, puzzled. What could *that* possibly mean? Just when I thought I had learned all of her bromides, she came up with a new one.

He sighed. "Aunt Martha, when Louisa and I decide what we're going to do, I will let you know. This is very fresh news." I heard him put his coffee cup down. "But one thing I do know, you can't abandon your family."

The truth was that we had stayed up late into the night discussing the contents of this telegram. I had no idea that my little cousin, Elisabeth, was even still alive. I hadn't seen her in years. She and her mother, my father's sister, had gone into hiding during the war. I had tried to find them, to send them care packages and money, but I never discovered a single clue of their whereabouts. Not one.

At first, I thought that might have been a good sign, that they were safely hidden. As time passed, though, I had an unsettled feeling about their safety. And here in Copper

Springs, I couldn't do anything about that worry. Well, other than pray, of course. I had never stopped praying for them.

Then came the telegram from the Red Cross. It stated that Elisabeth had just been released from a labor camp. From Dachau, near München, the first of the camps designed by Hitler. One of the worst. And there was no mention of her mother, which was definitely *not* a good sign.

How had the International Red Cross Tracing Service managed to locate me? I had come to the United States two years ago using a false name to hide my identity. It used to be false, anyway. Now it belonged to me. After Robert and I married, hastily, to avoid my deportation, I became Louisa Gordon, a citizen of the United States. And somewhere along the way, Robert and I fell in love.

That little slip of yellow paper that arrived last night stirred up many memories of Germany for me. Some good ones, many bad ones. As I gently screwed the cap back on to the top of the radiator, I knew for certain that somehow, someway, I was going to go to Germany to get Elisabeth.

And on the heels of that thought: while in Germany, I intended to find someone, *anyone*, who would help me track down Friedrich Mueller, the banker from Copper Springs. The man who caused my family, not to mention this town, so much damage. But I had no intention to confess that plan to Robert.

Robert refused to discuss Herr Mueller; it was the Gordon Way. It might be a closed chapter for Robert, but not for me. I hadn't stopped thinking about Herr Mueller— places he might have fled, ideas to track his trail. I was convinced Herr Mueller could be found and brought to justice. I just needed a little help.

Over the next few days, Robert and I spent hours discussing options of how to get Elisabeth here, what it might mean for us as a family to have her live with us, how it might change things. We were in complete agreement about bringing Elisabeth into our home, but we couldn't concur on how to get her here.

"Robert," I started one evening after Aunt Martha had gone to bed, "I can travel to Germany and back again in just a few weeks. I did it during the war, through blockades and occupied countries. Think how much easier it will be now with the war over."

"It's *not* safe. The war has only been over for a few weeks. It's not even over in the Pacific yet." He glanced up at me. "I recognize that look of maddening determination in your eyes, Louisa. You're *not* going alone. I won't let you put yourself in harm's way."

"But we've been over this. We can't bring William. One of us needs to stay here with him. He's too much for Aunt Martha to handle; she won't work with him on his lessons. And you can't leave the church. Please, Robert, be reasonable. I'm the logical choice to go."

"All of Europe is in chaos! There are shortages, railways have been blown up from air raids, Allied troops are everywhere. No. You can't go. There must be a way for someone to bring Elisabeth here."

"If we waited for a Red Cross escort—it could take months, maybe even a year or more. I speak the language; I know how to get to places. It's exactly what I did when I was working with the Resistance. There is less risk now than there was then. I can do this!"

"No." He wouldn't budge.

"Then what are we going to do?" I asked, frustrated.

"I don't know yet," he admitted flatly.

We faced an impasse. A stubborn, bull-headed, immovable impasse. That was, until our good friend, Judge Pryor, came up with a solution.

The judge knocked on the door of the parsonage one afternoon. As I opened the door, the judge took off his hat, wiped his brow with the back of his hand then replaced his hat before asking me to join him for a conversation in Robert's office. Blue eyes twinkling, he told me he had an interesting proposition to discuss with us. Curiosity piqued, I followed him over to the office.

We sat in front of Robert's desk in a rather formal meeting. Judge Pryor leaned back in his chair, taking his time, seeming to weigh his words. I shot a puzzled glance at Robert, who only shrugged a look back at me. Finally, the judge spoke. "You know that my nephew works in Washington D.C."

The judge's nephew was a figure shrouded in mystery. The judge spoke of him often, with evident pride, but never explained what his nephew actually *did* for the government. Clearly, he was someone of great importance.

I was convinced Robert knew more about this nephew but wouldn't tell me. "Louisa," he would lecture in a fatherly tone, "if you *needed* to know more, the judge would tell you." To which I would respond, "Robert, if I operated on principle, I would not have been a very effective Resistance Worker."

The judge cleared his throat. "Well," he continued, "you probably heard on the news that President Truman is heading over to Germany for a Conference with Churchill and Stalin. There will be a naval ship accompanying the U.S.S. Augusta as an escort, and in that ship will be the Press Corps. I made a call to my nephew, and it turns out that the Press Corps is in need of someone who can translate the President's press releases into German for the German population. The translator who was meant to go just broke out with mumps." He leaned back in his chair, watching Robert carefully, giving him time to absorb this information. "An amazing coincidence."

Oh no, it wasn't. Just last night I had prayed for God to send us some kind of miracle. I needed one. So did Elisabeth.

"So Louisa could travel with the Press Corps. Escorted each way." He turned to look directly at me. "But you'll only have a brief window to get down to Munich and fetch this child. You'll have to stay with the Press Corps to hitch a ride back. Miss that ride and you're on your own. Understood?"

I nodded, not daring to look at Robert.

"Now, it'll cost some to get Louisa to meet the ship in Virginia and then back again, but when she's on the ship, she'll earn her keep. And she'll be safe, Robert. There can't be any safer means of transportation than traveling with the President of the United States." He smiled. "Of course, my nephew will be on the ship, too," he added, pausing for effect, as if he had just made a piece de résistance.

The judge rose from his chair. "I need your answer within an hour. If you're going to do this, Louisa, you'll have to be in Washington D.C. by Friday." As he reached for the door, he turned back to add, "One good thing about traveling with the Press Corps. You can telegraph each other, and the telegrams will get delivered. They send out regular dispatches. One of the perquisites of politics." Then he closed the door behind him. The silence in the room was deafening.

Cautiously, I looked over at Robert. His head was bowed low, chin resting on his chest, scribbling something mindlessly on a piece of paper. I went over to stand behind his chair and wrapped my arms around his shoulders. "Please, Robert. I *have* to do this," I whispered. Couldn't he understand?

He was quiet for a long moment. Finally, he lifted his head and said, his voice raw, "I guess you'd better start packing."

Chapter Two

With only two days to prepare for a trip that would last at least four weeks, probably longer, I jumped into action. I spoke to each of my piano students to give them work to do while I was away. I prepared William's lessons so that Robert would know what to keep working on, borrowed clothes for the trip from my friend and neighbor, Rosita, and bought boxes of saltine crackers to take along for the sea journey.

The night before I left, Robert and I lay in bed, facing the ceiling, neither of us saying a word. Actually, Robert hadn't said much of anything in the last few days. Not since we had that conversation with the judge. I was so excited about the trip that I hadn't even noticed. Until now. "Robert, is something wrong?" I asked.

"No," he answered, typical of the Gordon Economy of Words.

"Are you worried about this trip costing so much money? Because I have some saved from my piano lessons. It's not much but it can help."

"No, Louisa. That's your money to keep."

"It's *our* money."

"It's not enough, anyway, to get you there and back again."

"Could we borrow money from Cousin Ada?"

"I do not borrow money. Not from anyone," he said sharply.

Of course not. How could I forget about his Scottish descent?

"I'll figure something out, Louisa. Let me worry about the money."

I turned on to my side and looked at him. Kind, generous, intelligent man that he was, he lived deep inside of himself. He could deliver a twenty-minute expository sermon on ceremonial law in the book of Leviticus but struggled to express his feelings. "Robert, please tell me what's troubling you."

He turned over to face the wall. "Nothing. Get some sleep. You've got a long day ahead of you."

I wasn't easily deterred. "Are you having second thoughts about taking Elisabeth into our home?"

"No. Of course not. Don't ever think that."

"Are you still concerned about my safety? Remember that the judge said nothing could be safer than traveling with the President."

"I remember."

"Then what is it? What's wrong?" I heard him take a deep breath, but he didn't answer me.

I could feel the brick wall between us, that same wall I had bumped into so many times before we married when I pushed him too far or asked questions that were too personal. He closed me off. I turned on my back and sighed. I hated to leave like this.

Quietly, he said, "So it's the first time you'll be back in Germany."

I turned on my side and propped my head on my elbow. *Of course!* How had I missed that?! "That's it, isn't it? You don't think I'm coming back, do you?"

He remained on his side. "From the moment I first met you, when you stepped off of that train two years ago, you were planning to return. I wish I had a dime for each time you asked me if I thought the war was almost over. I would be a rich man."

That was true. "But that was before we married. I've never mentioned returning to Germany since we married."

"But you really didn't have a choice. If you didn't marry me you would have been sent to a camp, either in the U.S. or in Germany. Or both. You didn't have a choice. Until now."

I lay back down, staring at the ceiling, thinking of how to answer him. "Robert, could you give me your left hand?"

He turned onto his back and held up his hand. I took his hand in mine and touched his wedding ring. "I should have asked you first about wearing this ring." I had surprised him with this ring at our wedding ceremony. It was my father's ring. Most men didn't wear wedding rings, but my father had, and I had given it to Robert. I'll never forget how his grey eyes filled with tears when he realized that the ring had been my father's. He had never taken it off since.

"Was your father wearing this ring when he...when he was..."

"Murdered?" I supplied the word for him. "No. It wasn't prudent to wear anything of value out of the house. He kept it hidden in the flour jar, but he always wore it when he slept. I do remember that." We were quiet for a while. "You must know what this ring means to me."

He gave a brief nod.

"Every day while I'm away, I want you to look at that ring and remember that I made a promise to you and to William and that I will be back. Just as soon as I can." I put his hand down and turned on my side to face him. "Please don't ever doubt that I am committed to you, to our marriage. But I *have* to do this. I have to go get Elisabeth."

He was quiet for a long while. Then he said, "Louisa, do you need to take care of the whole world?"

"No! Of course not. Only those whom God puts in my path."

Then he smiled and reached out to draw me close.

The next morning, Aunt Martha handed me a cup of coffee when I came downstairs. I waved a hand, refusing it. "Thank you, but I'm too nervous this morning to eat or drink anything."

Her forehead wrinkled in concern. "You can't start a train trip on an empty stomach. Eat!" She set a plate of scrambled eggs and toast on the table and ordered me to sit down.

I forced myself to take a few bites, but my stomach was churning.

"Louisa, I was wondering about something," Robert started, stirring cream into his coffee. "Would you mind if I read through the letters Sabine wrote to you about Dietrich?"

Sabine Bonhoeffer, Dietrich's twin sister, had married a Jewish man who had become a Christian. Before the war began, as the pressure against Jews increased in Germany, they emigrated to England. "No, not at all. But they're written in German."

He slapped his palm against his forehead. "I forgot."

"I could translate them for you when I get back. Is there a reason you want them?"

"I was just thinking...I'd like to see if I could write a magazine article about Dietrich. About the impact he had on others. I just...I just feel that his story should be told. I have some letters he and I wrote over the years, and I have notes from lectures he gave while we were at seminary. I need more information about the last few years, though."

I gazed at him fondly while he sipped his coffee; we shared a devotion toward Dietrich Bonhoeffer. When I first arrived in Copper Springs, I think the loyalty we felt toward Dietrich might have been the only thing that drew us together. We had absolutely nothing in common *other* than Dietrich.

Robert and Dietrich had become friends in seminary, during the one year Dietrich had spent in the United States. I had known Dietrich as a child. My father tuned the piano at the Bonhoeffers' home in Berlin. Later, after my father was killed by the Nazis, I joined Dietrich in the Resistance Movement. "Perhaps I could learn some more details about his experience in the camps when I'm in Germany. I might be able to locate his relatives and—"

"Oh, no, you don't." He set his coffee cup down with a clunk and leveled me with a stare. "You promised me you wouldn't put yourself at any risk, Louisa. I don't want you wandering around areas of the city that might be dangerous."

"I'll be careful."

He cast a suspicious glance at me.

"I promise! But if you really want those letters translated right away, perhaps Mrs. Bauer's mother-in-law could help you. She speaks German."

Aunt Martha snorted. "A few more of that woman's tent stakes have slipped loose. Last week someone found her in her bathrobe and slippers buying bananas in Ibsen's Grocery Store."

Robert frowned.

"What if I translated the letters for you while I'm on the train trip? I could mail them to you before I board the ship," I offered.

His face brightened. "You wouldn't mind?"

"No. It would give me something to do." And help me do something to dispel my nervous energy.

After breakfast, Robert left the house in his Hudson and was gone for hours. I was so busy finishing some last minute tasks that I didn't hear him come back inside. Later that afternoon, William, his big yellow dog named "Dog", Robert, and I left for the train station in Tucson. As I hugged Aunt Martha goodbye, she handed me a twenty-dollar bill. "Just in case of an emergency," she whispered, her face filled with worry.

Such a thoughtful gesture from a woman who was not overburdened with thoughtfulness! I knew how valuable that money was to her. The entire town had been wiped out by Herr Mueller, who had stolen assets and cash from every safe deposit box in the bank and copper from every mine he owned before he scurried back to Nazi Germany or to wherever it was he scurried. Like a rat to the sewer.

In our driveway sat the judge's car. "Where's the Hudson?" I asked, as I helped William and Dog clamor into the back seat.

"It needed some work," Robert answered.

"But I drove it yesterday and didn't notice anything. And I *didn't* strip the gears," I added defensively, conditioned to expect a lecture on improving my driving skills.

"No, nothing like that. Just an oil change," he said.

I glanced at him, curious. Robert usually changed the oil in the Hudson himself. He felt machines were more dependable and less complicated than his congregation so it actually gave him pleasure to work on his car.

"Look, Mom." Over the seat, William handed me his notepad from the Junior Spy Kit.

"Hmmm," I said, reading it over. "9:02 a.m. Aunt Martha hangs out laundry. 9:19 a.m. Aunt Martha comes back into the kitchen and turns on radio. 9:25 a.m. Aunt Martha dances in kitchen to radio. 9:27 a.m. Aunt Martha waves her arms at me to stop spying on her. 9:54 a.m. Aunt Martha takes cake out of oven. Puts cake on counter. 10:14 a.m. Dog jumps up on counter and bites cake. 10:16 a.m. Aunt Martha finds cake on floor and chases Dog outside with broom."

I turned all the way around to face him so he could read my lips. "William! What wonderful observations! I never knew Aunt Martha danced in the kitchen!" I said, laughing. I couldn't even imagine Aunt Martha dancing. *Anywhere!* "Take good notes for me while I am gone. I'll want to read your notepad when I get back. I want to read about everything that I missed."

"You shouldn't be encouraging him, Louisa," Robert tried to scold, but he couldn't hold back a grin. "It'll be interesting to see if that Junior Spy Kit is still around when you get back. I have a hunch Aunt Martha plans to confiscate it."

"What does that mean?" asked William, watching Robert's face in the rearview mirror. He hung on our words like a cat on a rope.

"It means that she will take it from you if you're not careful," I said, turning to face William so he could see me clearly.

William looked worried.

"Hide yourself better when you take observations," I advised.

"Louisa!" warned Robert, rolling his eyes.

I grinned at William.

"So you're going to have a chance to meet the mysterious judge's nephew," Robert said.

"Yes. I'm looking forward to it."

"Louisa," he sternly warned, "you don't need to know everything about everybody."

Yes, I did.

"Some things are best left alone," he added.

No, they weren't. But I nodded as if I agreed with him.

At the train station, Robert handed me an envelope fat with cash. "There should be plenty for you and Elisabeth."

I looked down at the envelope in my hands, puzzled, until a realization dawned on me. "You sold the Hudson, didn't you?"

He kept his eyes on William, who had been edging his way close to the greasy train wheels to examine them.

"But you loved that Hudson."

He turned to me with one of his straight-in-the-eyes looks that always made my knees turn to Jell-O. "But I love you more." Then he hugged me for a long time.

That act touched me profoundly. I swallowed back tears. "I am coming back. I will be back."

"Please do," he whispered in my ear, holding me so tightly I could hardly breathe.

"I love you." I kissed him and then bent down to pull William close to me for a hug. He reached into his back pants pocket and handed me a brown paper package. In it was his new Kodak Target 6-20 Mickey Mouse camera with two extra packages of film. He had used fifty cents of his Christmas money and one cereal box top to purchase this camera; he'd been saving for it for six months. He treasured this camera. And now, with his spy kit, he felt it was an essential ingredient to be a good spy. That camera meant as much to William as the Hudson meant to Robert.

"You could take pictures of Germany for Elisabeth, so that she'll remember it," he said solemnly.

How could a little boy have so much compassion in his heart? "I'll take lots of pictures for her. I'll take good care of your camera, William." I hugged him one last time and showed him the sign language signal that said I loved him. Just last week, the Copper Springs librarian had found a book on sign language for me from the traveling library; William and I were trying to learn basic language. "I love you" was our first and favorite sign.

I wrapped up the camera carefully as an idea popped into my mind. "Robert, perhaps I could photograph Dietrich's family home while I'm in Berlin." If it hasn't been bombed, I thought but didn't say.

Robert's face changed into a frown, looking worried, convinced I would be in harm's way if I ventured away from the judge's nephew. It seemed wise to say good-bye before he launched into a sermon about not taking undue risks. I climbed the steps to the train. Just before heading into the passenger section, I turned around again and called out, "I am coming back! Just as soon as I can!"

Robert held William up to wave goodbye to me at the window. Both of them had tears streaming down their faces. They both looked so sad. I felt guilty, because I didn't feel sad. I felt *thrilled*. I was finally, *finally* going back to Germany. Going home.

* * * *

My excitement grew with every passing mile of train tracks. It reminded me of being a Resistance Worker, when I lived with a deep-down thrill of knowing I had an important job to do. I had never felt so alive, so purposeful, so empowered, as when I was completing a subversive assignment.

The next three days on the train sped by. At every stop, I hopped off to exercise and to soak up the rapidly changing American landscape, including the added benefit of watching people at the train stations. Their faces were full of unguarded expression. Saying hello, saying goodbye; whole stories written on their faces.

Passing through the western states, I noticed the internment camps looked deserted. When I had first arrived in America, they had been filled with Japanese internees. Through southern Colorado, the farm fields had been filled with Japanese workers, working in the fields to supply needed labor. No longer. The war was over, and they were released to resume their lives. How much had changed for them during that time? I wondered. As much as it had for me?

It had been nearly two-and-a-half years since I left Berlin. I hadn't wanted to leave, but Dietrich had insisted. We were being watched by the Gestapo; he knew it was just a matter of time until we were arrested. Dietrich helped me to escape by driving me to the Swiss border. From there, I was chaperoned from village to village, country by country, with the aid of fellow Resistance workers. I arrived in New York City after a bumpy, lonely, bitterly cold trip on a freighter, and took a cross-country train trip to Copper Springs, Arizona, to stay at the home of the Reverend Robert Gordon. I only intended to stay until the war was over but, unexpectedly, I became an integral part of Robert and William's lives. We became a family.

I put a hand up against the cold window. How strange it felt to be returning to Germany.

On the third day, the train pulled into Union Station in Washington D.C. I had the address of where I would stay for the night, so I grabbed my small suitcase from the conductor and headed down the platform. Suddenly, I heard someone call my name.

"Mrs. Gordon? Is that you?" A younger version of the judge ran up to me breathlessly. "I'm Thomas Pryor, Judge Pryor's nephew. Have a good trip? Yes? Yes. Did I keep you waiting? No? No. Good. I was running behind, with tomorrow being such a big deal and all, you understand, I'm sure." He spoke in staccatos, never really giving me a chance to answer. He grabbed my bag and rushed toward the street. He turned his head slightly to call back to me, "My uncle made me promise to take good care of you. Uh, would you mind hurrying it up a little?"

"Please don't worry about me," I said as fast as I could. He was so far ahead of me that I had to shout, running to keep up with him. "I can take care of myself. But it concerns me that I'm only coming along as a favor to your uncle. I really want to be of use to the Press Corps on this trip."

He stopped in his tracks and turned to look directly at me, a sheepish grin spreading across his face. "Don't worry about being a freeloader, Mrs. Gordon. I already have a pile of papers waiting for you to translate. Trust me, you'll hardly even know you're on the ocean."

With my proclivity toward motion sickness, that sounded like a fine arrangement. "I was hoping we might be able to talk about locating Friedrich Mueller."

The judge's nephew gave me a sideways glance then looked at his watch. "Who?" I'd already noticed he checked his watch so often you'd think he was about to miss a train.

I explained the story of Friedrich Mueller as quickly as I could because I could tell he was not a man with a long attention span. I told him Friedrich Mueller was related to Heinrich Mueller, the head of the Gestapo, and that he had stolen money from the entire town of Copper Springs, Arizona to send back to Nazi Germany. I described how he had purchased copper mines before the war began and created a double-dip situation, where he sent the refined copper to Germany and sold the tailings to the United States, effectively exploiting both countries for his benefit.

"Uh huh, uh huh," the judge's nephew replied.

I could tell I had piqued a little interest, though he was zipping the car between lanes as if in a frantic hurry. I opened my mouth to describe more about Herr Mueller as the judge's nephew interrupted, "I remember a little about all of that. Something about a German refugee getting used as a hostage exchange by the Justice Department for American prisoners in Germany, right?" He veered the car sharply into a side street, causing me to grasp the handle to hang on for dear life.

"Yes! I am that German refugee!"

Now he turned to me, wide-eyed. "Aren't you a U.S. citizen?"

"Yes. Of course. I married an American."

He looked colossally relieved. "Okay then, nothing to worry about. Here we are." He pulled up to the hotel, jumped out of the car, grabbed my bag out of the trunk, and handed it to me. "You'll be fine from here, right? Good? Good. See you tomorrow. Eight o'clock sharp." And off he zoomed.

Our conversation about Herr Mueller, if one could call it that, would have to be continued at a later date, I thought, frowning.

As soon as I checked into my hotel room, I took a hot shower and lay down on the bed. After three days and nights sitting upright in a train, my neck and back felt like a question mark. I sank onto the bed, just for a moment; it felt like a mountain of soft feathers. I hadn't realized how bone-weary tired I was. It wasn't just the last three days; I had been exhausted for weeks. I must have fallen asleep because when I woke the room was dark. I rolled over and was just about to fade into sleep when a knock at my door startled me. It was a bellboy with telegrams. Telegrams from home. The first one said:

> *Louisa,*
> *Terrible shock. The judge's wife dropped dead.*
> *Love, Robert*
> *P.S. Can you play the organ?*

And the second one read:

> *Dear Mom,*
> *Aunt Martha called Dog the worst dog in the world. Please come home.*
> *Love, William*

I read the telegrams, re-read them then searched the desk in my room for hotel stationery so that I could mail a letter to them from the hotel lobby before the ships left tomorrow.

> *Dearest Robert,*
> *Your telegram was waiting for me when I arrived in Washington D. C. I was so happy to hear from you and William, too! The train journey went well; I met a number of interesting people along the way. It made the*

time pass quickly. The judge's mysterious nephew met me at the train station today. I'm sorry to hear about Mrs. Pryor. Though, as Aunt Martha often pointed out, quite often, in fact, she was a woman of deluxe-sized proportions. Please tell the judge how sorry I am. I really am. I didn't know her well, but she was a very loyal organist to the church.

I translated all of Sabine's letters for you and will include them in this envelope. I hope it gives you a start on your magazine article. I think Dietrich would have been pleased that you are writing about him. I'll try to recall more memories.

The ships leave tomorrow. I'm eager to get this journey on its way! I wish you and William were with me. Oh, and Aunt Martha, too.

All my love, Louisa

P.S. I'm sorry to say that I don't play the organ.

P.P.S. And I never plan to.

The next morning, I was getting ready to meet the judge's nephew to head over to the ship when a bellboy delivered another telegram from home. I didn't expect to hear from Robert. Once, he was gone for over three weeks on a trip to a General Assembly meeting of the Presbyterian Church. He only sent one postcard. One! Besides that, Robert was a frugal man. Telegrams weren't inexpensive. I opened up the telegram and smiled as I held it in my hands. This was *fun.*

Dear Mom,

Here is my spy log on Dad tonight: 7:00 p.m. Dad listens to news on radio. 7:22 p.m. Dad looks for book, goes to office to start typing on the typewriter. 7:23 p.m. Aunt Martha tells me that I have to take a bath and go to bed. When are you coming home?

Love, William

P.S. Aunt Martha said she wants to give Dog a one-way ticket to the Pound. What is the Pound?

I was amazed that Robert let William send such a long telegram, though, the more I thought about it, it was entirely plausible William bypassed Robert and collaborated with Ernest at the telegraph office to send out his missives.

I wrote William a quick letter to include in Robert's envelope. Hearing the clunk that the letter made at the bottom of the mail box gave me a catch-in-my-heart pang. It was my last letter sent from American soil. My last connection to William and Robert.

The judge's nephew drove up, a little late, quite harried, in a big black box of a car. I started to say I was sorry to learn about his aunt's death, but he handed me a gigantic pile of file folders and spent the entire car ride giving me instructions about translating the contents. He drove us over to a dock in Virginia, swarming with newspaper people taking photographs of the President and the Secretary of State James Byrne as they boarded the U.S.S. Augusta. This conference was going to be a significant one: three world leaders meeting to discuss the end of a world war.

On the dock, I waited to board the escort ship, the U.S.S. Philadelphia. I had a feeling I would be waiting often in the next few weeks. I paced the dock anxiously. Waiting was never my forte. Finally, after the President boarded his ship, the press contingency was allowed to board the escort ship.

A boyish looking sailor led me to a tiny room with two berths. He explained I would be sharing the room with the naval nurse assigned to the ship. By the looks of things, she had been living on the ship for quite a while. As the only female on the ship, she hadn't had reason to share her tiny quarters. Until now. Until me. I wondered if she would resent the intrusion.

I wouldn't have long to wonder.

"Bottom bunk is taken," bellowed a gruff sounding voice from the door behind me. "And don't turn over in your bunk in the night. The squeaks will wake me up. I don't take kindly to being woken."

I spun around and looked at my roommate. At first glance, she resembled a small, solid icebox, as wide as she was tall. For a split second, I wasn't sure if the Icebox was a man or a woman. Even her cropped-short hair had a no-nonsense look about it. She glowered at me. She reminded me of someone, but whom? I couldn't quite place whom.

"And keep your things in your suitcase. You're not here for long, you know." She eyed me up and down. "Doubt it's for any legitimate reason."

I opened my mouth to object to her rather rude accusation when she interrupted me. "Oh, I heard all about that translation excuse." She eyed me suspiciously. "Look, girly, I don't care why you're here. But I will tell you two rules. One...stay out of my way. And two...follow rule one."

Ah! Now I knew. She reminded me of a short and stout version of Aunt Martha.

After the Icebox left the room, the sailor knocked on the door to deliver more telegrams to me. I hoped Ernest was giving Robert a discount.

Louisa,
Counting days until you return.
Love, Robert
P.S. Organ getting tuned.

And the other:

Dear Mom,

It's hot and boring around here. Dad types at the typewriter, and Aunt Martha is cranky. Dog and I spied on Ernest, but he caught us. Ernest tried to teach me Morse code, but I couldn't hear the clicks. When are you coming home?

Love, William and Dog

P.S. Are you on the same ship as the President?

The Judge had never mentioned a need for brevity in my telegrams, so I decided not to worry about that. Brevity had never been my strong suit, anyway. After trying to find some room in the cramped stateroom for my things, I sat down to write before preparing to tackle the papers that needed translating.

Dear William,

Are you working on your coursework with Dad? Did you go to Mrs. Morgan for speech therapy? Why did Aunt Martha call Dog the worst dog in the world? Ask Dad about the pound. What did Dog do? Thank you for giving me your spy log on Dad.

I love you and miss you, Mom

P.S. I saw President Truman today! He's on a different ship. He is not very big, and he walks and talks fast.

Dear Robert,

The ship set sail yesterday. As the coastline disappeared from the horizon, I felt hit with a giant wave, missing you and William. But the judge's nephew gave me stacks and stacks of papers to translate, so my mind is busy. And off of being seasick. I love you.

Louisa.

P.S. Don't bother tuning the organ.

The Icebox so intimidated me that I spent the first night in the bunk lying stiffly in one position so I wouldn't wake her. Soon, it was apparent that only a stick of dynamite could rouse her from her sleep. I thought we were next to the engine room until I realized the rattle noise was her snoring!

The next night, I had trouble falling asleep. My mind was whirring about Germany and my cousin, Elisabeth. The Icebox hadn't come in yet, so I jumped off the bunk, dressed, and took a walk on the ship's deck. Tonight, the sea was still. The moon cast shadows over the water, smooth as glass. The stars were close enough to touch. The weather had been ideal. Sunny and warm, with just a little rain one night.

Ambling along the deck, I heard voices coming from the mess hall and poked my head inside. Seated at a table was the Icebox, losing badly in a card game with some of the other reporters. After throwing her cards on the table, the Icebox glanced up and spotted me. "What are you looking at?" she squinted.

"Just wondered what's going on," I answered.

One of the reporters pulled up a chair for me. "Playing a little card game, Ma'am."

"What game?"

"Twenty-one," said one of the reporters.

The Icebox flashed a wicked smile. "Care to join us?" she asked, raising her eyebrows. "Fresh meat," she whispered under her breath. Among other things, she underestimated my hearing ability.

Who could resist? "Why, thank you. I'd like that." I sat down in the chair. An hour later, after everyone folded their hands, I collected the pot of money and thanked everyone for a lovely evening.

Back in our tiny quarters, the Icebox glared at me. "Where did you learn to play poker like that?"

"My husband's cousin taught me. I'm not really cut out to be a poker player, but after my first experience playing with her, I found it was wise to become *extremely* proficient at the game." I climbed up to my bunk, hoping the Icebox didn't plan to knife me in the back while I slept.

As I lay there looking at the ceiling, my mind drifted to Robert. He had a way of softening the hardest people. I'd often watched him gently turn heated conversations into constructive ones during church meetings. Not just at church but at the parsonage, too, when Aunt Martha and I would be at a gridlock. I could imagine him frowning at me for acting so smug. I exhaled deeply and knew what I needed to do.

I poked my head over the side and asked, "Perhaps I could I give you a few pointers?"

And in the dim light, I saw the Icebox smile.

Chapter Three

Dear Louisa,
William and I spent day fixing clothesline after Dog incident.
Love, Robert
 P.S. Organ and piano are nearly same instrument.

I folded his telegram and put it in my pocket, loving the crackling sound it made when I moved. After supper, I would sit out on the ship's front deck and read it again. It still amazed me—this strange new sense of family.

Dear William,
Tomorrow, our ships will be docking in Antwerp, Belgium. Ask Dad to find Belgium on the map. It's only taking one week to cross the Atlantic Ocean. Perfect weather. Please put Dog on the tie-down when you are not with him.
Love, Mom

Dear Robert,
Today, I saw President Truman on his ship, walking on the deck. Tell William that tomorrow I will be flying with the President in a special transport plane known as the "Sacred Cow." It won't be long now until I am reunited with Elisabeth.
All my love, Louisa
P.S. Telling me the piano and the organ are practically the same instrument is like telling you that you can play the violin just because you play the guitar. Find someone else to play the organ!

I had actually caught sight of President Truman quite often. His ship was always a few hundred meters away, so it was easy to spot him on deck. Up at dawn, he took frequent brisk walks around the deck, chatting with the sailors. Someone said the President napped every afternoon and in the evenings he watched movies. Just like Aunt Martha!

Apparently, this was the smallest staff the President had ever taken on a war conference. Along with his aides, there were correspondents from the major news services, one from the radio networks, one still photographer, and two newsreel photographers.

I had hoped to find time with the judge's nephew to finish my conversation about Herr Mueller, but he was on the President's ship. Just what did that man do? I tried to find out from the reporters. They said if I could find *that* out, they would offer me a job.

So I decided to talk to the reporters about Friedrich Mueller, hoping they could think of someone who could track him down. They listened with mild interest, until one interrupted. "Mrs. Gordon, do you have any idea how many Nazi war criminals the Tribunal is trying to track down?"

I knew. I realized what he was trying to tell me. Friedrich Mueller was insignificant compared to others, for example, his cousin, Heinrich Mueller, head of the Gestapo.

But Friedrich Mueller was not insignificant to me.

Most of the sailors looked at me in the same way the Icebox looked at me, exchanging sly glances with each other as if I had more duties than merely translating. But one of the first things I learned in Resistance Work was to act more confident than I felt. "Whistling in the Dark," we called it. Not even the dark could quite overcome our courage, or at the very least, our belief that what we were doing was right. So far, that helped me.

There were moments when I wondered what I was doing here, too, but then I would think about Elisabeth. I lay in bed at night wondering what she was like and how she felt when she first heard I was coming to get her. If she had even been told yet.

I replayed in my mind the very last time I had seen Elisabeth. It was years ago, before the war, when my father and I had visited relatives during Christmas. Elisabeth was very small for her age and had a surprisingly bold manner. I was a teenager, and she was, well, a nuisance. One time, my father asked me to play a piece on the piano. In the middle of it, Elisabeth—probably only seven or eight years old at the time—jumped from her seat, scowling, and told me I was playing the piece all wrong. Then she waved me off of the piano bench, as if shooing the butler, and sat down to play it correctly. Magnificently!

Below me, the Icebox snorted in her sleep, not unlike a wild boar. I hadn't been sleeping well, but it wasn't entirely the Icebox's fault. I was seasick. My hands and wrists ached from so much typing. As I rubbed them, it reminded me of being a student at the University of Berlin, preparing for a piano exam, spending hour upon hour in the practice room.

Aside from not feeling well, my mind was working overtime. The closer we came to Germany, suppressed memories of my past kept popping, unbidden, into my mind. I had longed to return to Germany from the moment I left. Truth to be told, I had never stopped longing for Germany, though I never shared that sentiment with Robert.

At last the day came when our ship reached port. "Excited?" asked a reporter as we waited on the deck of the

U.S.S. Philadelphia until the President and the Secretary of State disembarked.

"A little," I lied.

I was prepared to feel great emotion as the ships approached the harbor near Antwerp, Belgium. Surprisingly, I felt numb. Antwerp, an important seaport, remained relatively undamaged. Belgium had fallen quickly when invaded by Hitler's Blitzkrieg. As the ship drew closer, I spotted clumps of fat cows in fields. Strangely peaceful.

But then we got off of the ships and into cars to go to the airfield in Brussels to fly down to Berlin. Indications of war were everywhere. Our convoy passed lines of tattered civilians, camping by the road, hauling anything they could find in wheelbarrows. One weary looking man dragged a child's red wagon. The refugees watched us as curiously as we watched them. Fierce looking Soviet soldiers stood guard at the crossroads, out of place against the sweet azure sky.

I had thought nothing could be worse than seasickness, but airsickness came close. I was only able to get my mind off of my churning stomach by looking out the window, absorbed in the scenery below the plane.

As we crossed into Germany, my heart rose into my throat. I had fled Germany before the Allies had started any air campaigns to bomb the country. Since then, Allied aerial bombing had damaged over half of the major cities of Germany. It was more horrifying than I could have imagined. Everywhere I looked was evidence of destruction. Shelled out buildings, heaps of brick and rubble. Scarred landscape. Lone chimneys standing amidst ruins. Charred remains from fires that followed the bombings.

The railway system had been targeted by allied air offensive. That knowledge was especially worrisome to me because that was how I had hoped to get down to Munich to get Elisabeth. Suddenly, the numbness I felt when we arrived at Antwerp wore off, a flood of conflicting emotions caught up with me.

And the last emotion of all, surprisingly, was joy.

For the first time in over two-and-a-half years, I was back in my country! A Germany freed from twelve years of tyranny. Yes, the sights of destruction were shocking, but it was over. It was finally, truly over! A reporter told me the Germans referred to May 8th, 1945, the day of surrender, as the Stunde Null, *Hour Zero*, in which life started again.

I took a deeply satisfied breath. Even the air seemed fresher. A new beginning for this wonderful country that had brought the world such light and goodness over the centuries—from Martin Luther to Beethoven and Bach. I would never understand how such heritage could have borne the evil of Adolf Hitler.

After arriving in Berlin, a military convoy took us to the secret location where the conference of the Big Three would be held. All that I knew was that it was to be held in an unbombed suburb of Berlin. Allied troops, made up of Americans, British, and Soviet soldiers, surrounded us at all times. I almost smiled as I thought of how relieved Robert would be to see the protection I was getting.

My lightness quickly faded as the cars pulled out, and I was able to observe, at ground level, the condition of Berlin. This beautiful seven-hundred-and-fifty year-old medieval city was in shambles. I had avidly followed the news stories. I knew that over half of a million Allied bombs had dropped on Berlin, most of them in the last six months. By Christmas of 1944, Berlin was being bombed around the clock. Bombs fell like rain. But the material destruction I observed represented something far more devastating—how many lives had been shattered? How many families had been destroyed?

The reporters had shared some basic information with me about Germany's current conditions while we were still on the ship. Still, I wasn't prepared for what I saw. The most serious problem that faced the Germans was how to survive. Emergency feeding stations were set up on city corners to provide meals to long lines of hungry Germans—mostly women and children, I noticed, with a few old men, standing passively, waiting for a meal. In the last weeks of the war, both state and economy had virtually collapsed. Store shelves were empty. Shortages were severe. Allied soldiers in weary uniforms covered the city by foot or by jeep to keep order and maintain a curfew. And yet there was an eerie quietness to the streets, belying the savagery of the prior few months.

One building looked as if it had gone through the war unscathed; the house next to it was a mountain of rubble. We passed by the stately and imposing Kaiser Wilhelm Memorial Church. It had been bombed out in 1943, and only its shell remained. From the street, I could look inside the church and see the roof rafters through crumbled brick.

Memories of Berlin started to flood my mind. I could hardly recognize this city I had once cherished. A part of me longed to find my home and, near to it, my Lutheran church, to see if my parents' graves remained undisturbed. But I wasn't really sure if I wanted to know the answer.

Seated next to me in the car, a reporter tapped me on the shoulder, pulling me back from a fixed stare out the window. He handed me a handkerchief. "Here, Mrs. Gordon. You're crying."

* * * *

The conference was held at the Cecilienhof, the palace of the last crown prince of Imperial Germany, though everyone involved roomed elsewhere, in villas around Babelsberg. A day or so later, Winston Churchill, Prime Minister of England, and Joseph Stalin, leader of Russia, joined President Truman.

By eavesdropping on conversations among reporters at meals, I knew that postwar Europe dominated the Potsdam agenda, but lurking offstage was the war in the Pacific. One reporter said Truman and Churchill were suspicious of the motives of Stalin, who already had a toehold—with a very large foot—of communism in the central European countries.

Not that I was privy to any details about the conference. Except for meals, I was stuck in a stuffy little room with a typewriter. It seemed as if every time I turned around, the judge's nephew sent over more stacks of press releases to translate so the German people would be duly informed. I worked so diligently I had to ice my hands each evening. Still, I felt that wonderful feeling I often had while in the Resistance. I was *doing* something for my country!

And in the few free moments I did have, I tried to talk to anyone who would listen about Friedrich Mueller. Military guards, workers at the Palace, even cooks in the kitchen. They listened, but no one offered to help me find him.

By listening in on conversations among the President's staff, I could tell there was a rising pressure for the three leaders to agree on *something* before July 26th, when England was having general elections for prime minister. Churchill left the conference to return to London for the election; he was expected to return a day later.

But Winston Churchill didn't return. He had been defeated. *Defeated!* The greatest Englishman who ever lived, ousted by his own country in a landslide vote! In his place, newly elected Clement Atlee arrived to continue the conference. From what I could overhear among the reporters, even President Truman was shocked at Churchill's defeat.

On July 26, 1945, the Potsdam Declaration—a demand for unconditional surrender—was broadcast to the Japanese by the Allied forces, but two days later, on July 28th, Prime Minister Suzuki announced to the world he would ignore it.

The last few days of the conference inched along; I couldn't wait to get to München to reach Elisabeth. Finally, on the last night, the judge's nephew knocked on my door. "Okay, Mrs. Gordon. You have one day to get your cousin and get back here again."

I still wasn't sure how I was going to accomplish that. On my desk were maps of Germany, with large X's crossing out routes I had considered but abandoned.

My latest plan was to "temporarily" borrow a military motorcycle. I was a little concerned because I had never driven a motorcycle. I tried to ignore images of Robert clasping his head in his hands, shouting, "Have you lost your mind?!" Still, I refused to be deterred. I was going to find a way to get down to München and back to Berlin again, even if I had to hitch rides as a last resort.

The judge's nephew walked over to my desk and looked over the maps, shaking his head. "You can't do it, Mrs. Gordon. Not by rail." He crouched down to look directly at me. "But…I do have an option. I've taken the liberty to assign a private to escort you. I've also requisitioned a jeep. He's going to drive you there and back again."

I looked at him, shocked. "You were able to get permission for that?"

"Well, let's just worry about little details later."

As Robert would say, this man had definite pull.

The judge's nephew grinned. "You've earned it. You've done a great job for us."

I fought back the sting of grateful tears. "When do we leave?"

"Tomorrow morning. Four a.m. sharp. And you must be back by noon the next day to catch the flight to England with the President to rendezvous with the ships." He winked at me, walked to the door, and turned around to say, "If you aren't back, you're on your own, even if your husband is a friend of my uncle's."

"But wait! Couldn't we talk about Friedrich Mueller?"

The judge's nephew looked blank.

How could he not remember what I had told him?! Why didn't anyone seem to care about bringing Herr Mueller to justice?!

In rapid speed, I gave him an account of Herr Mueller's crimes. For the first time, I realized, I felt free to share the story of my Resistance work and Dietrich's involvement with assassination attempts against Hitler. And I even told him that Mueller had stolen more than money from the Gordon home. He had charmed Robert's wife into going with him, promising her wealth and fame, then shot her in cold blood after she rescued William and me.

"I see," he replied, rubbing his chin.

He didn't.

"An interesting tale, Mrs. Gordon."

"But it's not just a tale. It's the truth."

"I meant that it is a fascinating story, but there are many other stories, similar to yours. With repercussions that were far more damaging than a little town in Arizona losing its savings. I'm sorry," he added, seeing the crestfallen look on my face. "We can only do so much right now, and our focus is on the Nazi war machine." He opened the door and turned back to me, "So four a.m. tomorrow morning, right? Good? Good."

The next morning, I was packed and waiting in my room at three a.m. I had hardly slept, so worried I might oversleep. Right at four a.m., there was a knock at my door. When I opened it, for a split second, in the inky dawn of morning, I thought it was my husband. This private looked like Robert— tall and lean, with a thatch of black hair. I fought a wave of emotion, of missing Robert.

"Ma'am? My name is Private Ryan Wheeler. I'm assigned to escort you to Munich. All ready?"

I couldn't be any more ready.

After facing the ruins of Berlin over the last few weeks, I had grown somewhat inured to the sights on the drive to München. Strange as it sounds, I was getting accustomed to destruction. We headed out on the A-9 then the A-10 and began the long journey to München.

At first the private would only answer my questions in one word responses. After living with Robert, I was accustomed to men with an economy of words, but that didn't stop me from asking. Finally, the private expanded to two words, then to three, then to four. After a hundred miles or so, he actually started to visibly relax. Or perhaps he was getting tired of the sound of my voice. "So where did you say you lived in the United States?" I asked again.

"All over."

"Why did you live all over?"

"My folks were in the military."

"Both of them?"

"Yes."

Another quality that resembled Robert. Trying to get information out of this man was painstaking. "Where are they from?"

"My mother is from some backwater town in Arizona." He grinned at me. "She opened the oven one day, when the temperature dial turned up high, and said that was hot it felt most of the year in Arizona. Like crawling into an oven."

I smiled back at him, understanding that kind of heat. But a backwater town? But there was no water in Arizona. "I live in a copper mining town, not too far from Tucson. Have you ever been to Arizona?"

"No, Ma'am."

"What do your parents do in the military?"

"My folks are doctors in the Army."

I looked at him in surprise. "Your mother, too? She's a doctor? A medical doctor?"

"Yes, Ma'am. She was determined to go to college and the military was her only ticket through. Her father didn't believe women should be educated, but she proved him wrong."

What an intriguing woman! "Are you considering becoming a doctor?"

"No."

"Do you have plans after you're discharged?"

"Yes, Ma'am."

"What sort of plans?"

"Seminary."

A minister? I looked sharply over at him. "What makes you want to be a minister?"

"Well, I'd be lying if I didn't admit that part of the reason is to make my folks mad. They've always thought religious people have small minds," he grinned at me, his first smile all morning, as he cast a glance at me. "But mostly, it's because I feel The Call."

I smiled back at him. "I wish you could meet my husband. He's a Presbyterian minister. You even remind me of him, a little."

Now that the private was finally talking, I asked what he thought of Germany since the war ended. I wondered if he hated the country and its people like the rest of the world did.

"Well, Ma'am, the most curious thing to me is to see folks come out of hiding. The news that the war is over is taking time to get broadcasted, maybe even to be believed. I've seen people coming like ants from an ant hole, entire families, from the tops of barns, out of cellars. Would you believe, even out of haystacks? I saw it with my own eyes! People living in haystacks for years, hidden by some kind-hearted farmer. So, Ma'am, I keep seeing that a lot of Germans tried to do what they could."

I could have hugged him.

The hours flew by. Before I knew it, I saw a sign for München. *Munich.* As the private exited the autobahn, *the highway*, I pulled out the map that directed us to the Red Cross facility where Elisabeth was sheltered. My heart began to pound in anticipation. What would she be like after enduring a labor camp? I didn't even know how long she had been there. Would she remember me?

The private parked the jeep in front of a makeshift Red Cross facility. The woman at the front desk took my information, then told me to sit and wait while she went to get Elisabeth's case worker. The private remained in the jeep, wanting to give me privacy with Elisabeth. I couldn't sit still. An eternity later, I heard my name called. I was led down the hall to another office and was given paperwork to fill out to prove that I was a relative to Elisabeth so that she could be released into my care. The Germans loved paperwork.

I was hurrying through the documents when someone entered the small office, turned and closed the door. I glanced up distractedly, then back down to shuffle through the papers. Suddenly, I felt a shock, as if an electric current passed through me. I put the pen down and looked up slowly. In front of me was the one man on this earth whom I could never forgive.

A man whom I once loved.

And now hated.

Chapter Four

"Hello, Annika," the man said, his voice gentle as he met my stunned gaze.

My chin snapped up, defiant. "Louisa," I corrected, feigning boldness. "Louisa Gordon." I hardly recognized my voice. It wobbled. I wanted it to sound strong. I wanted to appear unmoved by the sight of this man. Instead, my body betrayed me. My palms started sweating and my heart pounded so loudly I was sure he could hear it. Despite the summer heat, I suddenly felt very, very cold.

He nodded as if he understood. "Yes, I know. I was the one who discovered Elisabeth and recognized her. I was the one who traced you in the United States."

My mind raced with memories. Karl Schneider and I had been music students together at the University of Berlin. More than that. We had planned a future together, dreaming of sharing the concert stage, playing to audiences around the world.

Until that one night.

It started out a day like any other. My father came downstairs, heading straight for the flour jar. He slipped off his wedding ring and buried it deep down in the flour.

"One of these days I am going to forget about that ring and bake it in a cake." I smiled, handing him a cup of hot tea.

"Dearest, the way that last cake turned out, I'd just as soon you quit baking altogether and concentrate on the piano," he said, giving me a wink.

I pretended to be insulted as I picked up the satchel that held my music scores. "Don't wait up for me tonight. I'll be practicing late. Mr. Bach and I still are arguing about his fugue."

He put down his tea cup and looked straight at me. "How will you get home? You don't have Ausweis." Authorization.

"Karl does. He'll walk me home if he's finished."

"He won't be," he said under his breath.

I put down my satchel. "Vati, please. This is a very important competition. If I win, it will provide scholarship money so I can stay in university." We desperately needed that money. Work for my father was growing scarce as the Nazi noose tightened around the Jews.

"Then why is Karl competing against you?" he asked. "His parents can afford to pay for his schooling."

"You know why. Tomorrow's competition could open important doors."

My father's brows lifted. "I still don't know why he chose to compete against you. There are other competitions."

"He didn't choose it. We were both invited to compete." I took one last sip of tea from my cup and put it in the sink, avoiding my father's eyes. "I don't understand why you dislike Karl. You need to give him a chance. I think he's going to be around for a while. A long while." I picked up my satchel and hurried out the door.

"Wait, Annika! I'll be outside of your practice room at 7 o'clock."

I froze, my hand on the door. My father and I both knew he shouldn't be out after dark. It was past the curfew imposed on Jews. My father refused to wear a Star of David and it made me frantic with worry when he was out, especially in the evening. But I had to practice; I wasn't as polished as I hoped to be for the competition. The weight of my father's eyes on me made me acquiesce. "I'll be waiting."

"Remember, tomorrow is in God's hands."

I turned to him and smiled. "As always." I gave him a wave, and left.

Later that day, Karl met me for a quick shared lunch before my practice room was available. "How's it going?" he asked, offering me half of his sandwich.

"Not so well. I'm struggling with that one section in Bach's Fugue."

"You'll do fine," he said, reaching over to kiss my forehead. "Eat. You need your energy."

Gratefully, I took his sandwich and ate it quickly. "I'd better get back. I need to leave by seven. My father is coming to get me."

Karl gave me a sharp glance. "Why is he coming here?"

"He doesn't want me on the streets at night." I stood up and stretched.

Karl gazed at me with such sorrow that it melted my heart. I bent over to kiss him once, then twice. "Karl, it doesn't matter who wins tomorrow. We both win." I kissed him gently one last time before pulling myself away to get to the practice room.

Right before seven, I closed up the piano and went outside to wait for my father. Though it was spring, a chill had set in after sunset. I waited as long as I could bear the cold, stomping my feet to stay warm. Then I went back inside and knocked on Karl's practice door. Karl seemed agitated by the interruption. Trying to reassure me, he said, "Maybe a piano tuning job came up. Or perhaps he just forgot."

"That's not like him." I glanced at the clock on the wall. Nearly eight. It was much too late for my father to be on the streets. "Would you mind walking with me? Maybe we'll meet him on the way."

Karl looked nervously at the piano, then turned back to me. "I wish I could, but I need to practice. You understand, darling." His brow was sweating despite the evening chill.

I did understand. I was frustrated that I had lost valuable time practicing, too. But now I felt so anxious about my father that I knew I couldn't concentrate.

I said goodbye to Karl and hurried through the deserted streets, hoping to find my father along the way. As I turned the corner to my street, I passed two young men laughing as they joked with each other.

When I reached my house, I found the front door wide open. Cautiously, I entered the threshold, listening carefully. The only sound I heard was my heart pounding in my ears. The house was eerily silent. Panicking now, I called out for my father. I searched through every room downstairs, then raced up the stairs. Pushing open my father's bedroom door, I stopped abruptly at the sight on the floor.

It was my father's body. A cloth Star of David was pinned to his chest.

Snapping to the present, I tried to harness my spinning thoughts. "I came to get Elisabeth. That's the *only* reason I'm here, Karl."

"Yes, I know." His face looked pained.

"As soon as I am reunited with her, she and I are returning immediately to the United States. To be with my husband and son."

He gave a brief nod. "I understand."

"So would you please go get my cousin?"

"Yes, of course. But...Annika—"

"Louisa."

"Louisa," he said, his voice full of broken glass. "Please let me explain." He held his hands in front of me, palms up, as if offering me something.

How *dare* he! I narrowed my eyes. "Explain how you arranged my father's death?"

He looked as if I slapped him. "No, wait, please. I never intended for things to go so far. I only meant to distract you from the competition," he admitted flatly. "I never dreamed...I never imagined that... If I could only take back that day." He covered his hands with his face.

It's a curious thing to watch a strong man crumble. With his head bowed, I eyed him more closely. Karl was an attractive man, even more handsome than I remembered. Too handsome, my friend Deidre had often pointed out. His face and shoulders had filled out over the years and he looked mature, seasoned. Humble, even. Karl had *never* been humble. "What do you want from me, Karl?"

He cleared his throat as if afraid to trust it. "I want...I need...to have you forgive me."

I turned back to the paperwork and continued to fill it out. "You're overestimating me. I don't think that's something I can ever give to you." It would be easier for me to forgive Hitler.

"I did a terrible thing. I know that. As soon as I did it, I regretted it. I just never dreamed it would end like that." He winced, pleading. "Winning the competition was so important, Annika."

"Louisa."

"Louisa," he shook his head as if trying to cement that name in his mind. "It was my future. Our future. At least what I had hoped for us. *Please* try and understand."

I gave him an icy stare. "I'd like to see my cousin now."

He exhaled, resigned. "She's at the children's facility across town for processing. I can take you there if you're finished with the paperwork."

"Then I'll finish it and we can be on our way." My heart felt no softening towards this man. Not only did I lose my father, but I was betrayed by the man I thought I loved, all in one swift act. I'm sorry, God, but this is beyond my ability to forgive. I had tried, many times before, I *really* had, but I could still feel the bile stir within me. I had withdrawn from University abruptly after discovering Karl was responsible for turning in my father. I never saw Karl after that.

Karl's family was well connected with the German government. He was able to avoid active military duty because he performed piano concerts for Hitler's visiting dignitaries. Part of me wanted to ask him why he was here, volunteering for the Red Cross, but I thought better of it. I didn't want to reveal any interest in him, nor prolong any conversation between us. I wanted to get my cousin and leave München as quickly as I could.

Karl climbed in the back of the jeep. "Is everything in order?" the private asked, seeing the stricken look on my face.

I nodded, but remained silent. As we drove north to the facility, I saw a road sign for Dachau. I turned my head slightly back toward Karl. Without making eye contact I asked, "Do we pass by the camp?"

"Yes," Karl answered. "But I really don't think you should—"

"Private?" I cut Karl off. "Would you mind turning into the camp? I need to see it. I need to see what Elisabeth has endured these last few years."

Even the private cast me a sideways glance, as if he wanted to ask if I was really certain I wanted to go in there. I was dead certain.

He drove the jeep up to the gates. There in looming iron work were the words of the first great lie of these labor camps: Arbeit Macht Frei. *Work Makes You Free.*

Dachau was the first concentration camp built by the Nazis in 1933, the year when Hitler became chancellor of Germany, built to house political prisoners. In late 1938, large numbers of Jews, Gypsies, Jehovah's Witnesses, homosexuals, and other supposed enemies of the state were also sent there. Nazi doctors used many prisoners at Dachau for scientific experiments. If one could call torture and mutilation science.

Allied soldiers with stoic faces didn't stop us as we drove into the camp. Private Wheeler's uniform provided enough credentials. Karl chose to remain in the jeep. Barbed wire curled viciously on top of the fences, with guard towers positioned strategically so there could be no escapes. The structure of the camp was very orderly, very well planned. Very German. Private Wheeler and I walked toward the row of barracks, one of which I assumed had housed Elisabeth. The barracks were filthy, reeking of human waste, screaming of suffering.

We walked toward a low building around the bend, where large outdoor ovens were placed with long chimney pipes. I had heard stories of those ovens, now verified by Allied reports. I could sense, deep in my spirit, the evil residing here. It was palpable. Had my own aunt, Elisabeth's mother, been cremated in those ovens? I squeezed my eyes shut; I could almost hear her cries.

Suddenly, my stomach twisted and I vomited, right in front of the private. Private Wheeler held my head and gave me his handkerchief to wipe my mouth, as if it was the most ordinary thing in the world.

"I'm so sorry," I said, afterwards, tears streaming down my face.

"Don't be."

"They must have known."

"Ma'am? Who? Who must have known?"

"The villagers. How could they not have known? The railroad tracks go right through the town. They must have known. And they did nothing." Dachau was a medieval village, a tiny suburb of München.

I suddenly felt compelled to pull out William's Mickey Mouse camera and take pictures. I didn't take the pictures for

Elisabeth's sake; I doubted I would ever show them to her. But I felt it was important to document this horrible place. I took pictures of the trenches of mass graves, the blood stained walls where executions had taken place, the crematorium, the gas chambers, the mounds of empty clothing and shoes. Of the silent barracks, the guard towers, the barbed wire.

As I finished, the sun broke through leaden clouds, washing over my skin. I looked up at the sky. *At least they couldn't take that from them, Lord,* I prayed silently. At least they still had the sun.

We went back to the jeep where Karl waited, an uncomfortable look stretched on his face. We drove a short distance and arrived at a school that had been temporarily converted into a children's facility.

Private Wheeler stayed behind. Karl took the forest of documents I had filled out and handed it to a woman at the desk, asking her to get Elisabeth. Then he sat down next to me, handing me Elisabeth's release papers and travel documents and visa. He described Elisabeth's history, at least what he knew of it, that she was severely malnourished but didn't seem to have any diseases. "Many of the children have typhoid or diphtheria. Elisabeth has been fortunate."

Fortunate? After being imprisoned in Dachau? But I kept my face void of expression. "Did her mother die there?"

"I don't know. We have no knowledge of her mother. Elisabeth doesn't seem to know what happened to her, either. They were in hiding at a farm not too far from here, and one day, they were discovered."

"Discovered?"

Karl held up a hand to ward off my next question. "The farmer's wife turned them in." He glanced at the reception area, then back at me. "Please. Please. Is there anything I can do to make up for what I did to you?"

His eyes pleaded that he wanted things to be right between us. But why?

I felt a dull sense of loss and failure. And hatred, too. *Oh God, I just can't do it. I can't offer him forgiveness that I don't have.*

All of a sudden, a response slipped through the tunnel of my throat. There *was* one thing. I met Karl's eyes with a level stare. "Find Friedrich Mueller and bring him to justice."

With unmasked interest, Karl asked who he was and what I knew of him. I told him everything, without emotion, as if I were reading a newspaper.

Then a door squeaked open and a nurse brought my cousin Elisabeth to me. I barely swallowed down a gasp as I took in her tragic face, small and thin and white. Elisabeth's large brown eyes were huge and shiny in her face. She was so tiny, just skin and bones. Her hair was cut short, wispy and thin.

"Kannst du mich erinnert?" I asked her. *Do you remember me?*

"Nein," she said. Her voice was surprisingly bold. Loud, too. "Warum sind Sie hier?" she asked me. *Why are you here?*

I reached for her hand, as tiny and fine-boned as a bird. "Ich wollte, dass Du weisst, dass Du nicht alleine bist." *I wanted you to know that you weren't alone.* I pulled her close to me to hug her, feeling her sharp shoulder bones protrude through her thin dress. Her body stiffened under my embrace.

She stepped away and fixed her eyes on me thoughtfully. She studied me over the next few moments of silence. It was evident some kind of calculation was being made. Then, she asked, "Wohin gehen wir?" *Where are we going?*

"Nach Hause." *Home.*

She nearly spat at me. "Ich habe kein Zuhause." *I have no home.*

Surprised at her sharp tone, I released her hand.

She turned to Karl and asked him, "Darf ich Danny mit bringen?" *Can Danny come with us?*

"Nein, Elisabeth. Danny hat seiner familie. Ich muss sie finden, damit sie wieder vereint sind." *No, Elisabeth. Danny has a family of his own. I must find them so he can be reunited.*

She stared at Karl for a long moment, then finally turned to me, shrugged and said, "So, lass uns gehen." *So, let's go.*

I turned back to Karl for one agonizing moment. He met my eyes steadily. In his eyes lay the detritus of our painful history.

But I climbed into the jeep and never looked back.

Dusk was fading into full darkness as we reached the highway. I sat next to Elisabeth, hoping to ask her questions. Soon, it was clear she wasn't interested in answering questions. Only asking them.

"Ich kann ein bisschen Englisch sprechen," she said. "Danny brachte es mir bei." *I know a little English. Danny taught me.* "Dannys Vater war ein Professor. Er konnte viele Sprachen sprechen." *Danny's father was a professor. He knows many languages.*

I nodded. "Ist Danny Dein Freund?" *Is Danny your friend?*

"Ja. Sprechen Sie Englisch?" *Yes. Do you speak English?*

"Ja, ich ganz es fliessend." *Yes, I'm fluent in English.*

For the first time, she looked at me with a tiny flicker of interest in her eyes. "Dann, werde ich nur noch Englisch sprechen." *Then I will only speak English.* She narrowed her eyes. "Kein Deutsch mehr," she ordered. *No more German.*

"All right," I said, wondering why she wanted to give up German. A little disappointed, too. I was looking forward to having conversations with her in my native language.

Taking pains to enunciate clearly, she asked, "Vhere go ve?"

"We're going to Berlin, and tomorrow—"

"Langsamer!" she interrupted crossly. *Slower!*

"We're going to Berlin. Tomorrow, we're going to start on our journey to America," I said slowly, enunciating carefully, just as I did with William. Karl must have told her some information because she didn't seem surprised.

"Dos Amerikaners came to da camp," she said, slowly thinking out her words.

"Ja, ich weiss," I said. *Yes, I know.*

"Sprechen Sie Englisch!" she said severely, suggesting a thunderous temper. *Speak English!*

"Yes, I know," I repeated. I did know. The Americans had liberated Dachau on April 30th. I wondered what that had been like for her. Just an hour ago, I had seen where the Americans conducted on-the-spot executions of the Nazi S.S. guards. I wondered if Elisabeth had witnessed those executions, and how it felt to see those, who had killed so many, face their own death. There were so many things I wanted to ask her.

As Elisabeth stared at the sights along the highway, I took the opportunity to look her over. She was so small but looked so old. Her wrists looked like a tree stick. She flicked back her hand to swat a fly and I suddenly gasped. There on the inside of her arm was a tattooed identification number. She looked sharply at me to see why I gasped and then crossed her arms together against her chest. Her body positioning right now—arms crossed tightly—seemed a metaphor for the shape her soul was in.

We drove through the night. Elisabeth fell asleep but I tried to stay awake to keep the private company. Just before dawn, highway signs for Berlin finally started to appear. A hammer tripped in my mind and I remembered Robert's article about Dietrich. I had hoped I would have been able to track down more information about Dietrich, but I didn't have time nor opportunity to venture out on my own. Twice, I had tried to walk to the Bonhoeffer home but kept getting stopped by the American troops, grimly warning me to stay clear of the Russian soldiers. The Soviets were the first to surround Berlin in the last few days of the war and they were ruthless in how they treated Berliners, especially women. Entire sections of the city were closed off, condemned from damage.

This morning, I wondered if a military jeep, driven by an American uniform, might have better luck than I had on foot. I tapped on the private's shoulder. "Would you mind detouring through the city?"

He obliged me and drove down some streets, close to where my childhood home had been. The city was just waking for the new day. We maneuvered around mountains of rubble, shoved aside to allow passage by motor vehicles.

We drove down the street to find the Lutheran church that was the heart of my family's life. It was gone; leveled to the ground. All that remained were a few burnt floor joists. The cemetery was undamaged so I hurried over; Elisabeth, barely awake, rubbing her eyes, followed behind me. I found my parents' neglected graves, side by side.

"Dat ist Seine Familie?" she asked, mixing German and English together.

I nodded. "Auch Deine Familie," I answered. *Also your family.*

"Ich habe keine familie mehr," she answered solemnly. *My family is gone.*

"Aber ich bin doch Deine Familie. Nun sind wir eine Familie." I told her. *But I am your family. We are family.*

She only shrugged her frail shoulders. I looked at my parents' headstones, caught by the overwhelming realization that I would most likely never stand at this spot again. I bowed my head and prayed out loud. "Dear Lord, Thank You for my mother who taught me about Christ. For my father, who taught me how to live my life. I thank You that they are in Your Holy presence. Amen." I stayed glued to the spot for a long moment until Elisabeth yanked on my sleeve, wanting to go.

On the way back to the jeep, a man stopped me to trade his Oriental carpet for a loaf of bread. I looked into his eyes and smelled his desperation. "Nein, ich brauche das nicht." *I don't need it.* His eyes glistened with tears. I reached into my pocket and pulled out a chocolate bar and a package of cigarettes that I had been given by an American soldier. The man hugged me in gratitude. On the Black Market, cigarettes were like gold.

Suddenly, I heard someone shriek my name. "Annika? Bist du es? Meine liebe Annika?" *Annika? Is it you? My dear Annika?*

I spun around to face Else Kauffman, the baker's wife. She grabbed me and hung on to me, as if grasping for a lifeline. When she finally let me go, I saw her eyes dart down to Elisabeth, then recoil, shocked by the child's appearance. "Frau Kauffman, this is my cousin, Elisabeth." Quickly, she recovered and put a hand out to Elisabeth, who stared at her without expression. Our words tumbled over each other, trying to catch each other up on our lives. I asked about everyone I could think of, but soon, I had to stop asking. The answers were too difficult to hear.

"Annika, you have heard about Reverend Bonhoeffer?"

I nodded solemnly. Dietrich had been executed at Flossenburg, just weeks before the war had ended. Weeks before Hitler committed suicide. Weeks before Germany buckled in surrender. But that was all that I knew.

Frau Kauffman knew details about his arrest and imprisonment; she told me of the letters smuggled out of prison and the conditions to which he had been subjected. I tried to cement every detail in my mind to tell to Robert. When Frau Kauffman exhausted herself of information, she clapped her hands to her cheeks. "Will we ever be the same? Will Germany ever recover?"

I took her hands and made her look directly at me. "God has not changed, Frau Kauffman. He is the same yesterday, today, and tomorrow. He is still here."

I felt a hand on my elbow. Private Wheeler interrupted with an apologetic look. "It's time to go, Mrs. Gordon."

Hurriedly, I gave Frau Kauffman my address in Arizona. "Please, keep in touch. And know that I am praying for you. For all of you." I hugged her good-bye. "Don't ever forget, Frau Kauffman, Emmanuel! God is with us!"

A warm light returned to her eyes. "Ja, Ja, Annika. Ich habe nicht vergessen. Emmanuel." *I have not forgotten.*

On the way back to Potsdam, we drove past the Reichstag, the house of the German Parliament. Littering the walls were thousands of bullet pockmarks from the final hours of the war. It had been the location of the last stand of Nazi Germany. Five hundred meters away was the bunker where Adolf Hitler and Eva Braun had committed suicide and where their bodies had been burned, orders given to the Germans because Hitler feared what the Russians might do to his body.

When I saw the flattened Deutsche Staatsopera, where I had attended concerts with my father, where he had tuned many pianos in his career, I reached my capacity for mourning. All of this senseless loss was now numbingly familiar. I couldn't take another moment. I was ready to leave this war-weary country.

I took one last picture, using William's Mickey Mouse camera, of Private Ryan Wheeler next to his jeep. "God bless you," I told him, meaning it, as I said good-bye.

At noon, our plane left the runway to fly to England to join the President's ships, I watched Germany recede into the distance and let the tears fall. For the first time in two-and-a-half years, I was ready to leave Germany behind. Really, truly behind me. And really, truly ready to embrace my new life. I was finally able to release that tiny little part of me that secretly longed to return to Germany.

By August 2nd, we were back on the ships heading toward Virginia. The Icebox raised her wooly eyebrows and shook her head when she saw Elisabeth standing behind me. "Top bunk," she ordered. To me, she muttered, "I don't know who you're sleeping with, missy, but you must got some kind of magic." Then, to my horror, she gave me a sly grin.

Chapter Five

Elisabeth meant it when she said she was going to speak only English. Her intense determination reminded me of William, as he first started to develop language acquisition and lip reading skills. He had exhausted me, in a wonderful way. So did Elisabeth. She even practiced her English on the baffled sailors—who were already confused as to why a little skinny waif of a girl was on a Presidential Naval Ship. Soon, they grew weary of her halting questions and shooed her off, plying her with candy bars, apples and oranges.

At least, I *think* they offered her treats as a bribe to leave them alone. She had collected a rather large stash of food that she kept squirreled away in her satchel. I didn't let on that I knew about the stash; I wanted her to feel secure about her food supply. It was the one gap in her hungry soul that I could help to fill.

I still had work to do for the press corps but this time, I was translating German documents and newspapers into English. My brain ached, so did my hands from using the typewriter, and my stomach had yet to make peace with the ocean.

Every time I stopped for a break, Elisabeth would tell me about Danny. I was an eager listener. If I asked her any questions about the last few years, her eyes would narrow and her lips would tighten, as if I was trying to pry national secrets from her. But Danny was fair game.

I learned that he was a Jewish boy, a few years older than Elisabeth, who had been at the camp much longer than she had. Somehow, he had earned the respect of all of the prisoners, even some guards. While they worked, breaking up rocks during the day, Danny taught English lessons for all those who wanted to learn. He had such a remarkable ability for engineering that the prison guards asked his help to keep their cars running.

Probably what kept him alive, I surmised.

But more than anything else, Danny gave prisoners a sense of hope and purpose, a belief in looking to the future. "Danny sounds like Daniel in the Bible," I said to her.

"Ja! His mutter told him to be yust like Daniel. To help da people not forget God."

And Danny was only fifteen-years-old.

"Does Danny want to come to America someday?" I asked Elisabeth.

"Nein, um, no. He vants to go to Palestine. He vants to build rockets. Vhen he is alt genug, um," she shook her head as if to correct herself, "uh, old enough."

Many of the liberated Jewish prisoners hoped to emigrate to Palestine, and not just those from Germany. Displaced Russian Jews, Polish Jews, and countless others no longer felt as if they had a country to which to return.

"Danny will be pleased to know you're getting so good at English."

"Ja. He told me I vas..." she struggled for the right word.

"Smart?"

She looked at me, puzzled.

"Klug? Ich denke, dass Du sehr klug bist," I said. *Smart? I think you're very smart.*

Her eyes glinted at me. "Vell, you is not so klug. You speak in Deutsch venn I told you to speak only in da Englisch."

I rolled my eyes, accustomed now to Elisabeth's sharp tongue. I wondered how in the world Aunt Martha and Elisabeth would get along. They were both right about everything.

With no explanation, I was told I wasn't permitted to send or receive telegrams on the return trip. Something of import was transpiring. Tension on the ship mounted; an eerie quiet resonated until the reporters were finally briefed: Soon after President Truman arrived in Potsdam, weeks prior, he had received word of the successful atomic bomb test at Trinity Site, New Mexico. On August 6th, while the ships were skimming the Atlantic Ocean, an atomic bomb was dropped on Hiroshima, Japan.

As soon as the ships docked in Virginia and we were permitted to disembark, I hunted for a telephone booth to call Robert in his office but there was no answer. The judge's nephew drove us to Union Station to catch our train. As the judge's nephew grabbed our bags out of his trunk, I tried one more time. I knew this was my last chance to find Friedrich Mueller. "Did you know that some large fish are caught using small fish as bait?"

Distracted as always, the judge's nephew barely glanced in my direction. "Is that right?" he said, glancing at his watch.

I sighed. I would have to be more direct. "Did it ever occur to you that if you found Friedrich Mueller, you might just find a lead to Heinrich Mueller?"

The judge's nephew snapped his head around and looked me straight in the eyes. At last, I had found a hook.

I gave the judge's nephew a fat envelope filled with every piece of information I could remember about Friedrich Mueller. "No promises, Mrs. Gordon," he said, tucking the envelope in his suit jacket. Still, he did accept the envelope.

Now, I was ready to go home.

Before boarding the train, I hunted once more for a telephone booth. This time, Robert answered. "Robert? It's me, Robert. It's Louisa."

For a long moment, there was only silence on his end. Finally, he found his voice, husky with emotion. "Louisa! How *are* you? *Where* are you?"

We both started talking at once. There was so much to talk about! I didn't even know where to begin. "Robert, the bomb. So *many* people."

"I know. I know." His voice sounded like I felt, heavy-hearted and conflicted.

I glanced over at Elisabeth. She was sitting on the bench, watching people walk by, swinging her small legs. "Robert, I have to warn you. Elisabeth isn't what I expected."

"What do you mean?"

With a shock, I saw Elisabeth stealthily reach a hand into the purse of the woman seated next to her on the bench. She pulled out a candy bar and slipped it, unnoticed, into her pocket. "It might be wise to prepare Aunt Martha for a child who is starving for love but acts in the opposite manner."

"Like half the world."

The operator asked for more coins, so I fed in more until I had completely run out of change and we were forced to say a rushed goodbye. As I replaced the receiver on the hook, I smiled. It felt so good to hear Robert's voice. I wished I could have heard William's voice, too. I didn't think about his deafness often, but suddenly it felt like an enormous barrier between us.

I steeled myself to confront Elisabeth, intending to make her return the candy bar but the woman had left. The candy bar was eaten. Elisabeth smiled broadly, revealing chocolate-covered teeth. I sighed. Next time. Hopefully, though, there wouldn't be a next time.

The train trip was halfway to Arizona when the bombing of Nagasaki exploded on the pages of history. I had just witnessed such devastation I felt as if I didn't really feel what I *should* have felt. When would this strange numbness wear off?

America wasn't numb, though. She was celebrating! By August 14th, the Emperor of Japan surrendered and the war in the Pacific was over. This world war was over! It was *finally* over.

The last few days of the train ride were a sight to behold. In every town, celebrations filled the streets. Relief and joy were tangible. With each passing mile, I felt joy waken and seep back into my soul. Finally, the pages began to close on the most deadly war in human history.

As the train crossed the border into Arizona, I could hardly sit still; I just paced up and down the aisles. Elisabeth told me I was annoying and to go into a different car, but I wouldn't leave her. I had never felt so happy to be going home in all of my life. It really *was* home.

I saw Robert and William waiting for us on the platform at the Tucson station, in almost the same spot as I had said goodbye to them, nearly six weeks earlier. In fact, it was almost the same spot as I had first said hello to Robert, meeting him for the first time, two-and-a-half years ago. I dragged Elisabeth down the platform steps and flew into Robert's waiting arms. We hugged silently for the longest time, my face buried in his chest. Then I remembered my cousin. "Elisabeth! This is Robert. And this is William!" I hugged William so hard he started coughing.

"Look, Mom!" He pulled away from me and held out the amplifier around his neck. "It's the newest model. A Zenith Radionic A3A! Dad got it for me."

I admired his new amplifier. "Is it better?"

He nodded solemnly. "Dog barks too loud."

"Then it does work well, William! Dog *does* bark too loud!" I laughed. I turned to Elisabeth. "Elisabeth, this is my husband, the Reverend Robert Gordon."

"Hello, Elisabeth," Robert said, bending over to shake her small hand. "Welcome to Arizona. Welcome to our home."

She looked at him with serious eyes. As always, it was hard to read what she was thinking. "Vhat I call you?" she asked.

"Robert would be fine."

"No. I call you da Reverend."

"Whatever you prefer." He smiled at her. "What do you think of Arizona?"

"Too hot," she noted bitterly.

"You're absolutely right. It *is* hot. You're in a desert," Robert explained. "This is my son...," he glanced at me and corrected himself, "our son, William."

William handed Elisabeth a package of Bazooka bubble gum. She looked at it suspiciously and smelled it. I don't think she had ever seen such a brightly colored package before. "You chew it. And blow bubbles," he explained. He blew a huge bubble to impress her. She cocked her head at him, watching curiously.

"Guess what, Mom? Dad bought us root beer for dinner tonight!" William announced. "And Aunt Martha is making fried chicken!" He turned to Elisabeth. "You can have the drumsticks, if you want," he added generously.

William couldn't have realized that offering food to Elisabeth would charm her.

Robert tucked the suitcases under his arms as we walked to the parking lot, but not to the Hudson. "It's a 1934 Chrysler Airflow," he said with false cheerfulness. "I got a great deal on it. Really great."

The Airflow was an ugly looking car. A large steel box with a stubby front end that ended abruptly in an enormous grill.

I felt a pang of sadness, missing the Hudson. "Roomy, inside," I said, trying to find something positive to say.

Robert nodded appreciatively. "Bigger inside than the Hudson. A good size for our family. Power is supplied to the rear wheels by the front mounted in line eight engine," he explained knowledgably. "It's really an engineering masterpiece." He spoke to me as if I knew what he was talking about, but it seemed as if he was trying to reassure himself. He turned the key, but the engine wouldn't start. He frowned, and tried it again and again. Finally, the engine turned over. "It's...ahem...hasn't been a very popular car for Chrysler. There seem to be some...uh...reliability problems."

Normally just a two-hour trip from Tucson to Copper Springs, it took us twice as long because the engine kept overheating. Waiting on the side of the road for the engine to cool off gave Elisabeth time to get better acquainted with William, which didn't go as well as I had hoped.

"Dat boy is sick. He has a cold in his nose," said Elisabeth, pointing to William.

"No, Elisabeth, I told you he is deaf. When he talks, he sounds a little different. You'll get used to it."

"I can not understand him. He talks like his nose is full of yunk. It's da vorst sound."

"I can't understand you, either. You make too many v's," William shot back.

Elisabeth snapped her head to look at him. Then a sly smile toasted her face, as if she just decided she might have underestimated William.

"Dad, what does yunk mean?" asked William.

"I think she meant junk."

"So she doesn't make j's either?" William asked me curiously. "Or w's?"

Elisabeth scowled darkly at him. "I speak da English yust fine," she announced, which only got Robert and me exchanging a grin. "Vhat?" Elisabeth sputtered for words, temper flaring.

William started to tell her about Dog, and Elisabeth's eyes grew wide. "I do not like dogs."

"Why not?" asked William.

She wouldn't answer.

"I bet you'll like my dog. He's big and—"

"He is big?" She looked terrified.

"Yep. He's big and likes to jump up on you to say hello."

She crossed her arms tightly and lowered her chin to her chest, obviously troubled.

"Elisabeth, is something wrong?" I asked.

She shook her head but wouldn't look at me, withdrawing.

I remembered a story Private Wheeler had told me. He had heard it from some friends of his in the military who had liberated Auschwitz, another labor camp. In the evening, the commander would ask for a prisoner to be set free in the yard, and he would set his German Shepherd dogs on him, ripping the prisoner from limb to limb. Just for the sport.

I wondered if she had witnessed similar atrocities. Gazing now at the tension in her face, I knew that she had.

"We won't let Dog scare you, Elisabeth," I assured her. "We'll keep him away from you until you're ready to make friends with him." But a part of me felt concerned that she may never be ready. I knew how hard it was to get over some of the atrocities I had witnessed during the war. I still suffered from occasional nightmares, though less and less.

We pulled into the driveway to see a black nose pushed against the large parlor window. Dog was waiting for us. Hurriedly, I tied up Dog on the line out back, trying to avoid the disappointment in Dog's woeful face. "We all have to make sacrifices, Dog," I whispered in his ear as I scratched his big neck.

Aunt Martha was in the kitchen making fried chicken and roasted potatoes for a homecoming dinner. I had to look twice at her. Ever since President Roosevelt had died, she had only worn black. Today, though, she had returned to her uniform of a long print dress and sensible brown shoes. Remarkably, she barely registered shock on her face when she saw Elisabeth, though she wasn't very warm, either. Nor to me, but I was accustomed to that. A good sign, I thought.

Aunt Martha appraised me with critical eyes. "Louisa, I believe you've gained some weight on that trip," she decided. She was right. Just this morning, I hadn't been able to button the top of my skirt. My skirt felt tight. Very, very tight.

"She has not fat," announced Elisabeth in a loud voice. "She has baby." I whipped my head around to look at her, astonished. I had never told her I was pregnant. I hadn't told anyone! Aunt Martha's sparse eyebrows flickered up. Slowly, I turned to Robert.

"What? Dad, what? What did she say?" asked William, pulling on Robert's shirt sleeve, trying to understand what had just transpired.

Cupping her hands around her mouth, like a football coach yelling plays to his team from the sidelines, Elisabeth shouted, "I says she has da baby in her!" She pointed to my tummy.

"Louisa?" asked Robert, with a shy look of delight on his face. "Could this be true?"

Immediately, my face turned red. He came over to me and gave me a bone crushing hug, right in front of everyone, right in the kitchen, a rare display of public affection. Just then, William understood what Elisabeth had announced. He shouted so loudly that he shook the foundations of buildings as far away as Phoenix. Dog started to bark and howl in excitement from his tie-down spot after hearing William's yelps.

"Dat Dog is too big," pronounced Elisabeth, peering out the kitchen window to make sure Dog was tied up. "Da dogs in da camp vere big like dat. Dey vould eat me if dey could."

"Dog doesn't have a mean bone in his body," reassured Robert. "He'll never hurt you." But Elisabeth remained unconvinced.

Later that evening, after dinner, as she was brushing her teeth, I asked her how she knew that I was pregnant.

She spit out the toothpaste in the sink with a flourish. "Dat nurse on dat ship told me. And I know tings. I vatch. I see you sick." She made a vomiting sound, clutching her stomach with dramatic flair. "On da ship, I see your stomach get bigger and bigger vhen you change da clothes." She put her hands out in front of her as if I was enormous.

"I would have liked to have told Robert that news myself."

"So vhat? Now he knows."

"But it was my news to tell him."

"So?"

I sighed.

"Everyting vorks out."

I found Robert outside on the porch, watching the sky change from lavender to inky black. The stars seemed especially bright tonight. When he saw me, he held out his hand. I smiled and squeezed it.

"So how did it feel to be back in Germany?" he asked.

I leaned against the railing to face him. "Conflicting. I had been so excited to go—"

"I know," he interrupted. "I know you couldn't wait to go."

It was true. I thought I had masked my feelings a little better, but I've never been one to hide my emotions. It was one of my worst faults. "But it is a broken land. I can't even begin to describe some of the sights."

"I'd like to hear about them."

"I will. I can't talk about them right now. Soon, though."

"Just tell me one thing." He gave me a straight-in-the-eyes look. "How did you feel about coming back?"

I knew how important this answer was to him. "I felt as if I was finally, really ready to let go of Germany and come home. To my home. To you and William."

He reached out to draw me close.

"Oh, and Aunt Martha," I added, over his shoulder.

"There's something I want to talk to you about."

I pulled back and looked at him curiously.

"I think there's more than just a magazine article about Dietrich. I think it could be a book."

I smiled. "Tell me more."

"I know it could be a book."

"I found out more about Dietrich's imprisonment while I was in Berlin. It was providential, actually. I didn't have much extra time, but I bumped into one mutual acquaintance with information about his arrest and...execution." Dietrich's death, by hanging, was still so hard for my mind to grasp.

"I want to hear everything. When you're up to it, that is." He leaned against the porch railing, hands in pockets, and gave me a shy sideways glance. "I've already had some interest by a publisher. I have a friend who has a friend...that sort of thing. They want to see the first draft. Soon."

I looked at him in astonishment. "Robert, I am *so* proud of you." I was, too. He kept surprising me.

When I had first arrived in Copper Springs, I would never have expected Robert to be a man who was willing to take such a risk. To even tackle a difficult subject. Certainly not from the pulpit. Yet I'd seen him grow as a minister beyond my expectations. Suddenly I realized *this* was the man whom Dietrich Bonhoeffer saw, deep inside, when they were at seminary together years ago. Dietrich *knew* that Robert could be this man. As I looked at Robert's profile in the twilight, my heart felt full. *Lord, tonight my cup overfloweth*, I prayed silently and happily.

He turned to face me. "So, you wouldn't mind helping me edit?"

"Of course not!"

"Typing, too."

Oh no. My hands still ached from the press corps translations. "I can start tonight," I offered bravely.

"Not tonight," he said, putting his arms around my waist. "Besides, first thing to work on is just a proposal." Modestly, he gave a quick glance around the neighborhood to make sure no one was watching us. Then he leaned toward me to kiss me tenderly.

Chapter Six

The next day was Sunday. Sunday was a day apart, a day that felt different. Slower. After church, we sat down to a light lunch. My happiness from the night before carried over as I gazed around the noisy table.

"Dad planted a bodacious smooch on Mom on the front porch last night," announced William, spreading peanut butter lavishly on a piece of bread.

Robert nearly choked on his coffee. "William, where did you learn that expression?"

"What expression?" he asked, carefully folding his bread in half.

"You know very well what expression I mean, young man," Robert said sternly, a warning look on his face.

"Ernest said he is going to plant a bodacious smooch on Miss Penelope someday."

"Didn't I tell you, Robert? That boy spent too much time at the telegraph office this summer," scolded Aunt Martha.

Robert ignored her. "William, *stop* spying on people."

"But...," he defended, "it was for my spy log!"

Robert scowled at me as if to say, "See what you started?"

I looked down at my plate. Elisabeth mumbled to William to pass the bread but he didn't realize that she was talking to him.

"Elisabeth, you need to look directly at William when you speak so that he can read your lips. Use expression," I pointed out.

She looked at me, puzzled.

"Mit der Gesichtsausdruck." *With facial expression.*

"Oh. Okay," she said earnestly. Then she looked straight at William, and shouted, "Pass dat d--- bread!"

We froze. Aunt Martha gasped, as Robert and I just stared at Elisabeth, stunned.

"What, Dad? What did she say?" asked William, tugging on Robert's sleeve, aware that something interesting had just transpired.

Quietly, Robert picked up the bread and passed it to her. "I don't think that's what Louisa meant by adding expression, Elisabeth."

To my astonishment, a look of mirth flitted through his eyes. Then he tucked his chin down against his chest, trying to cover a broad grin. He was trying so hard not to laugh that he had tears streaming down his face.

I could count on one hand the number of times I had ever seen Robert laugh with abandon. Once he started laughing, he couldn't stop himself. Finally, he broke into gales of laughter.

Robert's amusement with Elisabeth's faux pas only fueled Aunt Martha's aggravation. She stood up, glared at him, and marched upstairs. I'd *never* seen her mad at Robert! Often with me, but never at her beloved nephew. Robert could do no wrong in her eyes. As soon as she was out of hearing range, I started giggling. It felt so good to laugh after the seriousness of the last few weeks. We needed to laugh more often.

Later that evening, I was getting ready for bed and heard mumbled voices down in the kitchen. Mildly ashamed of myself, I unscrewed my radiator cap and listened in. "That child's language must not be tolerated, Robert! To think that a word like that was uttered at your father's table."

"Now, now, Aunt Martha. She'll learn."

"You've got to nip it in the bud," countered Aunt Martha. "Soon enough William will be picking those words up, too."

"Aunt Martha, it's not as if we haven't heard cuss words before. I think most of my congregation leaves half of their vocabulary outside the sanctuary before entering on Sunday."

"Don't joke about this, Robert. I wouldn't expect Louisa to do anything..."

Pardon me? *What* did she mean by *that* remark?

"...but I would certainly expect you, a minister, to hold to higher standards and not laugh at the child. It only encouraged her!"

I screwed the top back on the radiator pipe, not interested in hearing any more of Aunt Martha's parenting advice.

* * * *

On Monday morning, I took Elisabeth to Dr. Singleton for a check-up. Peering at the advanced-in-years doctor, Elisabeth asked in an overloud voice, "Yust how old *are* you?"

Frankly, I had often wondered the same thing because he seemed to be heading into his second or third century. He had more lines on his face than a street map of Tucson. Still, Elisabeth's bluntness was uncalled for. Just as I started to correct her, Dr. Singleton said, "Old enough, young lady." He looked her up and down, frowning. "Well, well. This is going to take some work."

Afterwards, Elisabeth was sent out to the waiting room while the doctor asked to speak with me in his office. "Mrs. Gordon, I've never seen anything like this. She's severely malnourished. Her growth has been stunted. She needs calcium, especially. Her bones, her teeth...well, I just don't know."

"But she'll be all right, won't she?"

"Let's just say it's a good thing you got her out when you did. I'm going to have my nurse draw up a chart that will instruct Martha about how many calories she needs each day. "

"She eats like a horse," I said, quoting Aunt Martha's observation of Elisabeth at last night's dinner.

"Good. Keep her eating. Fatten her up. Lots of bread, cakes and cookies. High calorie food. I'd like to check her again in a month. And she'll need to see a dentist. Soon. Her teeth are in bad condition." He snorted. "The Reverend will be making Dr. Klein a rich dentist!"

I failed to see the humor in that remark.

"So, I want to see her again in a month."

I nodded slowly and started to get up to leave.

The doctor surprised me by saying, "Whoa there, little lady. Not so fast. I understand that you need to have a check-up."

I looked at him curiously.

"Your husband called me this morning."

Ah. I was discovering a new side to Robert. In fact, when I came out of the doctor's examination room, he was waiting, hat in hand, in the doctor's office.

Robert looked worried. "Is everything all right? Is Louisa all right? I mean, with the sea journey...and..."

"Relax, Reverend. Your wife is fine. Your baby is fine."

Robert's face relaxed into a delighted grin. He reached over and squeezed my hand. "Did you hear that, Louisa? Everything is fine." He was beaming. "So I guess the baby is due around March—"

"January," the doctor interrupted.

"Excuse me?" Robert leaned forward in his chair. "When did you say this baby was due?"

"Sometime in late January, I would say."

Robert turned and looked at me curiously. Then he shifted back to the doctor. "Just how far along is Louisa?"

"Four to five months."

Uh oh. I could see the wheels in Robert's mind start to spin.

On the way home, Robert faced the road ahead, hands tightly gripping the steering wheel. "Louisa, did you know that you were...with child...before you left for Germany?"

"I didn't know for sure," I supplied slowly, hoping to ward off follow-up questions. A feeling of dread intensified.

"But you suspected."

Oh dear. "I might have wondered. Once or twice." Or thrice.

Then his face fell dark and set. As he pulled into the driveway, Elisabeth jumped out of the car before Robert cut the engine. As I put one hand on the door handle, Robert turned and said, "Wait a minute, Louisa. Were you ever planning to tell me?"

"Yes. Of course. Soon."

He pierced me with his angry eyes. "This is my baby, too, Louisa. It's one thing to risk your own life by returning to Germany—something I was reluctant to let you do—but you also risked my child's life. You had *no* right to make a decision like that without me. To not let me know."

"I wasn't *trying* to deceive you, Robert. Please don't doubt that."

But he looked at me, and I knew he did. A dark cloud settled between us.

* * * *

Robert had often been irritated with me, quite often, actually, but never angry with me. In fact, I don't think I had ever seen him truly angry. A man with a great deal of self-control, he usually acted as the peacemaker in any conflict. But finding out I knew I was pregnant before I left for Germany sparked an icy response in him. It was like living with a glacier.

He hardly spoke to me. He hardly looked at me. He slept on the davenport in the parlor. Even Aunt Martha, not known for her sensitive streak, noticed his frosty treatment of me. Nothing I could do seemed to thaw him out. We went on for four more days in a similar manner. It should have been a happy time for us, a wonderful homecoming as it had begun, but instead, we steered clear of each other.

One afternoon, I spilled out the telegrams on my bed that he had sent to me on the trip to Germany. I used to read and re-read his telegrams so often during those weeks. I remembered the joy when a new telegram would arrive. Those telegrams helped me to long for my home and my husband. Those telegrams spurred me home.

Hmmm. I picked up a telegram and turned it over. What if I wrote a letter to him even now? I took a piece of paper and started.

Dear Robert, I know you are upset with me, but I feel we should try and discuss this rather than ignore the great gulf between us. Would you be willing to talk? Or maybe to write to me? Love, Louisa.

I put it on his desk when I knew he was out of the church office.

Later that afternoon, I prepared for a piano lesson with Arthur Hobbs. As Aunt Martha saw me lift the piano lid, she announced, "That Arthur is a hopeless case, I hope you know."

"No one is a hopeless case, Aunt Martha," I said with great sincerity. Although privately, I had my doubts about Arthur. He was a music teacher's greatest challenge. He had absolutely no talent whatsoever, nor any interest in music, but his ambitious mother was convinced he was the world's next Mozart.

Just last spring I held a piano recital for my pupils. When it came time for Arthur's turn, he was nowhere to be found. After a frantic search, we found him up in William's tree house, throwing balls down for Dog to chase.

After a great deal of persuasion and a threat of a spanking by his father, Arthur reluctantly agreed to come down from the tree house and play. He marched up to the piano, right in front of everyone, and just stood there.

"Arthur, where is your music?" I asked with a sinking feeling.

He reached a grimy hand into his overalls' pocket, pulled out a balled-up page of music, and sat down to play Bach's *Minuet in G*. Badly. I offered up a silent apology to Mr. Bach, high up in heaven above, hands clapped over his ears, no doubt. It actually hurt to listen to Arthur, but his music put his mother into rhapsodies of happiness.

What really worried me was that Arthur had two younger brothers. Six-year-old twins.

Today, I went to the piano and was surprised to find a letter waiting for me from Robert. I smiled. A promising sign. Perhaps we were finally getting somewhere.

Louisa, I'm just not ready. Robert

I slumped my shoulders and released an audible sigh.
There was a part of me that wanted to write him back:

Dear Robert, I might have replied, you might be annoyed with me, but I am annoyed with you, for being annoyed with me. Am I not a grown woman? Have I not proven myself to live a life of common sense? Good heavens, I was a Resistance Worker. I did not take any undue risks. And I still would make the same decision, to go to Germany for those few short weeks to bring Elisabeth home. I simply could not miss that opportunity.

But I didn't write it to him, and we remained stuck at an impasse.

On the fifth morning after our argument, Robert and Aunt Martha were in the kitchen, talking. I went over to the radiator pipe and unscrewed it. Today, I did not feel a single twinge of guilt. "Crick in your neck, Robert?" asked Aunt Martha.

"Oh, it's that horsehair davenport. If I ever have some spare change, I am getting a new sofa. My mother bought that davenport secondhand when I was in college. I don't know *what* she was thinking."

"She was thinking that there's no reason to keep a stubborn man sleeping too comfortably on the davenport," Aunt Martha responded back tartly.

Then silence descended upon the kitchen. I could just see Robert stiffen his back in the Gordon Way. I couldn't hold back a grin. *Good for you, Aunt Martha!*

A few days later, before the heat of the day was upon me, I started turning the soil for a fall garden. My garden had expanded to a rather sizeable portion of the front yard. I had expected Aunt Martha to object as Robert built more beds for me and hauled in better soil, but I think she enjoyed the compliments the parsonage was getting.

Our neighbor and friend, Ramon, stopped by with his daughter Esmeralda. "Hello, Louisa! Esmeralda wondered if Elisabeth might like to come to play."

"Really? Oh, I think she'd love it! Go in and ask! She's in the kitchen."

Esmeralda scampered up to the front door and burst right in. I turned back to Ramon and smiled happily.

"You feeling well, Louisa?"

William had appointed himself the Town Crier, broadcasting news of our baby to every citizen of Copper Springs whether they were interested or not. "I am. Very well. Thank you for asking."

"Robert must be proud."

I cocked my head. "I hope so."

Ramon raised an eyebrow, but remained quiet.

"I just...well..." Before I knew what I was saying, I spilled out the story.

Ramon listened patiently, nodding at all of the right places. Scratching his chin, he quietly offered, "If my memory serves me right, the first Mrs. Gordon had a habit of not telling him things."

I leaned back on my feet. My heart dropped into my stomach. I had never once linked how Robert might have felt about my keeping something from him, after what Ruth had done. The sting of her betrayal lingered. I shook my head in dismay. *How* could I have missed that? "Thank you, Ramon. You've helped me immeasurably."

Esmeralda and William came out of the house together. "Where's Elisabeth?" I asked.

Esmeralda shrugged.

"She wouldn't come out to play," William volunteered.

I sighed. I should have realized that *nothing* would be easy for Elisabeth, including making friends.

"Another time, Louisa," Ramon said reassuringly, as he followed the children home.

I went in to the house, wrote another letter to Robert, this time with a sincere apology, and a promise to not withhold information from him again. Later that afternoon, I found another letter on the piano.

Dear Louisa, Why don't you start by telling me your real name? Sincerely, Robert

This time, he added a salutation. Perhaps the glacier was thawing.

I went over to the study, knocked on the door and opened it. He looked at me without expression. "Annika. Annika Schumacher. That's the name I was born with. When I went to University, I took my mother's name so I wouldn't be identified as a Jew. Jews weren't allowed to attend University." I turned and opened the door to leave, then turned back again. "But my *real* name is Louisa Gordon." And I closed the door quietly and left.

Later that night, as I was reading in bed, I heard a gentle knock on my door. He poked his head in. "I can't sleep on that lumpy sofa another night."

I leaned over and pulled back the covers on his side of the bed. Robert was half-smiling, a good sign. Our fight was over.

* * * *

"I don't vant to go to no d--- school." Until that improper remark, there had been a resonant peace in the parsonage this morning.

Robert nearly dropped the orange juice pitcher he was holding, Aunt Martha spun around on her heels with jaw wide open, and I, accustomed to Elisabeth's colorful language, darted my eyes nervously between them. Only William remained unperturbed, reading the comic strips in the newspaper. "Elisabeth! Stop using that word" I scolded.

"Vhat vord?" she asked innocently, eyes wide open.

Aunt Martha threw the spatula in the kitchen sink and went outside to hang laundry, slamming the door behind her.

I frowned at Elizabeth and hurried behind Aunt Martha. "I'm sorry."

"Don't say I didn't warn you," replied Aunt Martha, pressing her lips together in that way I loathed. "Where did she learn those awful words anyway?" She glared at me accusingly, as if I had taught her them myself.

"From the sailors on the ship. She was so eager to learn English that she picked up every word she could remember from them."

Disapproval radiated in waves from Aunt Martha. "Can't you do something about her English?"

"Her English?" Was she serious? What about Elisabeth's temper? Or her pain? Or the fact that she didn't trust anyone? Or that she never laughed? Or cried? I walked closer to Aunt Martha and picked up a clothespin that she had dropped on the ground. "There are so many things about Elisabeth we need to do something about. It's overwhelming. She needs time, Aunt Martha. Time to understand what a family is like."

She put the clothespins down and looked straight at me. "And how do you expect her to learn when you kowtow to her every demand?!"

Kowtow? What did that mean? I refused to give her the satisfaction of asking. Unfortunately, she caught the puzzled look on my face.

"I meant that you spoil her."

"Well, right now she needs some spoiling."

With that, Aunt Martha rolled her eyes to heaven.

"I'm trying to develop a relationship with her. I'm not ignoring her behavior. It upsets me, too."

She glared at me. "I'll tell you what else upsets me. Her voice."

"I know." It was true. Elisabeth's German accent coloring her broken English was very guttural and throaty. "German can be a harsh sounding language."

"Do you mean to tell me that entire country talks like they're clearing phlegm from the back of their throat?"

I had to look down to keep from grinning. "Well...I guess that's one way of describing it."

"Thank goodness you don't sound that way."

Thank goodness, indeed! I'm not sure I could have coped with one more category of displeasure from Aunt Martha.

Later that morning, I took fresh coffee in a thermos over to Robert's office. Wincing, I filled his coffee cup and said, "I'm sorry about breakfast."

He only smiled. "Well, Elisabeth has a way of jumpstarting the day." He took a sip of coffee. "Can you stay for a few minutes? I have some gaps about Dietrich I hope you can fill."

I poured a cup of coffee and sat down across from him.

He had a pen and notepad in front of him. "Dietrich and I became acquainted in 1931 while he spent the year at Union Theological Seminary. What happened when he returned to Germany?"

I nodded. "He taught in Berlin until he was forbidden to teach in 1936. After that, he directed an underground seminary for the Confessing Church—a secret community of German pastors who opposed Hitler. He had a profound influence on others. He wrote quite a bit during that period, too. But when the seminary was discovered, the students were immediately inducted into the army."

He leaned forward in his chair, interested. "So is that why he ended up back at Union Theological Seminary?"

"Yes. The invitation came just at the right moment. Many were encouraging Dietrich to leave Germany. He was being heavily censored. He was forbidden to preach or teach or publish. So he went to New York." I tried to think of the dates. "I think that was 1939."

He scribbled down a few lines on his notepad.

"No sooner had he arrived when he decided to return to Germany, no matter what came of it. He took the last ship to sail for Germany before the war." I stopped for a moment, swirling the coffee in my cup. "He felt that unless he was right alongside the German people during the war, he would have no right to lead them after the war." It made me sad to think of Dietrich during this time. If only he had stayed in the United States. If only he hadn't returned to Germany.

"I saw him right before he left," Robert said, interrupting my muse. He poured a second cup of coffee, raising the thermos to see if I wanted a refill. I shook my head.

Curious, I asked, "What were you doing in New York?"

"We were..." he hesitated. "The timing...it was just a coincidence that brought us...me...to New York."

Us? Could he have meant Ruth? Robert *never* spoke of her. Could that mean Dietrich had once met Ruth? I cocked my head to listen carefully.

He swirled in his chair a little so he wasn't facing me. "I had a call to serve as a minister to a church in New York City, so I agreed to go and deliver a sermon." He glanced sideways at me, as if he wasn't sure if he wanted to continue. "Dietrich happened to have been in church that day, so we went out to lunch afterwards. That was when he asked me if I would sponsor someone from Germany, if he ever needed my help."

I remained silent, profoundly touched at how God had been weaving our lives together, years before we met.

He cleared his throat. "So I was offered the pulpit."

I nodded.

"But...I turned it down." With that, Robert ran out of steam. He didn't need to say anything more.

I could guess how this story played out. Ruth wanted Robert to live in New York. She wanted a more exciting life than the one they had in humble Copper Springs. I could imagine how angry she must have been with him when he turned down that opportunity. Not much later, I realized as I started to add up the years, William was born. And soon after, she began a relationship with Friedrich Mueller.

"Maybe I'd better go see if Elisabeth and William are annoying Aunt Martha." I could see it was difficult for Robert to remember back to those years, for his own reasons, and recalling memories of Dietrich during that deteriorating situation in Germany churned me up inside. I picked up the empty thermos and kissed him on the cheek. "Perhaps we can only manage brief discussions about Dietrich."

He gave a short nod of agreement but reached out to squeeze my hand.

After lunch, I told Elisabeth to hurry and brush her teeth so we could go.

"Vhere go ve?" She looked up at me from her bed where she was reading.

"Where are we going?" I corrected. "That's how you should ask that question. Not 'where go we?' You can't translate an English sentence from German construction."

She scowled, but she paid attention. Elisabeth was trying very hard to learn English; she had already made huge strides. On the ship, she mixed German and English in sentences when she didn't know the English words. Now, even if she didn't get the right word, she rarely resorted to German anymore. I couldn't help but admire her determination.

"So vhere are ve going?" she asked.

"Over to Rosita's. She has some hand-me-downs from Esmeralda to give you for school."

"Vhat is dat?"

"Hand-me-downs?" With delight, I realized it was the first American colloquialism that I'd ever used. Frankly, the first one I understood. "Dresses that Esmeralda has outgrown." Even though Esmeralda was younger than Elisabeth, she was much taller and filled out, more like her mother's generously sized figure.

I sat on a bed while Rosita cleaned out Esmeralda's closet, tossing outgrown clothes into a large pile on the floor. Esmeralda was downstairs trying to teach Elisabeth and William how to play "Go Fish" with a deck of cards.

"So how is it going, Louisa?" asked Rosita.

"Harder than I thought it would be," I answered honestly.

"She looks like a tough cookie."

"She is. Inside and out. I hope her looks will soften when she starts to put some weight on. And when her hair grows. We've already been to the doctor. He's put her on a diet to gain weight."

"I didn't know there was such a thing!" Rosita laughed, patting her round bottom.

Just then, the girls came upstairs. Elisabeth's eyes grew as round as saucers as she saw the pile of clothes on the floor. She looked up at the closet, which was still overflowing with clothes. "Dat is a sin!" she announced, pointing at the pile of clothes.

The very Catholic Rosita gasped. "*What* is a sin?" Quickly, she pulled out her Rosary beads from her skirt pocket.

"To make such vaste. Is a sin!"

"Elisabeth!" I scolded, but she turned and ran down the stairs and back home. I looked at Rosita. "I'm so sorry. She doesn't know...she's been in such a terrible environment...please don't take that comment seriously. She doesn't understand how she can hurt people."

The pained look on Rosita's face crumpled into the big toothy grin I loved so well. "Louisa, welcome to parenthood."

We gathered up the clothes into a few bags, and William helped me carry them home.

"Did Elisabeth say something bad?" he asked, looking up at me.

I stopped to look directly at him. "Not bad. Just not...good."

"I think she does that a lot."

I smiled. "I think you're right."

"But I found something good."

"Really? What?"

"Aunt Martha hasn't said anything mean about Dog since Elisabeth came to stay with us."

It was true. Aunt Martha had been so busy complaining about Elisabeth that she had hardly noticed Dog's latest indiscretions. Just last night, he had rummaged through the garbage can, but all that Aunt Martha said was, "You'd think no one ever fed that creature."

Thinking about Dog filled me with sadness. It was starting to look as if we might have to find a new home for him. Elisabeth was terrified whenever he came near her, so we kept him outside, on the line. When I mentioned my worry to Robert, he looked stricken. He said he would keep Dog with him in the church study during the day. But that wasn't fair to Dog. He was meant to be a boy's dog, not a minister's footstool.

I didn't know what to do about this situation; Elisabeth's fears were very real. She had already had a few bad dreams about Dog, waking up in a cold sweat, shouting "Das hund!" *The dog!*

I looked down at William's sandy-blond head, holding two big bags of clothes in his little arms. He had a way of catching me in the heart. "William, do you know you're my boy?"

He nodded up at me solemnly. "And Elisabeth is your girl."

I gulped. I really didn't feel much love for Elisabeth, only a sense of familial obligation, and a steadily growing annoyance. But love? Not yet, but I was working on it. To William, I nodded enthusiastically.

When we got home, I took the clothes and a box of straight pins into Elisabeth's room. "I'd like to have you try these on so I can tailor them to you. School starts in just a few weeks, so I'll need to get busy adjusting them for you."

She acted disinterested but got up to see the clothes. She pulled off her shirt and pants to try on one dress. I forced my eyes away from her body. It was nearly skeletal. I could count her ribs, and her scapula looked more like chicken wings than shoulder blades. It melted my heart toward her.

As I pinned up the hem on one dress, I said, "This reminds me of when I first arrived in Copper Springs. Rosita gave me clothes to wear. I didn't have very many, and the ones I brought with me from Germany were threadbare."

"Dey are rich," she announced.

"No. They're not rich. They're like we are."

"Den vhy she give me da clothes?"

"Rosita is extremely generous. Kind-hearted, too. She has provided a great help to you, Elisabeth. Did you know we haven't even been able to buy new shoes in America?"

"Vhy not?"

"There was a ban on shoe making and all kinds of other things so every resource could go toward fighting the war. You wouldn't have these shoes to wear if it weren't for Esmeralda."

She looked down at the secondhand shoes on her small feet.

I glanced up at her. "Don't you think you should apologize for telling her she sinned by having so many clothes?"

"No. She did sin. People in da vorld need da clothes, and she has too many."

"Elisabeth, you're not in the camp any more. It's over."

"Sprichst du nicht davon!" she spat at me. *Speak not of it!* She clapped her hands on her ears and scowled darkly at me.

O Lord, give me patience! I prayed silently. I finished adjusting the rest of the clothes and then left her alone.

At dinner that evening, William said, "Pass that d--- spinach, please."

Aunt Martha nearly suffered a heart attack. Robert froze his fork in mid-air. He glanced at me and raised an eyebrow. Then he said, "William, please don't use that word."

"What word?" William asked.

I glared at Elisabeth, who had an angelic expression on her face. When she felt my eyes on her, she quickly looked down at her plate and put her hand over her mouth to hide a grin.

Robert cast a glance at Aunt Martha. "We'll discuss it later."

"Okay." William returned to eating then remembered something in his pocket. He pulled out the log from his latest spywork and showed me his notes. "Is this the kind of thing you did when you worked with the Resistance?" he asked me.

"Vhat?" interrupted Elisabeth.

"Elisabeth, didn't you know Louisa was part of the Resistance Movement?" asked Robert.

"No," she said, cocking her head as she looked at me. "So you did do someting to fight the var. Not yust sit here in America and read da newspaper stories?"

I didn't think this day could get any harder with Elisabeth, but it just had. I couldn't stand being at the same table with her another moment. I pushed my plate away. "Please excuse me," I said. "I need some fresh air." I went outside on the front porch, leaned against the railing, and watched the evening sky, fighting back tears.

Robert came outside. He put his arm around my shoulder and pulled me close, tucking my head under his chin. "You can't let her get to you, Louisa. She wants to upset you."

"I know," I said. "But I think I might have made a mistake bringing her here. I think she's upsetting the entire family."

"Actually, I kind of get a kick out of her."

I leaned my head back to search his eyes. "Really? You don't mind her?"

"No. There's something rather endearing about her. And I can't help but admire her. Imagine surviving a camp like that. That takes someone with an astonishing amount of inner strength."

He was absolutely right about that. "I'm glad you can see something good in her. Aunt Martha says she's as mean as a snake."

"Well, she isn't rude to me like she is to you. You're the lucky one," he added.

I frowned at him.

"Look at it this way, Louisa. She knows you're committed to her. She knows you're her family. You went all the way to Germany to prove that to her. She feels safe with you. She's counting on you. Ironically, that's why she treats you badly."

"Do you know what bothers me the most? She acts as though she's the only one who has suffered in that war. And to be fair, she has suffered more. I can't deny that."

"I think she wants us all to feel some of her pain."

"I worry that she has been hobbled, that she'll never be whole again. Sometimes I think there's a part of her that's missing now. She has no understanding of anything or anyone except how it affects her."

"I don't think it's missing. I think it's frozen." He watched the changing sky for a few moments. "Have you ever told Elisabeth that you tried to find her and her mother?"

"No. Any time I bring up it up, she puts her hands on her ears and tells me she doesn't want to hear it."

"I wonder if that could be why she seems so angry with you. She thinks you could have saved them if you had tried."

"But I *did* try."

"I know that." He brushed some wisps of hair off of my forehead. "Did you ever meet that boy she talks about so much?"

"Danny? No. I wish I had. I didn't realize how important he was to her."

"No kidding. Sounds as if he gave her the determination to survive the camp."

"I've had the same thought. All I know about him was what—" I stopped abruptly. I had never mentioned Karl's name to Robert and had no plans to. "The case worker said they were still trying to locate a relative of Danny."

"Hope they find one soon. Everybody needs family." Robert turned to go inside. "You know, Louisa, you treat Elisabeth as if she's made of spun sugar. I think she's a lot tougher than you're giving her credit."

I stayed outside a little longer, watching the sunset. *Lord, take over,* I prayed. *Remove this tension and frustration. Fill me with your peace and power.* As the sun slipped behind the mountain, the Lord did not disappoint me.

* * * *

The next day, after receiving a few more blunt remarks from Elisabeth that punctuated breakfast, Aunt Martha looked out the kitchen window at Elisabeth and William as they hung laundry outside on the clothes line. "She's da vorst," said Aunt Martha.

I burst out laughing. "You're right! She is da vorst." Laughter was a tremendous gift. How ironic that Aunt Martha, a woman of little humor, reminded me of that.

All day, I mulled over Robert's remark that I treated Elisabeth like spun sugar. I decided that I was going about this the wrong way. Trying to love Elisabeth through unbending kindness wasn't working. In fact, it only made her sharp tongue a little keener. Loving Elisabeth meant giving her clear limits.

At breakfast, she gave me a chance to try my new parenting method.

"Who made dis pancake?" Elisabeth demanded.

"I did," I shot back. "Don't you like it?"

"It's da vorst," Elisabeth said vigorously. "Yust like eating a tire."

I leveled my eyes on Elisabeth's and stared straight at her. "Don't eat it, then."

Robert and Aunt Martha watched the exchange between us in astonishment.

"I did not say I vould not eat it. I only said it vas da vorst pancake ever." Nonchalantly, she resumed eating. "Maybe da vorst pancake in da vorld."

Afterwards, as Aunt Martha washed dishes, she turned to me and asked, "Weren't you a little hard on her?"

"I think the time has come," I answered, putting the glass milk container back in the refrigerator.

"Hmm." She turned back to the sink. "And to think I thought you couldn't mash a mango."

"I would have no trouble mashing a mango, Aunt Martha. Any mango," I replied with great confidence. I would have to remember to look up "mango" in the dictionary later.

After that morning, I noticed a slow, glacially slow, improvement in Elisabeth's behavior. I felt quite encouraged, thinking we were actually making some progress. That feeling of well-being lasted just a few days, evaporating when I heard Aunt Martha shriek hysterically. I ran upstairs. Aunt Martha was in Elisabeth's room, pointing at the bed as if a dead body might be stuffed underneath. "Look! Look what's there!"

Gingerly, I crouched down and reached under the bed, pulling out a pillow case full of rotting food. "Oh no." My heart sank. Elisabeth had hoarded food on the ship, too, but I thought it was just an isolated situation because she was in such a temporary environment.

"That girl is the limit! She is the *limit!* Such waste! No wonder Dog is always trying to get in here."

Out of the pillow case I pulled bruised apples, shriveled oranges turned green with fuzz, moldy bread.

"When has she been getting this food?" asked Aunt Martha.

I cringed. "I thought I've heard someone downstairs in the night."

"What would make her behave so peculiarly?"

"Not so peculiar when you remember that she spent the last year starving."

I looked under the bed again and found another filled pillow case. Aunt Martha took the pillow cases and emptied them into the garbage, with a flourish.

I went into my bedroom and took out newspapers that I had saved from my trip to Germany. They had pictures of the camps, taken by American news reporters as they followed Allied soldiers into the camps. I also had a transcript from Edward R. Murrow as he went through Buchenwald just after it was liberated.

"Aunt Martha, this is very upsetting, but please read this over. Buchenwald was where Dietrich Bonhoeffer had been held for a while. And look at these pictures I took of Dachau with William's camera. That's the camp where Elisabeth was imprisoned."

She frowned at me but sat down at the kitchen table and read the following:

Edward R. Murrow's Report From Buchenwald

Legendary CBS reporter Edward R. Murrow described the scene at Buchenwald when he entered the camp after liberation:

There surged around me an evil-smelling stink, men and boys reached out to touch me. They were in rags and the remnants of uniforms. Death already had marked many of them, but they were smiling with their eyes. I looked out over the mass of men to the green fields beyond, where well-fed Germans were ploughing...

I asked to see one of the barracks. It happened to be occupied by Czechoslovaks. When I entered, men crowded around, tried to lift me to their shoulders. They were too weak. Many of them could not get out of bed. I was told that this building had once stabled 80 horses. There were 1200 men in it, five to a bunk. The stink was beyond all description.

They called the doctor. We inspected his records. There were only names in the little black book - nothing more - nothing about who had been where, what he had done or hoped. Behind the names of those who had died, there was a cross. I counted them. They totaled 242 - 242 out of 1200, in one month.

As we walked out into the courtyard, a man fell dead. Two others, they must have been over 60, were crawling toward the latrine. I saw it, but will not describe it.

In another part of the camp they showed me the children, hundreds of them. Some were only 6 years old. One rolled up his sleeves, showed me his number. It was tattooed on his arm. B-6030, it was. The others showed me their numbers. They will carry them till they die. An elderly man standing beside me said: "The children were enemies of the state!" I could see their ribs through their thin shirts...

We went to the hospital. It was full. The doctor told me that 200 had died the day before. I asked the cause of death. He shrugged and said: "tuberculosis, starvation, fatigue and there are many who have no desire to live. It is very difficult." He pulled back the blanket from a man's feet to show me how swollen they were. The man was dead. Most of the patients could not move.

I asked to see the kitchen. It was clean. The German in charge...showed me the daily ration. One piece of brown bread about as thick as your thumb, on top of it a piece of margarine as big as three sticks of chewing gum. That, and a little stew, was what they received every 24 hours. He had a chart on the wall. Very complicated it was. There were little red tabs scattered through it. He said that was to indicate each 10 *men who died. He had to account for the rations and he added: "We're very efficient here."*

We proceeded to the small courtyard. The wall adjoined what had been a stable or garage. We entered. It was floored with concrete. There were two rows of bodies stacked up like cordwood. They were thin and very white. Some of the bodies were terribly bruised; though there seemed to be little flesh to bruise. Some had been shot through the head, but they bled but little.

I arrived at the conclusion that all that was mortal of more than 500 men and boys lay there in two neat piles. There was a German trailer, which must have contained another 50, but it wasn't possible to count them. The clothing was piled in a heap against the wall. It appeared that most of the men and boys had died of starvation; they had not been executed.

But the manner of death seemed unimportant. Murder had been done at Buchenwald. God alone knows how many men and boys have died there during the last 12 years. Thursday, I was told that there were more than 20,000 in the camp. There had been as many as 60,000. Where are they now?

I pray you to believe what I have said about Buchenwald. I reported what I saw and heard, but only part of it. For most of it, I have no words.

If I have offended you by this rather mild account of Buchenwald, I'm not in the least sorry...

Edward R. Murrow - April 16, 1945.

Aunt Martha finished reading and looked at me with a grave face. "I...knew it was bad...but...I had no idea."

"I know. Not many people knew about these camps. And not many people want to know about them." Including Aunt Martha. She had heard news reports just like I did, but she just hadn't given it much thought. Until now.

"Have you shown this to Robert?"

"Robert saw all of this when I returned. I should have shown you when I first arrived. It's just...terribly hard to stomach. I don't even want Elisabeth to know that I took those pictures." I gathered the papers and turned to go upstairs. "I'll make sure she doesn't hide food in her room anymore."

Aunt Martha stood up and went over to the kitchen window, gazing outside at Dog, tied up to the tree, looking woeful as Elisabeth and William played hopscotch on the driveway. Then she turned back to me and said crisply, "Just make sure she doesn't hide food that needs to be refrigerated."

I glanced at her, astonished. For once, she sensed the spirit behind the rules. "I'll do that, Aunt Martha."

I had found something else under Elisabeth's bed. It was one of Esmeralda's skirts, but not one that Rosita had given to us. One that Elisabeth had taken without permission. When Elisabeth came back inside, I was waiting for her upstairs. "We have to have a talk." I held up the skirt.

Her eyes darted to the skirt. "No talk. I'm tired. My stomach hurts," she said, flopping on her bed.

"Elisabeth, you took something that didn't belong to you."

"So vhat? Dey are rich."

"They're not rich. They're our friends. And it doesn't matter whether they're rich or whether they're our friends. You *stole* something."

She sat up slowly on the bed and fixed her eyes with a level stare. "I not steal noting. I organize tings."

"What are you talking about?"

"I vas da organizer in dat camp."

I sat down on the bed next to her. "What do you mean by organizer?"

"I found tings for people."

Oh! She was the *scrounger*. That shouldn't have surprised me. She was a clever and observant girl. Shrewd, too.

"I organized da lunch from da guards. I could have been shot."

"You were hungry."

"So vas dat stealing?"

I looked at her large, inquisitive brown eyes. "Elisabeth, you *needed* food. There's a difference between wanting something and needing it."

She pointed to the skirt in my hands. "I need dat."

"No. You *want* that skirt. You have to take the skirt back to Esmeralda and apologize to her. And tell her that you won't take anything from her again."

She narrowed her eyes. "Vhy did you come and get me?"

I clapped my eyes on hers. "Don't you remember? I told you I wanted you to know you are not alone."

Elisabeth glared at me, but she got off the bed and we went over to the Gonsalvez' to confess the day's crime.

Chapter Seven

The judge had been coming around the parsonage rather frequently, even if Robert wasn't home. He would drink coffee in the kitchen and chat while Aunt Martha would iron or wash dishes, a part of the family. Robert thought he was just lonely, but I had a feeling there was more to his visits.

Tonight, as the judge walked into the kitchen just in time for dinner, he sniffed the air. "Martha, I don't believe incense in a cathedral could be any more pleasing than the scent of chocolate lingering in the air."

Aunt Martha cast him a shy sideways glance and blushed. She *blushed!*

We actually had a surprisingly insult-free evening with Elisabeth, who loved Aunt Martha's chocolate cake. Aunt Martha even gave her two slices. "Tante Marta, you are da best cook." Eyes glinting, she added, "But Louisa is da vorst cook."

"True, but not reassuring," I agreed, laughing with the others.

"You're absolutely right, Elisabeth. We'd be up the creek without a paddle if we didn't have Aunt Martha," agreed Robert, humor lighting up his eyes.

"Well, I'm not going anywhere," chided Aunt Martha, looking pleased.

Afterwards, Robert and the judge sipped coffee at the table while Aunt Martha and I washed and dried dishes. William and Elisabeth had gone upstairs.

"You're quiet tonight, Judge," Robert observed, passing him the cream pitcher.

The judge stirred cream into his coffee. "For the longest while, Elisabeth reminded me of someone but I couldn't quite place whom. It just hit me. She reminds me of Alice."

Aunt Martha dropped a glass into the sink, shattering it. Robert shot a warning glance at the judge, whose eyes went wide with surprise and concern, as if he suddenly realized the magnitude of his remark.

"Who's Alice?" I asked, pulling a dry tea towel out of the cabinet. A reasonable question, it seemed.

Robert kept his eyes on his coffee, frowning. His mouth tightened; finally, he said, his voice flat, "Alice was my sister."

Now I nearly dropped the dish I was wiping dry. "Your sister? You have a sister?"

"Had. I had a sister."

"Now, Robert," said Aunt Martha.

"I need to get some work done tonight," he said abruptly, departing quickly through the kitchen door.

I looked at Aunt Martha. "Don't look at me," she warned. "She's his sister."

I turned to the judge, who only shrugged and made a quick exit.

Briefly, I thought about leaving it alone. I *really* did. But then I dismissed it. I put down the tea towel and walked over to Robert's office, knocking gently on the door before opening it. He didn't look up as I came in. I stood behind him and wrapped my arms around his shoulders.

He settled into a cautious smile. "I know what you're thinking," he said, although I hadn't said a word out loud. "You're after information. I know these things. I'm married to a Resistance Worker."

"And one who is particularly skilled at overcoming Gordon Resistance."

He laughed. An encouraging sign! "Robert, why didn't you ever tell me you had a sister? Is she buried in the cemetery? I've never seen another Gordon grave." I had looked with great interest when I first arrived. Information about this family was always given in short supply, sparsely handed out on a need-to-know basis.

Robert sighed. "I didn't mean to keep it from you. I just...don't really think about her anymore."

"When did she die?"

"Well, she...didn't."

I stood straight up. "She's alive? And you don't keep in touch with her?"

He spun around in his chair to face me. "Exactly why I didn't tell you! I knew you would badger me to find her."

I crossed my arms and scowled at him. "Would that be such a bad thing?"

"Alice *chose* to leave home as a teenager." He peered at me. "A pregnant teenager. She ran off, married the father of her baby, and she's never been back."

"And you haven't tried to find her?"

"Louisa, I'm the one who *hasn't* moved. *She's* the one who left."

"When did you last see her?"

"The day she left home. I sent her a telegram when our parents died, hoping she would come to the funeral, but she never responded. So I gave up."

"Was she older or younger than you?"

"Older. By a year or so."

Mentally, I quickly calculated their ages. It must have been nearly twenty years since they had seen each other. I leaned one hip against his desk. "Does Elisabeth remind you of her?"

Robert gave me one of his straight-in-the-eyes looks. "Remarkably so. Argumentative, pugnacious, and combative."

And probably the very reason he was so fond of Elisabeth.

I scooted up onto the desk. "Do you realize you've never really told me what your parents were like?"

He leaned back in his chair, hands folded behind his head as he decided how to answer me. "My mother was kind, but shy as a deer. Completely intimidated by my father. He was very responsible, very proper and very, very sure he was right about everything."

I tilted my head but said nothing, hoping he would continue.

"My father raised us up to fear the Lord, and for a long time, I did just that. I did only that. Truth be told, I think it was through meeting Dietrich that I first started to understand there was more to God than fear."

Then he grew quiet, as if he had said all that he wanted to say. He looked up at me. "About my sister, Louisa, please drop it. It was a long time ago, and some things are best left alone."

"It just surprises me."

"Well, I suppose I should have told you. Her behavior was just not something I was very proud of."

"Oh, I understand. People make mistakes. It's you, though. You surprise me."

He looked puzzled. "Why? What have *I* done?"

"You've always been a peacemaker, Robert. You build bridges between people. I've seen you do it again and again. Why wouldn't you want to do it in your own family?"

He stiffened his spine.

"You can't abandon your own family."

"I didn't abandon anyone," he said curtly. "Did it ever occur to you that she doesn't want to be connected with her family? That this was her choice? Not *everyone* wants to be found, Louisa."

"You're wrong, Robert. Everyone wants to belong to someone."

He looked down at his desk.

"So her name is Alice?" I looked at him, waiting for him to fill in the blanks. "Alice...?"

He eyed me suspiciously. "Alice O'Casey. She married a Catholic boy—one of my father's chief objections. But that marriage didn't last. And she has since remarried."

I hopped off his desk. "Your father would not have approved of me, would he?" I looked at him carefully to read his response.

Robert's face looked pained. "No. He wouldn't have approved of you, being half-Jewish. Maybe even worse is the fact you're German. He had fought in World War I and never forgave the Germans."

It just seemed so unfair. For a moment, I had a glimpse of Elisabeth's life. Blamed by everyone.

Robert took my hand and sought my eyes. "But if he would have been willing to get to know you, he would have loved you."

What he was really saying was that his father would never have been willing to get to know me.

"My mother was softer."

I gave him a half-smile. "So what is Alice's new name?"

"I honestly don't know her new married name."

I looked at him skeptically.

He released my hand. "I really, truly don't know, Louisa."

"What about her baby?"

"A boy. I don't know where he is now."

"Well, would you mind if I tried to find Alice?"

He folded his arms on his desk and clunked his head down on his arms in despair.

I turned and left, taking that for a "yes."

When I returned to the kitchen, Aunt Martha had already gone upstairs to bed. To avoid me, no doubt. She probably wasn't going to divulge any information that Robert hadn't told me. Even though I now shared the Gordon name, Aunt Martha did not view me as one of her clan. I knew she cared about me, in her own way, but I was still an outsider.

I gathered my facts. Alice would be in her mid-thirties now. I assumed she had married a local boy, which meant that there might be a family in town who had a connection to Alice, her husband, and her baby. And there was only one person in this town with a network of connections. I would have to look for a moment alone with the judge.

* * * *

"Mail's here," Robert called as he came through the front door. "Elisabeth, there's a letter for you!"

Elisabeth flew down the stairs and grabbed the letter from him. "Von Danny!" she screamed at the top of her lungs. She flew back up the stairs and slammed her bedroom door shut.

Robert's eyebrows shot up when he heard the door slam. "Good thing you thought to give Danny our address," he said, heading into the kitchen.

But I hadn't. Karl Schneider must have given it to him.

Suddenly I heard a shout from the kitchen. Waving a letter, Robert had a broad smile on his face. "It's been accepted! They want to publish my book!" He grabbed me for a hug, lifting me off of my feet, not even caring that William and Aunt Martha were watching.

* * * *

A few days later, school began for Elisabeth. Dog's respite could finally begin. He would be allowed off of the line in the backyard and given his freedom, at least until three p.m. when she was due back home. Elisabeth was still terrified of Dog. The night before school started, she peered at him out the window and said, "Dat dog has yaws as big as eine krokodilklemme." *That dog has jaws as big as a crocodile.*

I had enrolled her in eighth grade a few days earlier. We walked around the school three times so she could find her classrooms. She laid out the clothes she wanted to wear, changing the outfit every few hours. On the first day of school, she woke me at dawn to help style her hair. There wasn't much I could do, it was still so wispy and short, but I tried my best. She didn't want me to go to school with her, so Esmeralda agreed to walk with her.

As the girls went down the street together, my heart ached. The contrast between them was shocking. Esmeralda looked happy, relaxed, arms swinging at her side. Elisabeth looked unhappy, tense, arms clasped against her abdomen as if her stomach hurt. I prayed for her as I watched her head down the street. I prayed that the other children would be kind to her, that her teachers would be merciful. I prayed for her confidence, her peace, her joy. *Give her joy, Lord.*

As the girls turned the corner out of sight, I shifted my attention to William. His head was bent over the newspaper, much like Robert's habit, reading every detail of the sports page. His mind was still a sponge, soaking up any and all information. I needed to keep his mind busy, but was starting to feel concerned about how to keep ahead of him.

My curriculum came out of the library, where we were reading through books on any and all subjects. "William?" I asked, gently patting his elbow so he would look at me. "Today is your first day of school, too."

Aunt Martha was upstairs, changing bed sheets. An opportune time for a science experiment. "Science, first!" I pulled out the baking soda and vinegar, and found a plate. "We're going to study chemistry. Cause and effect." I piled up the baking soda and had William spoon drops of vinegar on top, eliciting a hiss and sizzle.

His eyes were transfixed. "That's the best thing I've ever done!" he said. "We have to show Elisabeth when she gets home." We added more vinegar to the baking soda for added fizzles, then quickly cleaned up. I opened the kitchen door to air out the sour vinegar smell.

"Time to get to the library," I told him, hoping to leave before Aunt Martha came down the stairs. Dog's ears perked up when I picked up his leash. He liked to stand sentry guard at the library door.

On the way to the library, William said, "Did you know that Josiah was only eight-years-old when he became king?"

I stopped and looked at him, amazed. "How did you know that?"

"I was in Dad's office yesterday when he was working on a sermon. He told me all about Josiah. Can you believe it? I'm almost eight!"

Just nine months to go, I thought, grinning. "Josiah was a good king, too."

"I know. Dad told me. His father and his grandfather were bad, but Josiah was good."

I nodded.

"I think that maybe I'll be a minister someday. Like Dad."

I smiled.

"Think I could?" he asked, searching my eyes for my response.

"I think you could be whatever you want to be."

His eyes looked solemn. "But do you think I'd be a good minister?"

"You'd be a wonderful minister, William."

He nodded earnestly. "But I might be a professional baseball player. Maybe for the Cubs." The Chicago Cubs were his favorite team. He was counting on them to go to the World Series this year.

It would snow in July in Copper Springs before that would ever happen, Robert told me.

At the library, we quickly settled into our routine. After picking out a book, I sat in front of William and read it aloud as he watched my lips move. Then he would read the text aloud to me, as I corrected his pronunciation. Then I would read the text again, as he watched me, so he could practice. We had been doing this for months, instructed by William's tutor in Bisbee.

This morning, I noticed that he rarely interrupted me as I read aloud. Just six months ago, I was reading very slowly; he would stop me, every few words, to check the words in the book to see what I was saying. His lip reading had galloped along into a high level of proficiency this summer. Just last week, his tutor labeled him a champion lip reader.

Afterwards, he searched through the shelves for interesting books. I gazed at him, amazed at how tall he had grown this summer. I wondered how long that irrepressible cowlick on his forehead would last. He hardly resembled the little four-year-old boy I met when I first arrived in Copper Springs, who peered at me with large, serious eyes and stole my heart the night he slipped his hand in mine as we watched the sun set. When we came home for lunch, I kept one eye peeled on the kitchen clock.

"Watching that clock won't make it turn any faster," said Aunt Martha. "You're fidgeting worse than a dog with fleas."

I sighed. "I know. I just keep wondering how she's doing."

"She'll do just fine. She needs school to keep her mind off of complaining."

True, but I had an odd, sinking feeling about whether the school needed her.

Finally, three o'clock rolled around. Elisabeth burst into the door, stomped up the stairs and slammed her bedroom door. William, Aunt Martha and I watched helplessly.

A few minutes later, Robert came in from the office. "Louisa, the principal called and wants to see you. Right now." He gave me a concerned look. "Shall I come?"

"No, I'm sure it's nothing. Probably just paperwork," I said hopefully.

I walked to school, grateful for a few quiet minutes in the day to collect my thoughts. There were, to be sure, a few concerns.

Principal Olasky was a woman who looked perpetually worried, as if wild dogs were following her. She met me with a grim face. We sat facing each other in her office as I braced myself for the litany of complaints.

"Mrs. Gordon, the day did not go well with Elisabeth."

"How so?" I asked.

"Oh, where to begin?" she answered as her hands flew up in the air in despair. "First, she has a number of gaps in her knowledge, significant gaps, not to mention that her English is quite poor."

I relaxed. These were not unexpected problems. "She understands more than you might think. It's just not easy for her to speak yet. But she's made remarkable progress in just one month's time," I said.

The principal ignored my defense. "And secondly, her behavior is a problem."

My eyebrows flickered up. "What kind of behavior problem?"

"She's extremely rude. In first period, she told Mrs. Graham she was fat! In second period, she told Mr. Koops, her history teacher, that he was incorrect in his knowledge of world politics. And in physical education class, she refused to change clothes with the other girls. Then, during lunch recess, she whacked a boy with her book pack."

Oh dear. This was worse than I feared. "Do you have any idea why she hit him?"

"It doesn't matter. We can't tolerate violence."

I bit my lip, trying to listen patiently. "Anything else?"

Mrs. Olasky frowned. "Isn't that enough for one day?"

"Well, it was only her first day. We need to anticipate an adjustment period. She's not exactly a typical student from Copper Springs."

"Mrs. Gordon, I need to have some assurance that this kind of thing won't be happening every day. Frankly, I'm not even sure she is ready for this grade level. Perhaps she should be at a lower grade. She might be more comfortable. She's so small, too. It might be a better fit for her to be in grade six. Or maybe even grade five."

Obviously, Mrs. Olasky was not concerned about Elisabeth's best interests. "Would you mind doing me a favor?" I asked, which immediately ratcheted Mrs. Olasky's perpetually worried-look up a notch. "Tomorrow, after school, I'd like to speak to Elisabeth's teachers."

She hesitated, which I took to be a yes and quickly made my exit, promising to return tomorrow afternoon.

The next morning, I stood at the kitchen window, staring down the dawn of a new day. And still I didn't know what I was going to do.

At three o'clock that afternoon, I put on a neat navy skirt and crisp linen blouse. I brushed my hair smooth. I was armed and prepared for battle. Robert volunteered to come with me for moral support.

At the school, I faced Elisabeth's teachers, already seated. One man radiated disapproval, but there was a young woman—who was no more than twenty-one-years old—who watched me with interest. I took a deep breath, trying to sound braver than I felt. "I am Louisa Gordon. Most of you know my husband, Robert." The faces turned to look at him. "Elisabeth is my cousin from Germany. I realize she is not a typical student for you."

"I'll say," said the disapproving man, whom I quickly surmised to be Mr. Koops. "Today she told me that I should change the boundaries on my map of the Middle East because Israel is going to become a nation." He looked at the other teachers, shaking his head, as if to say, "Can you imagine trying to teach a child with ideas like that?"

Actually, I wanted to say, Elisabeth was correct. Just last month, the Zionist World Congress had approached the British government to discuss the founding of Israel. But Robert stepped next to me and flashed me a warning look, trying to convey that now was *not* the moment to point out Mr. Koops' error. Robert was right; I had a more important task at hand. "Elisabeth has been rescued out of a concentration camp in Germany." I paused. As expected, they looked at me blankly.

"Don't you mean a labor camp?" asked a rather generously proportioned woman, whom I quickly deduced to be Mrs. Graham. "Like the internment camps for the Japanese?"

"No. *Not* like the internment camps for the Japanese- *Americans*," I added for emphasis. "The Nazis created the concentration camps to imprison the population of Jewish people, as well as others, whom they wanted to annihilate. They killed millions of innocent men, women and children in these camps."

"Mrs. Gordon," said Mr. Koops with an air of condescension. "Those news reports are greatly exaggerated. There are conflicting reports."

A surge of anger rose inside me toward this ill informed man. I deliberately avoided Robert's eyes. "Mr. Koops," I said, slowly and carefully, as if I was speaking to a dense child, "I traveled to Germany this last summer to get Elisabeth and went through the very camp where she had been imprisoned."

I opened the file in my lap and took out the pictures I had taken of Dachau, including those of stacks of corpses. One by one, I handed them to the teachers and let the pictures tell the story. The room was silent, punctuated by gasps now and then. Two teachers reached for a handkerchief. Mr. Koops barely glanced at the pictures, passing them quickly down the row.

"I also have newspaper articles taken by first hand sources, if you would like to read them." I put the file on the desk. "Somehow, Elisabeth survived in that camp. She *survived*. One of her jobs was to separate soles from used shoes. When I picked her up at the Red Cross Center, her hands were still raw from picking at stitching and pulling at the leather. On her left forearm is a tattoo. That was her identification at the camp. She wants to save up money to have it removed. She wants to forget everything about the camp. She won't discuss it; I ask that you respect her wishes. In fact, I think it would upset her to know that I was here today. We are trying to help her gain back her health and her strength."

I paused for a moment to gauge their reaction. "Mrs. Rimer, the reason Elisabeth doesn't want to change clothes in front of the girls is because she's so self-conscious about her body. She weighed only sixty-seven pounds when I found her this summer. And Mrs. Graham, the reason she asked you about your..." *Uh oh. How should I word this?* "Well, she's trying so hard to gain weight. She didn't mean to insult you. Elisabeth's feisty nature, what you're seeing in your classes, is what helped her to survive the camp. If you will give her a chance, she will meet your expectations. But she needs time and patience."

The teachers nodded sympathetically. All but Mr. Koops. "Why was she in a camp?" he asked.

"She is Jewish." And then, in his eyes, I saw it. A flicker of hostility.

Mr. Koops looked at the other teachers. "A child like Elisabeth will take an enormous amount of work for these teachers, not to mention the fact that she disrupts the rest of the classroom with her impudence. Personally, I think she has the kind of personality that asks for trouble."

"Meaning what?" I asked, frustration rising in my voice.

"Meaning she'll never fit in. She won't make friends."

"There is nothing *wrong* with Elisabeth. She has been cruelly mistreated and needs time to recover." My temper was teetering on the brink of explosion.

He stood and narrowed his eyes. "That girl is Germany's problem. Germany started this. Germany should finish it. It shouldn't be up to the American government to try to educate her. If she even can be educated! You can't shovel out a load of work for the rest of us by sending a child like her to school and expect us to fix her."

That *did* it! I took a deep breath and started to collect my thoughts to give Mr. Koops a full and complete understanding of what was wrong with him when Robert squeezed a warning on my arm.

"Her immigration paperwork is in order, Erik," Robert answered in a calm voice. "She's in the United States legally on a student visa."

Mr. Koops was unimpressed. "Nonetheless—"

"I believe your parents were immigrants, weren't they, Erik? Wasn't your father about Elisabeth's age when he arrived in America from Holland?"

Mr. Koops frowned.

"I remember hearing stories about how your father struggled with the English language. Even came to school wearing wooden clogs. And look at him now. He owns his own hardware store. Best hardware store in the county."

Mr. Koops's face lost that tight tension. "That's beside the point."

"But that's exactly his point, Mr. Koops," said Miss Howard, the young teacher who smiled at me when I walked in. "Mrs. Gordon, I'll do everything I can to help Elisabeth."

The other teachers took Miss Howard's lead and offered to give me books to work with Elisabeth at home, to help fill in her gaps. They even thanked me for taking the time to tell the story about Elisabeth. Everyone except Mr. Koops.

On the walk home, Robert took my hand.

"Nice work, Reverend." I squeezed his hand. "Your ability to calm troubled waters never ceases to amaze me."

"You're the one who organized the meeting. All that I did was to save Mr. Koops from a fierce tongue lashing by an irate German hausfrau." He shuddered at the thought.

I tried to scowl at him but couldn't hold back a grin. "Think it will help?"

"You bought her some time. And she needs that right now." He stopped for a moment. "You never told me that her job was to separate shoes."

"She told me about it once, on the ship, when she woke up from a nightmare." Thankfully, the Icebox wasn't in the room at the time. "Elisabeth said Danny used to make up stories about the former shoe owners. One pair used to belong to a jeweler. Another to a concert violinist. It was a creative way to distract her."

Robert lifted his face to the cloudless sky. "We owe a great deal to Danny."

I nodded solemnly, wondering if Karl Schneider had ever located a relative for Danny. And if not, what would happen to him? Where would he be sent? We started walking again, until I asked, "Robert, does Mr. Koops remind you of a Dutch version of Friedrich Mueller?"

Robert shot me an aggrieved look, a warning to not get started on my theory of Friedrich Mueller. There were times that I would have liked to discuss Herr Mueller, and Ruth, Robert's first wife, and the terrible crimes they had committed together. Crimes against Robert, against William, against this town. I didn't like the way Robert pretended it was over and done with, never to be discussed again. Even William had taken his mother's picture and put it away. That seemed to be the Gordon Way.

Friedrich Mueller had a powerful and damaging affect on Robert's family, but pretending he didn't exist didn't change anything. Ignoring terrible things in one's life, bottling them up and pretending that they weren't real, only allowed those damaging events to continue to cause pain. Yet I knew enough about the Gordon Way by now to realize that I couldn't change them. At least not in one conversation.

I squeezed his hand. "Well, anyway, thanks for putting Mr. Koops in his place." The awkwardness lifted between us.

Robert turned to me and asked, "Would you mind if I borrowed those newspapers clippings and pictures you brought back?"

"Not at all. Any particular reason?"

"I don't know. I guess I'm wondering if it might give me some insights into Dietrich's experience over the last few years."

"How is the book coming along?"

"As slow as molasses on a January morning," he said, quoting Aunt Martha, "but I am enjoying the process."

When we arrived home, I went upstairs to find Elisabeth. She lay on her side on her bed, legs curled up. She looked miserable. I lay down on the bed next to her. "Is your stomach hurting again?" On the ship, she had often experienced stomach cramps but I thought it had been because she was eating different food. More food, too.

She nodded. "And deeze." She pointed to her teeth. She suffered a great deal of pain from dental caries. We had appointments lined up with the dentist for months ahead to fill the cavities.

I took her small hand and placed it on the small ball of my belly. "If you wait for a few minutes, you might be able to feel the baby kick. He's kicking all of the time now." After a moment, Elisabeth pulled her hand away, bored. "Is school that bad?" I asked her gently.

"I hate der schule. I hate da kids. I hate dat Mr. Koops."

"Miss Howard?"

"I do not hate dat Miss Hovard."

"Why do you hate the kids?"

"No one vould sit vit me at lunch. Dey make fun of me. Da vay I look and da vay I talk. One bad girl told me to say someting and vhen I did, she laughed and told her friends. Den, dey laughed at me, too."

"What did she ask you to say?"

"Vonderful wiolin."

I clapped my hand over my mouth to stifle a giggle.

"And one bad boy said I looked like a monkey."

Probably the boy whom she whacked. Sounded well-deserved! But she did look a little like a monkey. Large eyes that dominated her face, tiny ears that poked through her wispy hair. Still, I suffered a deep ache in my chest, climbing up to my throat. It was a sad truth of life that ranked people, especially children, primarily by looks. Tenderly, I patted her hair. Soon, I hoped her hair might shape into the bubble-cut that was popular among girls.

"Vhen I got home, dat dog stayed outside of my door and breathed underneath it." She made a loud rasping breathing sound to imitate Dog. "And he left a apfel vit his bite marks in it. He has done dat two times."

Worried that Aunt Martha would find them, I asked, "What did you do with the apples?"

She gave me a look as if I was very dense. "Ate them."

I had forgotten to put Dog out on the tie-down line in my haste to get to the principal's office. "I think Dog is trying to make friends with you, Elisabeth. Dogs are like people. Some are bad, and some are good."

She rolled over and looked at me curiously. "Dat commandant vas bad. Dos guards vere bad."

"Yes," I agreed.

"But Danny vas good."

"Yes."

She rolled back on her side, deep in thought. "Sometimes, Danny vould give me half of his potato."

"Really? Even though he was hungry, too?"

She nodded.

"And he is only a fifteen-year-old boy?"

"But Danny is a man," she added thoughtfully.

A wave of compassion swept over me. I knew she suffered still. Nothing could ever give her back what she lost, but I wished I could do more for her. Suddenly, I had an idea. Maybe there was one thing I could do to help. "William goes to a tutor in Bisbee for speech therapy. She helps him to speak clearly. Would you like her to help you, too?"

Elisabeth rolled on her back. "Maybe."

A good sign.

"But I don't vant to sound like I got dat yunk in my nose like Vilhelm."

I reached over and smoothed the wisps of hair on her forehead. "Do you remember why I came and got you in Germany?"

"So I vould know I vasn't all alone."

I kissed her on her temple. For the first time, I felt like I was starting to love her. I stood up and walked to the door, remembering something. "What did Danny's letter say?"

She waved her hand as if shooing away the butler and said, "None of your beesvax."

I said I was *starting* to love her, not that I loved her.

Chapter Eight

As we were cleaning up the kitchen after dinner, Aunt Martha pointed out to Robert, "That Mattie Osgood has designs on the judge. It's the third casserole she's brought him in one week. She looks at him as if he hung the moon."

"Well, would that be so bad?" he asked reasonably. "I sort of hope the judge will find someone. He's got a lot of living left to do."

"He wouldn't be doing much living with that Mattie Osgood."

"Aunt Martha, don't tell me you haven't buried the hatchet from your tiff with Mattie Osgood over that bake sale for hymnals? That was years ago!"

"Oh, I buried the hatchet all right. But I marked the spot."

I smiled at the two of them. Many conversations carried on like that between the two. Aunt Martha complained, while Robert patiently tried to point her to a better way.

Elisabeth came stomping down the stairs to find Robert. "I need newspapers articles about dat Goddard man."

"About Robert Goddard? The rocket scientist?" he asked, surprised.

"Danny vants me to send him everyting I can find about dat man."

Robert raised his eyebrows, impressed. "Not many people know about him." Robert Goddard, the father of rocketry, had died on August 10th, just a few weeks ago. "Danny must really be interested in rockets."

"I told you dat. Someday, he is going to build a rocket to travel to da moon."

Watching this interchange, William said, "Dad, is that possible?"

Aunt Martha gave a snort.

Robert glanced in her direction and frowned. "Hard to imagine, but it might just happen someday."

"And cows will have five legs," muttered Aunt Martha.

He ignored her, stood up and walked over to the top of the icebox where today's newspaper sat. "I think I even noticed something in today's news about rockets, Elisabeth. There's a group of German rocket scientists who surrendered to the Americans and were brought to Texas to work for the Army." He opened the paper up and spread it on the counter, then pulled out a drawer to find scissors.

"Dad, what makes a rocket fly?" asked William.

Robert turned to him, a puzzled look on his face. "I honestly don't know, son. We'll have to do some reading on the subject."

I was relieved I wasn't included in that assignment.

On a sunny afternoon in late September, William and I came out of the library only to find that Dog had left his post. We hurried to the parsonage to see if he had gone home, but Aunt Martha hadn't seen him. When I knocked on Robert's office to see if he had seen Dog, he waved me in, talking on the phone to someone. "Uh, uh, well, thank you, Mrs. Olasky. Someone will be right down to get him. Again, my apologies for the interruption."

Oh no.

As Robert replaced the receiver, he shook his head. "Dog," he said. "Problem at school."

"I'll go," I volunteered and hurried out the door.

In Mrs. Olasky's office lay Dog, tethered to the leg of a heavy table with someone's necktie. In a chair, Elisabeth sat tall and pleased. Mrs. Olasky, I noticed, did not look quite as pleased.

"I'm so sorry, Mrs. Olasky. I won't let Dog wander again." I grabbed Dog by the neck-tie and motioned to Elisabeth that we should leave. *Fast.*

Later, as I was finishing up the dinner dishes, I looked out the kitchen window and saw Elisabeth throwing the ball for Dog. A miracle! I went outside to join her.

"You and Dog seemed to have worked out an understanding," I said, curious.

"Maybe he is not such a bad dog after all," she answered. After a while, Dog keyed in on a squirrel and, an evil thought in his head, took off to chase it.

I watched Elisabeth watch Dog. "Did something happen to change your mind about him?"

She gave me a wicked grin. "Dat Dog came to school at lunch, yust when dat bad boy stole my lunch and tossed it in da bushes. Dog went in da bushes and brought my lunch back to me. Everybody laughed at dat dumb boy."

I gazed at Dog with keen admiration. Such a noble canine! How could he have known that the key to Elisabeth's heart would be food?

"Would you sit with me a few minutes?" I asked her, patting the step next to me.

Robert had encouraged me to tell Elisabeth about my father's murder, about my work in the Resistance and fleeing the country. Now seemed like an opportune moment. Elisabeth was softer tonight. I told her everything, though I avoided the part about Karl Schneider's involvement in my father's death. And when I was done, all that she said was, "Still, you vere not in da camps."

"No. I wasn't."

"You vere lucky. Your God smiled on you."

"Why do you think He smiled on me?"

"Because you're only half-Juden. God does not hear dem Juden's prayers."

"He hears your prayers."

"Da time I vas in da camp, God did not hear me. And He didn't hear da prayers of da people vhen dey cried to Him on da vay to da shower."

I didn't know how to respond. The room that was called the shower was actually filled with sprinklers that sprayed toxic fumes on the prisoners, killing them within minutes.

Elisabeth never mentioned her mother, but was it possible that she had seen her deathwalk to the shower? *Oh God*, I prayed silently and boldly, *give me Your wisdom. Give me Your words.* "Elisabeth, I believe everyone's life has purpose and meaning. I believe that every one of those individuals, every single one, who was led to the showers, mattered to God. Their life mattered, and their death mattered. They were significant to God. There's a verse in the book of Psalms that says 'Precious in the sight of the Lord is the death of His saints'."

She listened, head bent low. "You sound yust like Danny. He said not to blame God for da camps. He said ve must not blame God for man's...man's..." she struggled to find the right word.

"Depravity?"

"Ja! Dat's da vord. Danny uses da big vords. Er ist sehr klug." *He is very smart.*

"I can tell. I think he's right, too. One thing I know, Elisabeth. No one can hide from God; He's there whether we like it or not, whether we know it or not. Everyone will have a day of accounting before God."

"Vill your God punish dat Hitler?"

Dog came barreling up with a ball in his mouth, dropping it on my lap. I picked it up, threw it, and wiped my hand on my skirt. "There's another Bible verse that says people like Hitler are like wandering stars, and that the blackest darkness has been reserved forever. Someday I'll read to you from the book of Jude. It's only one chapter long. The entire chapter feels as if it was written with the Nazis in mind. For how God will punish those who give themselves over to evil."

"Dat blackest darkness is still too good for dat Hitler."

I heartily agreed. "I wish I had simple answers to give you. All I really know is how God has dealt with me. He has shown me mercy over and over. I know God loves me."

She looked at me accusingly. "How do you know dat?"

"How do I know that God loves me? He brought you to me. Sometimes I think *you're* a miracle, Elisabeth."

"Vhat do you mean?" she asked, interested. Skeptical, but interested.

"I think God helped you survive in the camp. He brought Danny into your life to give you encouragement. And somehow He connected you to me even though I lived seven thousand miles away. I think, no, I *know* that God has a special plan for your life."

She kicked at a tree root sticking out of the ground, quiet for a moment. "I still don't vant to be Juden no more."

"Do you not want to be Jewish or do you not want to believe in God?"

She wouldn't answer that question. But she did toss something at me. Enclosed in a recent letter from Danny was a sealed envelope from Karl Schneider, addressed to me.

My dearest Annika,

I am diligently working to find leads on Friedrich Mueller. Would you be so kind as to write to me about the information that you shared with me back in August? Include as many details as you can remember, especially any people and places he might have associated with. I will not fail you this time. I hold hope in my heart that you have forgiven me.

Sincerely yours, Karl Schneider

My stomach turned inside out as I read it.

"Vhat does he vant?" asked Elisabeth, watching my face. "You look mad." She scrunched up her face as if she had just stubbed her toe.

I folded it up tightly and put it in my pocket. "He wondered if you were doing well," I lied.

Lately, memories of Karl came unbidden, like a gusty wind carrying me away to other times and places.

The funeral service for my father was held a few days after he had been murdered. Friends from our Lutheran church helped to make arrangements. My father was buried next to my mother. I went through the motions, numb, as if this had happened to someone else and I was just a bystander.

Karl had been so sweet, so attentive to me this week. Throughout the funeral, he had stayed close to my side, watching me with worried eyes. "Are you going to be all right? I need to get back to University to meet with some people about...well...about making some plans." Karl had won the competition handily after I had forfeited my spot. But neither of us seemed to care. I certainly didn't.

"I'll be fine," I said.

Karl wrapped his arms around me. "Life will get good again, you'll see."

I felt comforted by his arms, by his presence, but I knew my life would never be the same.

"Where will you be?"

"For now, I'm staying at Diedre's. I just can't go back to the house."

"Maybe we should get married sooner, especially if I'm to travel with..." He pulled back from me with something on his mind to say. "Annika, there were some important people at the competition."

I smiled sadly. "I know. I'm glad you won. I really am."

He bit his lip. "Very important."

I tilted my head at him. "Who was there?"

"The Chancellor."

I stepped back as if I had just touched a live wire. "Hitler was in the audience?"

Karl nodded. "Yes."

"Did you know that he was going to be there?" My face must have shown the disgust I felt.

"Lower your voice." Karl pulled me over to the side and looked around to see if anyone was listening to us. "I had heard a rumor but...you know how that goes." His eyes scanned the crowd before he whispered, "I was sent word he wants me to play for official government events."

My blood froze. "You are going to perform for Hitler?"

Karl gazed at me. "It's just an opportunity, that's all. Besides, how am I supposed to turn it down? You don't turn down the Chancellor. I would be sent to the Russian front faster than I could play a C scale."

My hands clenched into tight fists. "Hitler was the reason my father was murdered."

Karl's eyes were on my shoes, not my face. "Annika, you don't know why he was murdered. It might have just been a break-in. Those stories are becoming common."

"There was no robbery. Nothing was taken." My hand slipped in my pocket to touch my father's wedding ring, the one hidden in the flour jar. "Someone intended to kill him."

"Maybe it just got out of hand. Maybe your father fought back. I could see him doing that."

"There was a Star of David pinned to his chest, Karl. Not to his shirt, to his bare chest!"

Karl winced.

Suddenly, I was hit with my first wave of grief. Fighting tears, I asked, "You would really play for Hitler?"

Karl cupped my face with his hands, a conciliatory look on his face. "Darling, these aren't normal times. We have to do what we have to do. Think about it—if I do this, I can avoid active military duty. That's what we both want, to be together, yes?" He kissed me tenderly, told me he would call me later, and left.

* * * *

In mid-September, Robert came in to the kitchen while we were eating breakfast, holding the morning newspaper. "Elisabeth—look at this! The first Jewish Miss America!" Bess Myerson from the New York Bronx was chosen to be Miss America for 1945 in Atlantic City, New Jersey.

"Vhat is dat? Vhat is Miss America?" Elisabeth asked, looked puzzled.

"It's a beauty pageant for young women. They receive scholarships for college, and travel around the country as a public servant. It's very symbolic that a Jewish woman was chosen, Elisabeth. It shows that our country is becoming more understanding of other races and beliefs."

Aunt Martha read the headline over his shoulder. "Do you think it's going to be easy for her, Robert? That poor woman will be mistreated all over America. Look at that one paragraph." She pointed to it. "They've already tried to get her to change her name."

131

"But she refused," Robert said, impressed. "I think she's up for the job."

"I thot dat America liked da Juden. I thot it vas yust da Nazis who hated da Juden," Elisabeth asked.

"Well, ahem, well," stammered Robert. "There are many people in America who still have ignorant ideas."

Elisabeth peered at him thoughtfully. "Like dat Mr. Koops."

"Exactly," Robert answered.

Elisabeth cut out pictures of Bess Myerson and taped them onto her mirror in her bedroom. As I was putting away her laundry one day, I told her that if Bess Myerson came to Arizona, we would try to meet her.

She played with her hair, flipping it behind her ear. "I tink dat someday I will be da Miss America."

"What a good idea," I said, sitting down on her bed. "But you'll need two things."

"Vhat?"

"First, you'll need to become a citizen of the United States."

"How do I do dat?"

I really didn't know. I came into the United States illegally, and then I married Robert, so I had stumbled onto a shortcut. "We'll have to ask Judge Pryor."

"So vhat is da next ting?"

"You'll need a talent."

"Like vat?"

"Hmm, well...didn't Bess Myerson play the piano in the pageant?" I rose to leave without saying another word.

The next afternoon, William and I were coming back from the library. Aunt Martha was at the market. As I drew close to the kitchen door, I heard Elisabeth playing the piano. I leaned against the door jam; the sound took my breath away. I motioned to William to go throw the ball for Dog while I listened. We went unnoticed until William threw Dog's ball so high it got stuck in a bush and Dog barked at it. I heard Elisabeth slam the lid of the piano shut and scurry up the stairs. I went over to the bush, retrieved Dog's ball and said crossly, "Dog, you cut short the concert." But inwardly, I breathed, Thank you, Lord, for letting me hear her play.

The next day, the milkman stopped at the kitchen door to chat with Aunt Martha. "I don't know what's going on," he said, as he handed her two milk bottles. "Almost every day I've been getting complaints that people ain't getting my milk! A different house each time. And I know for a fact that I've delivered it."

Robert and I exchanged a concerned look. Could Elisabeth still be "organizing?" I shook my head. No, no, it was impossible.

One morning in mid-October, I stretched out in bed and waited for the now familiar baby kicks to begin. After the first nudge or two, I got up, threw on my robe, and headed for the kitchen, stopping at the door. There on the floor was a tattered letter from the school that Elisabeth needed, signed and returned. A request for a conference from Mr. Koops.

Oh no. This was no way to start a day.

I dreaded meeting with Mr. Koops. He and Elisabeth were at constant odds. I tried to convince Robert to go in my place, but he had a meeting with the Elders. When the appointed time arrived, I sat on a child-sized chair. Mr. Koops sat authoritatively at his desk. I felt small.

"Well, Mrs. Gordon," he started with his customary scowl, "things are about as I expected them to be. Maybe even worse. Elisabeth is nearly failing my class. The work is too difficult for her. She has trouble keeping up."

"She's still mastering English, Mr. Koops. Look at how much progress she has made in just a few months."

He ignored my remark. "And she antagonizes her schoolmates."

"How so?"

"For example, she taught Peter Harwood to say 'Ich bin ein dumkopf.' She told him it was a very, very, very bad word. So, of course, he taught all the other boys to repeat it."

I had to bite my lower lip, hard, to keep from smiling. Unfortunately, as usual, I didn't conceal it very well.

"I *know* what that phrase means, Mrs. Gordon," he said, eyes narrowing suspiciously.

Well, Peter Harwood was hardly a scholar.

"And there are other concerns about her judgment. She's become friends with another child who doesn't fit in."

"Everyone deserves to have a friend, Mr. Koops. Everyone." I tried to mask my annoyance. I really did. Robert had given me a lecture about holding my tongue with Mr. Koops. He pointed out that losing my temper with Mr. Koops would only make things harder for Elisabeth.

"Yes, well, you know what they say."

"No, Mr. Koops. What do they say?"

"Peas in a pod."

I looked at him as if he was speaking another language.

"I meant that trouble finds trouble."

"Who is this friend?"

"Tanya Myers."

I hadn't heard anything about Tanya from Elisabeth, but that was no surprise. She didn't volunteer information, only her sour opinions about the shortcomings of Copper Springs. "I'm not concerned, Mr. Koops."

He raised an eyebrow at me. "The Reverend might be. His aunt certainly would be."

How patronizing! How pious! "So, you said Elisabeth is passing your class."

"I said *nearly* failing."

"That sounds like passing to me." I had heard all I needed to hear from Mr. Koops. I stood up. "Please excuse me. There's another teacher whom I should meet in a few minutes."

I went over to Miss Howard's room and waited, leaning against the wall, until her conference had finished. She looked surprised when she saw me but asked me to sit down. "I don't have another conference scheduled today," she said, pointing to an adult-sized chair for me to sit in.

A minor but symbolic act, it seemed. We were seated eye-to-eye.

I took a quick breath. "You didn't request a conference for Elisabeth."

"No need."

Trying not to sound too eager, I asked, "So is Elisabeth doing well in your class? Or well enough?"

"She's coming along very well. She's really trying. To be truthful, she's not up to grade level, but I love her effort."

I bit my lip. "May I ask you about Tanya Myers?"

"I know who she is but I don't have her in any of my classes."

"Do you know anything about her?"

She hesitated. "Just that it can't be easy for her."

"What do you mean?"

"Well, her father was killed in the war. Her mother cleans houses to make ends meet. I think they live with a grandmother. But it can't be easy being the only Negro child in this school."

Now I understood Mr. Koops' comments. The *nerve* of that man! And to make an assumption that Robert wouldn't want Elisabeth to be friends with Tanya. He obviously didn't know Robert.

I stood, silently suggesting that God strike Mr. Koops with a bolt of lightning. Then I informed Him that I was going to go tell that man exactly what is wrong with him! Instantly, I felt an inner prompting to do the opposite: to keep my mouth closed. Frustrated, and now annoyed with God as well as Mr. Koops, I went over to the window for a moment, trying to calm down. As I turned back to Miss Howard, I noticed an old piano in the corner. "Do you play?"

"No. I wish I did. The students only have music twice a week and we need to practice the songs for the Christmas musical. We *really* need the practice," she emphasized.

"Elisabeth plays beautifully," I said sadly, "but I don't think she's ready." I had only heard her play that one time. As far as I know, she hadn't touched the piano since.

Miss Howard came over to stand near me by the window. "Mrs. Gordon, there's one thing you should know about Mr. Koops. His younger brother was in the army. He was held as a POW by the Germans and executed as he tried to escape."

The fire passed out of me, as fast as it came. *Oh Lord. For once, I listened to you before I spoke.* "No. I didn't know that. Thank you for telling me."

Reluctantly, I stopped by Mr. Koops' room. He was seated at his desk, correcting papers. He looked irritated when he saw me at the door.

"I just found out about your brother. I'm sorry."

He visibly tensed up and his eyes narrowed into slits. "My brother was killed because of trying to save those Jews."

"It wasn't *Elisabeth's* fault," I said slowly, pointedly.

He turned his attention back to his papers on his desk.

"But I am very sorry about your brother, Mr. Koops." I turned quietly and left.

On the way home, I stopped at Rosita's restaurant. It was just a small restaurant, only eight tables, but she was a wonderful cook and it was nearly always full, at least on weekends. I found her in the kitchen, skillfully rolling small balls of dough to make corn tortillas. "Where are Esmeralda and Juan?" I asked her.

"Esmeralda took him home for a good nap. That boy is making me loco en el coco." She pointed to her head and made a stirring motion. "Crazy. Here. Sit. I get you some dinner."

I sat on a little chair, watching her bustle efficiently in the kitchen. She placed a plate in front of me with enchiladas, rice and beans. "Double portions. You are eating for two, you know."

Gratefully, I started eating. Lately, I was always hungry. But I had another reason to stop by. "Rosita, has Esmeralda ever said how Elisabeth seems to be settling in to school?"

She stopped rolling the dough and looked up at me, startled. "Oh yes. She is doing great. Just great. Lots of friends. Everyone loves her." She nodded with exaggeration.

Rosita was a lovable, big-hearted, sweet-to-the-core person, but she was a terrible liar.

Chapter Nine

One evening, I sat down at the piano. I had been working on Beethoven's Sonata No. 8 in C Minor. Suddenly, Elisabeth burst out of her room and flew down the stairs, shouting, "No! No! Vhy do you alvays do it dat vay?"

I looked at her blankly, but I knew. I had played it incorrectly to see if she would catch the mistake. The second movement had a suspension at the end. Instead, I resolved it up. I stood and swept my hand at the bench in a be-my-guest gesture.

She stared at me accusingly. Then she sat down at the piano and played it correctly. "See? Da melody repeats twice before da song goes to da B section. Den twice again. Don't you see? Can't you hear it? Vhat is da matter vit you?"

I nodded. "Oh, oh, *now* I see."

With an air of disgust she jumped off of the piano bench and clomped back up the stairs.

Leaning against the door jam to the kitchen, arms folded against his chest, Robert said, "Well, well, well. Ever thought of a career in child psychology?"

I grinned. "It's a start, don't you think?"

* * * *

Later in the week, Dog disappeared. My concern grew after Elisabeth returned home from school and he still hadn't returned.

Just before dark, Mrs. Bauer knocked on the parsonage door. As Robert opened the door to her, Dog charged through, a little pink leash dangling from his collar.

Mrs. Bauer was a very active and overly opinionated member of the First Presbyterian Church of Copper Springs. She stood at our door, hands planted firmly on her hips, and told us she would call the dog catcher if Dog showed himself around her darling poodle Mitzi one more time. "And what breed is that dog anyway?" she sniffed.

"Well, Mrs. Bauer, he has a questionable lineage," Robert explained.

A little gasp escaped from her lips. "You had better pray that there will not be any...repercussions, Reverend!" Abruptly, she spun on her heels and left.

I patted Dog's head as I unclipped the pink leash from his collar. "We really should have him turned into a eunuch, Robert."

Robert eyes went wide as his jaw dropped open. "*Louisa!* Don't *say* such a thing around him. Don't even use that word!"

I handed him the leash. "What word should I use?"

"Well, that he should be neutered. But still, don't even *think* such a thought. That's a very serious operation. I'm not sure that we even want to...consider...changing him. Why...it's unthinkable!"

Dog stared at me soberly, as if he understood the conversation and was deeply disappointed in me.

"It's not his fault, Robert. It's just his nature to go roaming. After all, he is a dog."

"We just need to keep a better eye on him," he objected.

I rolled my eyes. "Then you can return the leash and do the explaining to Mrs. Bauer the next time Dog gets a little wanderlust."

The next morning, over a bowl of Cheerioats, I asked William, "What are you doing with your spy log?"

"Nothing," he answered glumly. "This town is boring."

"What if you started to take pictures along with your observations? You could develop reconnaissance skills."

"What? What's that?" he asked, looking at me carefully, unsure of the word I had used.

"Reconnaissance. Let me spell it out for you." I took a piece of paper and wrote it out carefully. "You gather evidence of observations. It's a military strategy. The Navy pilots took aerial reconnaissance. From an airplane, they would take pictures of where they wanted to drop bombs, so they would hit factories instead of villages."

William's interest was growing. "Maybe I'll be a Navy pilot one day."

"See? That's why you need these skills," I said encouragingly.

"*Louisa!* Why on *earth* do you keep trying to turn him into a spy?" Robert called out from the parlor where he had been reading the newspaper.

I walked over to the parlor door. "I'm just trying to keep him interested in new things. Trying to keep his mind occupied is a full-time job."

Robert put down his newspaper and frowned at me. "Why can't he take pictures of sunsets? Why does he have to be gathering data on our friends and neighbors?"

I thought about that for a while. "Excellent point." I went back and sat next to William and asked what he thought about taking pictures of sunsets.

"Boring," he answered.

"What if we did sunsets *and* sunrises, so you could compare how the light changes the sky?

He cocked his head and scrunched up his face, deep in thought. "Okay."

In the dusky light of evening, William took pictures of the sunset. Early the next morning, I woke him up at dawn to catch the sunrise, before it climbed over the craggy cliffs in the east and flooded the valley.

Afterwards, William wanted to finish up the roll, so I suggested that he walk down the street and take a few pictures of the church, just as the sun fanned the buildings. I hoped he might get an interesting view of the church that we could frame for Robert for Christmas. William handed me the roll of film to drop at the film store the next time we went to Bisbee. I tucked it in my sweater pocket and promptly forgot about it.

At dinner, Elisabeth said that she had to write an essay for English class about what book she would take with her if she were shipwrecked on a deserted island.

"Can you take the *Bible*?" asked Robert.

"No. Dat Mr. Koops said no *Bible*. So vhat odder book?" she asked him. She was stumped. She didn't enjoy reading. She still labored with her English and needed a dictionary to do most of her homework.

"Hmm," he said, rubbing his chin. "Well, I'd probably take along Oswald Chamber's *My Utmost for His Highest*."

"I think I would take along *The Christian's Secret to a Happy Life* by Hannah Whitall Smith," pondered Aunt Martha. Written by a Quaker in the 1800s, it was a classic devotional. Still, I thought that was an interesting choice for Aunt Martha, who could never be accused of oozing happiness.

"What about you, Louisa?" asked Robert, helping himself to another portion of the meatloaf.

"Just one book?" I asked.

Elisabeth nodded.

"What a difficult choice."

She rolled her eyes. "So vhat book?" she asked in a louder voice.

"I think I might choose a play by Shakespeare." I had been trying to help Elisabeth read through *King Lear.*

Elisabeth looked at me as if I had lost my mind. "Dat man is too hard to understand. He says he is using English but I can't understand a vord of him. Shakespeare is da vorst."

"What about you, William?" I asked, tapping his arm so he would know I was speaking to him. "What book would you take with you if you were shipwrecked on a deserted island?"

William looked at me carefully to read my lips. Then he reached for the butter plate. "Can Dog come with me?" he asked.

"Okay," I said.

"So vhat book?!" Elisabeth barked, losing patience.

"I think...," he said, adding pats of butter into his steaming baked potato. Butter was becoming a staple in homes after rationing had eased and William couldn't get enough of it. He had never accepted Oleo as a reasonable substitute. "I think...I would bring a book about how to build a boat if you get stuck on a deserted island." He added another pat of butter, then watched the butter melt into little rivers in his potato.

With a catlike smile, Elisabeth went back to eating with renewed gusto.

Before Thanksgiving arrived, I wrote two letters. One to Alice, Robert's sister, inviting her to come for a visit. The judge helped me to locate the O'Casey family and I hoped they would forward the letter to Alice.

I also hoped that if she were to be found, Robert would welcome her warmly.

Well, so I hoped.

The second letter I wrote was to Karl Schneider. He had enclosed two more notes in Danny's letters to Elisabeth and then had sent me a letter directly. Despite feeling strangely unsettled about communicating with Karl, I finally decided that if he was willing to help locate Friedrich Mueller, I should accept his offer. I had yet to hear a single word from the judge's nephew. I had nowhere else to turn. But I did ignore Karl's repeated pleas for forgiveness. And I signed the letter: 'Cordially, Mrs. Robert Gordon'. I underlined my name for emphasis. *Twice.*

Too soon, it was Thanksgiving. Cousin Ada was due in, which meant Aunt Martha was cleaning the house from top to bottom in a frantic fall cleaning mode. William and I stayed outdoors as much as possible. Even though my abdomen was rather pronounced, I still gardened, turning over the dirt and preparing the soil for my fall crops. Robert had built a compost box for me that we kept hidden on the side yard to create amendments for my garden. Little by little, my garden was taking over the entire front yard.

Rosita stopped by on her way to her restaurant one morning when she saw me out front. "What are you going to plant now, Louisa?"

"Well, broccoli, carrots, lettuce, onions, cabbage in those beds." I pointed to the side yard. "And closer to the front of the house, in the bed next to the roses, I'm going to plant flowers. This year, I'm going to put in narcissus bulbs so the house will smell of spring." It would smell like springtime in Germany, I hoped. "I've got the bulbs in the icebox right now."

"The icebox? Flower bulbs in the icebox?

"Bulbs need a cold storage period. Arizona is much too hot for bulbs, so I'll dig them up when they finish blooming and put them back in the icebox."

"Doesn't Aunt Martha mind bulbs in her icebox?" Rosita asked, familiar with Aunt Martha's fussy ways.

"Why, yes! She minds quite a bit! But she does like my flowers."

Rosita smiled and sat down next to me. "How are you feeling?"

I leaned back on my heels. "Good. Wonderful. The baby moves all of the time now."

"Just don't hurt yourself, doing all of that bending."

"I'll be careful." I patted my middle. "Aunt Martha says I have peasant stock in me."

Rosita looked at me, confused. "Is that good?"

I sighed. "Probably not."

Her face stretched into a big gap-toothed grin as she headed off down the street toward her restaurant.

After dinner that night, a loud, "Elisabeth! Get down here!" bellowed from the parlor. Robert walked into the kitchen, holding up the daily newspaper, which had large holes cut out of it like Swiss cheese.

Elisabeth flew down the stairs. When she saw him, her eyes grew wide. "I had to cut news for Danny! About rockets! And about Israel and Palestine and dat United Nations! You said it vas okay!" She looked worried. Robert had never raised his voice to her.

Robert frowned. "Well, could you at least wait until I am done reading it?" He went back into the parlor, shaking his head.

* * * *

A few days later, Ada came sweeping into our house in her usual "roar in, roar out" style. Sensing the excitement, Dog dashed down the stairs and skidded up to Ada, jumping up to lick her face. I hurried to get Dog under control. "I'm sorry,

144

Ada!" I said, as I held back his wiggling body with both hands. "He takes greeting very seriously."

"That mutt is as welcoming as a swarm of bees," groused Aunt Martha, as she came in from the kitchen to greet her cousin.

Dramatically, Ada brushed off her new red wool suit with fox fur trim. "I don't know what it is about dogs, but the more I dislike them, the more they seem to like me."

Hearing the commotion, Elisabeth came downstairs. She watched Ada ooh and aah over everyone. Ada couldn't get over how tall William had grown. He wiped his cheek down with a flourish after she had finished covering him with wet kisses. Then she patted my swelling abdomen and pronounced that this baby was a boy, no doubt, from the way I was carrying it.

Inch by inch, Elisabeth slid into the parlor to investigate. She peered at Ada with an odd look on her face.

Suddenly, a horrible realization flooded over me. I felt as if I was in a dream, running in quicksand. *Don't say it, Elisabeth, please don't say what I think you're about to say!*

"How in da vorld did you get so fat?" she asked Ada.

A deafening silence filled the room.

"Why, just too much good living, little girl!" Ada grabbed Elisabeth for a smothering hug. "And we're just going to have to fatten you up, too, little Lizzy," she claimed. She continued to hug Elisabeth, rocking her back and forth. When Ada finally released her, Elisabeth looked dazed, as if she'd never encountered anyone like this before in her life.

Regarding Ada, I shared those sentiments.

Robert came through the door with multiple suitcases tucked under his arms, including a cat crate. Setting them down, he rubbed his shoulders and muttered, "They nearly took my arms from their sockets." Dog began sniffing and didn't stop until he had sniffed every square inch of the place, finally locating the source of that smell, hackling and growling as if he had just found dinner. Quickly, William put on his leash and dragged him outside, where Dog resigned himself, mournfully, to a long stay on the tie-down line.

A music aficionado, Ada often asked me to play the piano for her. One afternoon, I had just finished playing a Mendelssohn selection for her when Elisabeth walked through the room. "Elisabeth is an even better piano player than I am, Ada," I whispered.

Elisabeth heard me and stopped abruptly, just as I had hoped. She narrowed her eyes at me. "Dat's right. Louisa makes mistakes. Lots and lots of mistakes."

"Oh, really?" asked Ada provocatively. "What kind of mistakes? She sounded perfect to me."

With great enthusiasm, Elisabeth explained how I often was off tempo. "She never knows vhen to push da timing or vhen to hold back. And her crescendos should be in tree notes," she held up three fingers, "but she is alvays off. Off, off, off!"

I nodded. She was right.

Ada wisely feigned ignorance. "I'm not quite sure what you mean, Lizzy dear. Would you mind showing me?"

Elisabeth scrunched up her face, contemplating whether she would accommodate Ada's request or not, but she couldn't resist an opportunity to show me up. I raised my eyebrows at Ada, impressed with her perceptiveness.

Elisabeth sat down at the piano and played the piece I had just played with astonishing precision. As she drew to the final few measures, she stopped. She looked down at the piano, pressing one key over and over. It was stuck. She jumped off the stool, and pointed furiously at the keyboard. "You call dat a piano? Dat is not music! Dat is da vorst piano in da vorld!" She shook her head stormily and stomped off.

I glanced quickly over at Robert, who was playing chess with William at the kitchen table. Robert had surprised me with this piano when I had first arrived in Copper Springs, knowing how I loved to play. "It's a wonderful piano, Robert. There's just one key that sticks a little. That's all. I can try to fix it."

Ada hurried to the kitchen. "Do you realize the talent in that child? Why, she's a wunderkind!"

"Yes, of course we realize that," Robert answered.

"But we must develop it!" she said.

I came into the kitchen behind her. "It's not that easy, Ada. That's the first time I've heard her play for anyone since she came. She associates the piano with her past, and she doesn't want to be reminded of it."

Ada shook her head. "Something must be done, Lulu. It would be a crime to neglect that kind of talent. A crime!"

Later that day, the judge joined us for dinner. Ada shifted into high gear when she discovered he was a widower. It was a curious sight to behold. Ada, flirting outrageously with the judge, Aunt Martha, lips pressed tight, shooting daggers at Ada.

Just as I had suspected!

A little undercurrent of romance *had* been blossoming with Aunt Martha and Judge Pryor! Once, I had noticed Aunt Martha softened her hairstyle from that tight little knot of a bun symbolic of her personality.

Another time, I noticed that she was wearing lipstick. *Lipstick!*

Ada wasn't even aware of Martha's injured feelings. Nor was the judge. Unfortunately, he seemed rather dazzled by Ada. It was understandable. Ada *was* dazzling.

This situation needed drastic intervention.

I kicked Robert under the table. "Ow!" he yelped.

"Robert, isn't this dinner wonderful? Aunt Martha is such a wonderful cook," I said.

Robert completely missed my cue and rubbed his shin, glaring at me as if mortally wounded. Clearly, he was not going to be of any help.

"We would really be up a river with our paddles if we didn't have Aunt Martha," I said.

Robert looked at me curiously. "Do you mean, up a creek without our paddles?"

"Yes. That's just what I said," I answered, frowning at him.

"Well, Louisa, if you're going to start using colloquialisms, you need to get them right," he informed me in a patronizing tone. "They only work if they're said correctly."

I glowered at him, silently vowing to never use one of those silly expressions ever again.

That night in bed, I kept trying to read a book, but couldn't stop thinking about the dinner. "Robert, I think Aunt Martha has a fondness for the judge. But it seems that so does Ada."

He put down his book. "What? Is that why you spiked me under the table? I think you broke skin."

"I *gently* nudged you and you *completely* missed my hint," I corrected.

"Well, it's ridiculous thinking, anyway."

"Why is it so ridiculous? Aunt Martha and the judge would make a wonderful match."

"Not if Ada has already set her cap on him." Yawning, he switched off his bedside light.

Robert was probably right. It seemed to be a lifelong pattern between the two women. Aunt Martha remained a spinster, while Ada had gone through three husbands and was on the hunt to find husband number four.

Well, I had other problems to worry about. "I'm sorry Elisabeth said the piano was bad."

"Don't give it another thought. I understand. She has a low frustration point. She actually played beautifully."

She did, too. Achingly beautiful. "Life has certainly changed, hasn't it?"

"Yes, with more changes to come." He stretched one hand tenderly on top of my rounded belly.

It should have been such a happy time. I should have been looking forward to the birth of this baby. Instead, I was filled with consuming worry about Elisabeth's health and well-being, trying to close the gaping holes in her education while helping William continue to develop skills. I wished the days could slow down. How could I manage those two with a newborn added in the mix? I was starting to fear what lay ahead of me.

I glanced over at Robert in the dark. Sometimes I wondered how he really felt about having Elisabeth with us. Too kind to say otherwise, I was sure there were moments when he regretted it. I know for a fact Aunt Martha did.

When I first arrived at their home, nearly three years ago, I was astounded by the peace and order in this household. They didn't even consider having a telephone installed in the parsonage; they considered it an interruption in the sanctuary of the home.

Interruptions. I sighed. That's what I was, an interruption, when I arrived as a refugee. I brought my own fair share of upheaval into their lives.

And now, Elisabeth wreaked havoc. Not a week had gone by that we weren't apologizing profusely to someone for her behavior. Other things had gone missing in the town, too; communion bread at the church, a crate of bananas behind Ibsen's Grocery Store. Always food, which led to one source: my little "organizer."

Ada's remarks about Elisabeth's undeveloped talent hit me hard, because I knew she was right. Elisabeth *should* be taking piano lessons, from someone more skilled than I, *if* she would ever want them. That would probably mean finding a music teacher in Tucson, nearly two hours away. On top of that, our dentist and doctor bills for Elisabeth were already steep and climbing.

I glanced over at Robert. He lay on his back, staring up at the ceiling, a serious look on his face.

He turned on his side to face me and propped his head on his elbow. "I'm grateful for all you brought into this silent home."

He had read my mind. "Even the worry and aggravation and the stack of unpaid bills?"

He smoothed wisps of hair off of my forehead. "No one ever said children would be easy," he said, adding with a grin, "I think trouble comes with the territory."

* * * *

The following week, an enormous truck arrived in front of the parsonage. Robert saw it from his study desk and went out to meet the driver. From the parlor window, William and I watched the two men conversing. I touched his elbow. "William—can you read their lips?"

"I'm trying. The driver says there is a delivery for Reverend Gordon."

Robert kept looking at the front door and shaking his head.

"Dad says it won't fit in the door," added William. "What is it?"

"I have no idea. Let's go find out."

We went outside and listened to Robert and the driver discussing the problem. "There's no way it can fit," said Robert. "You'll just have to return it."

"No can do, Reverend," said the driver. "What if we turned it right side up and took off its legs?"

"But even if you got it through the door, it can't fit *in* the house. The dimensions would take up the entire parlor."

All of a sudden, I knew what the delivery was. A new piano. A burst of generosity from cousin Ada. Knowing her, it would be a grand piano, not even a baby grand. Leave it to Ada to send us a grand piano when we couldn't even pay the dentist's bill. The two men went to the back of the truck, puzzling over this impractical gift.

William scurried out to investigate. "I think the only doors it would fit through are the church doors," said William, looking at the piano in the truck.

"William! That might just be a perfect solution!" exclaimed Robert happily.

And so it seemed. The movers moved it into the pulpit area, near the choir. "You could give lessons here, Louisa," Robert offered. "I wouldn't mind. I can close the study door."

Oh, how Aunt Martha would *love* that arrangement! She wouldn't have to listen to Arthur Hobbs any longer. Just last week she said his playing grated on her like splintered oak.

Robert signed for the piano and walked the delivery men to their truck. He came back into the church with a look of awe on his face. "The driver told me that Baldwin hasn't been making pianos since '42, when the War Production Board ordered all piano building stopped due to the war effort. So this is one of the first off of the new production lines. They just started making pianos again, this year."

He walked up to the piano and lifted the lid. He waved to William to join him. "He also told me Baldwin had such woodworking expertise because of their piano business, that they manufactured wings and fuselage parts and center sections for training and cargo planes." He crouched down to William's level. "They even manufactured parts for fighters, bombers and gliders. Think of that, William. A piano company!"

William's eyes grew wide. He had his father's aptitude and interest in mechanical things.

Robert's face grew animated as he described the inner workings of this piano. "So the lessons they learned in the construction of the multiple-ply aircraft wings became the basis for this very piano. It uses forty-one ply maple pinblock. Apparently, it has exceptional tuning stability and strength." He glanced over at me. "Amazing, isn't it? How one invention leads to another?" He pulled out the piano bench for me to sit down. "But the proof is in the pudding."

"What?" I asked him as I adjusted the bench. "What does pudding have to do with it?"

He tried to stifle a grin but didn't quite make it. "I meant, let's see what it sounds like."

I sat down and played a melody, impressed by the rich tone that poured out. How could I ever go back to Mrs. Drummond's piano with the sticky key?

The phone rang in Robert's study, interrupting us. Robert answered cheerfully, but grew quieter and quieter as he listened. He came back into the church with a grim look on his face. "That was the principal from the grammar school. She wants us to come in for a meeting immediately."

Our lighthearted mood skidded to a halt.

"What do you think she's done now?" Robert wondered aloud, as we walked up to the school.

In the principal's office was Elisabeth, sitting in a chair, wearing her usual aggressive frown. Next to her was Tanya, looking as if she might be ill. In the other chair was a very sour looking Mrs. Bauer with her daughter Trudy. It was clear that the cause of the general unhappiness in the room had its source in Elisabeth.

"Reverend and Mrs. Gordon, apparently there is a misunderstanding about Trudy's coat," began Mrs. Olasky.

"There's no misunderstanding, Mrs Olasky. That child stole my daughter's coat!" hotly contested Mrs. Bauer.

"I didn't steal noting," growled Elisabeth.

"I didn't know she took it, Mrs. Olasky. I *really* didn't," said Tanya, big brown eyes filling with tears.

Mrs. Olasky held a hand up to ward off emotion. "Let's just consider the facts for now. We've determined that Elisabeth did take Trudy's coat."

"Is that the coat?" I asked, looking at a blue jacket on Tanya's lap.

"Yes," answered Mrs. Bauer. "And now it's ruined."

"I did not steal it," said Elisabeth, furrowing her brow.

I looked at her. "Elisabeth, if you didn't steal the coat, why *did* you take it?"

"I vas organizing."

My shoulders fell. I shot a knowing glance at Robert.

153

Using his pulpit's voice, which added a nice touch, Robert said, "We need to explain to you what Elisabeth means by the term organizing." He described her habit carefully, though he avoided any mention of the camp. Elisabeth kept her eyes focused on the ground and kicked the floor. "My guess is Elisabeth realized that Tanya was cold this winter and knew that Trudy had a number of coats to keep her warm. So, in her logic, she organized it. Not unlike a modern day Robin Hood." He gave Elisabeth an encouraging look. "Does that sound about right, Elisabeth?"

Chin to her chest, she gave a brief nod of acknowledgment.

"Nonetheless, Reverend Gordon, it still isn't right," said Mrs. Olasky.

"No, it isn't," he agreed. "Even if the intentions were right, the means were wrong. Elisabeth is learning all about that lesson this year. Tanya, if you don't mind, would you please return the coat to Trudy?"

"No!" gasped Mrs. Bauer, casting a sharp glance at Tanya.

Her look unveiled why she had said the coat was ruined. My temper flared. "Then we'll pay for the coat, Mrs. Bauer, and let Tanya wear it." So Trudy can have *another* new one, I thought. Even Mitzi, her prize poodle, whom Dog had taken an inexplicable fondness for, wore a coat.

"Fine," she sniffed. "It cost $10."

Robert took the money out of his wallet and handed it to Mrs. Bauer, who accepted it without a thank you.

Dramatically, Mrs. Bauer took Trudy's hand to march out of the principal's office. As Trudy dragged behind her mother, she leaned over and whispered to Elisabeth, "Vonderful wiolin."

Pain shot across Elisabeth's face.

Robert turned back to the principal to ask, "Anything else?"

"No," she said, looking as defeated as I felt. "Not today, anyway."

The four of us left the principal's office and walked out to the front of the school. Tanya took the coat off and handed it to me. "Ma'am, I don't need that coat."

I smiled. "Tanya, please wear the coat all winter and enjoy it. Consider it a gift from your friends." Her face broke into a smile. "Tanya, would you be able to come to dinner one evening?"

"I'll have to ask my mother," she answered shyly.

After Tanya turned off on her street, the three of us walked home in silence. Just as we passed the church, I said, "Please, Elisabeth, no more organizing."

She scowled at me. "Dat rich girl has too many coats. She left dat coat on da playground three days ago and forgot all about it until today. She should share."

"Well, what would you think if we just did a better job of organizing?" Robert asked.

Elisabeth and I looked at him curiously.

"Wanting to help people is a good thing. I don't want you to stop. But there's a right way to do it and a wrong way." He stopped on the sidewalk and faced her. "What if we put a list of needs and blessings in our church bulletin each week? So if someone needs a blanket, then another person, who might have an extra blanket, could be the one to share it? What do you think of that idea?"

It's a wonderful idea! An inspired idea! A way to show Elisabeth how to help others and to teach the congregation how to care for each other. Why, it was just like the early church of Acts! I smiled appreciatively at Robert.

Elisabeth was looking at Robert with serious eyes. "Den I need someting," she said.

"What?" asked Robert.

"I need new shoes," she announced. "Da ones I have are ugly."

* * * *

The Needs and Blessings List was so readily accepted in the church that families became motivated to clean out their attics and garages, listing the unused items in the blessings page. Mr and Mrs.Hobbs offered an old sofa, which happened to have just the right fabric to suit Betty Drummond's home. Tom Bunker dropped by the parsonage one night with a used crib. "My missus thought you could use this, Mrs. Gordon. She said she's plumb worn out havin' babies and to git that crib outta here."

She was, too. Barb Bunker had eight children.

"Thank you, Tom. I hadn't even thought about a crib yet. I could really use this." I didn't have much set aside for the baby yet. I put my hand along the side of the crib. A little sanding and new paint and it would be as good as new.

But despite the success of the Needs and Blessings List, more things continued to disappear in Copper Springs. Strange things. The blankets in the back of the milk man's truck were stolen before dawn one day. Laundry went missing off of Barb Bunker's clothesline. I studied Elisabeth's face suspiciously as she ate her cereal and read the comics page of the newspaper, but she looked completely dispassionate.

That wasn't particularly revealing; she often looked dispassionate.

I'd even noticed that it seemed as if someone was thinning out my garden during the night. Tomatoes were gone, carrots pulled up, onions yanked from the earth. When I complained to Robert, he said it was most likely a raccoon. "I was worried about that compost pile attracting animals," he said.

He was probably right. I did hear Dog bark in the night every so often, as if he heard something. But I kept a closer eye on Elisabeth, just in case there was no raccoon in my garden. Just in case Elisabeth couldn't give up her organizing habit.

Robert was equally concerned about the things gone missing in town, too. He found me in the garden one morning and sat down on the ground, leaning on his elbows. "Someone has been getting into the church kitchen and taking food. Someone who knows his or her way around the church."

I sat back on my heels. "What makes you say that?"

"I've always locked up the kitchen at night, but a lot of people know where the key is." He had something more to say but hesitated. "The Ladies Altar Guild paid me a visit this morning. Last night, Mrs. Bauer had put a tray of sandwiches in the icebox for their meeting, but today, the icebox is empty." He frowned. "Mrs. Bauer stirred up the ladies, telling them the culprit is probably Elisabeth."

"What?! It couldn't be her!" I'd like to give that Mrs. Bauer a lecture on Christian charity. "Besides, when Elisabeth organizes things, it usually means that someone else finds the things they need. Well, like the Chinese ladies. Remember how they said they needed a new hose for their garden and Elisabeth stole one from the Dunbars' and put it on the Chinese ladies' front porch?

"I remember," he moaned, thinking of how expensive it was to replace the Dunbars' garden hose.

"And when she overheard Flora O'Dean talk about needing new glasses, she took Ernest's extra pair and left them in Flora's mailbox."

He nodded, a troubled look growing on his face. He rubbed his chin. "I've thought about locking up the church at night."

I hated to consider that option. I could tell Robert hated the thought, too. A church should always be open to people. I thought back to how often, seeking solace, I had slipped into my church in Berlin.

I kept an even closer eye on Elisabeth after that and searched her room for any evidence of organizing. But there was nothing. Nothing suspicious in her behavior, no contraband in her room. I wanted to believe in her, I *really* did. But no one else seemed to. I could feel the suspicion in people's faces when Elisabeth was around. One day we were in the grocery store and Mr. Ibsen stayed right alongside of us the entire time, as if he anticipated shoplifting. Another time, Elisabeth and I were in the hardware store, and I overheard old Mrs. Koops mutter to her husband, "Batten down the hatches. Here comes Miss Sticky Fingers."

Thankfully, Elisabeth didn't have any idea what she meant. But I did. We turned and left. I would wait to purchase new batteries for my radio for a trip to Bisbee. Maybe it was my pregnancy, maybe it was Elisabeth's organizing, but I was starting to lose patience with certain people in this town. Robert pointed out that I never had much patience to start with, but, lately, I had even less.

On Saturday night, I went into Robert's office while he was polishing his sermon. I looked at the books for a while, then out the window, then back at Robert, then at the books.

Finally, he put his pencil down and said, "What? What's on your mind?"

I went over and sat on his desk. "I did something terrible today. Something I can't believe I did. I'm deeply ashamed of myself."

He looked at me with concern. "Tell me what happened."

"At the Peterson wedding today—"

He looked puzzled. "Something happened at the wedding? I thought it went well."

"It did. It was a wonderful wedding. It was later, in Fellowship Hall, during the reception—"

He eyed me suspiciously. "What happened at the reception?"

I took a deep breath. "At the reception, Arthur Hobbs and his twin brothers were ahead of me in line, looking over the food that everyone brought."

"And?"

"And they were complaining about all of the choices. They sounded like spoiled children, Robert."

"And?" he said, looking at me as if I was to blame.

"So Arthur finally decided on bread to create a sandwich and he saw a large bowl of mayonnaise and spread a lot of it on his sandwiches. Quite a lot. The size of a baseball."

"What's so bad about that?"

"It wasn't mayonnaise."

"What was it?"

A fresh wave of remorse flooded over me again. "It was horseradish."

Robert's eyes grew wide. Then he started laughing so hard that tears started to stream down his cheeks. Between gasps he choked out, "And you didn't stop him?"

"No. That's what I felt so badly about. I should have! I know better. Goodness, I'm a grown woman. But I just couldn't resist. He's such an incorrigible boy. Last lesson, he left his bubble gum inside of my metronome!"

That only made Robert laugh all the harder.

"Robert, you're no help at all. You shouldn't laugh at someone giving confession. It isn't right."

Now he was doubled over. I started to smile. Watching Arthur Hobbs's face turn bright red with a mouth filled with spicy horseradish gave me a deliciously satisfied feeling. Even now, just thinking about it.

After Robert finally stopped laughing and caught his breath, he said that as long as I was there, he needed to ask me more about Dietrich's time in prison.

Over the last few months, we had discussed Dietrich's work in the Resistance, but one topic we hadn't covered was Dietrich's arrest. I think we both dreaded it. I sat down on the chair across from him, and rolled up my sweater to support my back. I was starting to have a lot of back aches.

"Comfortable?" he asked.

I nodded.

"Okay, then. What more can you tell me about Dietrich's arrest?"

I had left Germany just a few months prior to Dietrich's arrest, back in 1943, so the bits and pieces I knew of his arrest came through letters from his sister, most of which Robert knew. "You knew that the Central Bureau for Security of Reich was collecting evidence about him. It had suspicions about Dietrich's involvement in plots to assassinate Hitler. But he was arrested because money was traced back to him for smuggling Jews out through Switzerland." My lighthearted mood quickly evaporated. "Just like he did with me."

"He was held in Berlin for a while, wasn't he?" Robert prompted.

"Yes, in Tegel, a Berlin prison, for nearly two years. The charges were vague. At least the guards were friendly; they helped to get Dietrich's papers to family and friends outside. But in September of 1944, the Zossen papers were discovered."

"What were the Zossen papers?" asked Robert, scribbling down everything I said.

"Documents and diaries that incriminated Hans, Oster, and Canaris."

"Slow down a minute, Louisa. Who were those men?"

"Hans von Dohnanyi was Dietrich's brother-in-law. Admiral Wilhelm Canaris was in charge of the Abwehr, the German Military Intelligence. He appointed Major General Hans Oster as his second-in-command."

Robert had an incredulous look on his face. "Louisa, these are the people you worked with in the Resistance? Why haven't you ever mentioned them before?"

"I suppose because you never asked. You have only asked me about Dietrich."

"I never realized...it never occurred to me that you were working with men at such a high level of government. Almost like double agents."

"No." I shook my head adamantly. "They weren't double agents. They were trying very hard to protect Germany from Hitler's insanity. Yet if their plans were too obvious, they would lose their ability to influence events."

"So were they arrested along with Dietrich? When those papers were discovered?"

"Dietrich was doomed from that point. In October, he was transferred to Gestapo prisons. First Buchenwald, then Schönberg, then Flossenbürg. All contacts with the outside world were severed."

I paused for a moment. This was *so* hard. "And the conditions at those camps were atrocious." Probably as bad as Dachau. I slipped my hands under my thighs. "Even though Hitler knew that his Reich was collapsing, he drew up a list of prisoners who must be executed. Dietrich's name was on the list."

I couldn't say another word; I didn't need to. Robert knew the rest of this story. On April 9th, just after leading a worship service for the prisoners, Dietrich was led out into a courtyard, naked, to a scaffolding and hanged. His body was instantly cremated. His ashes mingled with the seventy-three thousand other bodies who died at Flossenbürg. He was only thirty-nine-years old. There was no grave.

Chapter Ten

The week after Thanksgiving, Elisabeth stopped coming home directly after school. She told me she was working on a school project at Tanya's house. She returned in time for dinner every night. A good sign, I hoped. I was feeling somewhat encouraged about Elisabeth.

Well, until the end of the week, anyway.

That feeling vanished the moment I bumped into Tanya's mother at the grocery store. "Thank you for having Elisabeth over so often," I called out, waving to her over a stack of pears.

Tanya's mother gave me a blank look.

"In the afternoons," I prompted. "Elisabeth said that she and Tanya were studying together."

Clearly, she had no idea what I was talking about. My heart sank.

"Mrs. Gordon," she explained, "my Tanya comes to work with me every afternoon."

That evening, as soon as Elisabeth burst in the kitchen door, I told her about meeting Tanya's mother and asked her where she had been.

Her lips tightened. She fixed me with defiant eyes. "None of your beesvax," was all that she said before running up the stairs and slamming the door.

"You should *not* let her talk to you that way," snapped Aunt Martha. "I would've been drawn and quartered if I had spoken to my mother that way."

"Aunt Martha, I didn't *let* her talk to me that way. I will deal with it, but in my own way." Open battles with Elisabeth never worked. Besides, I was trying to elicit information, not cause her to clamp her lips shut even tighter than they usually were.

"Your way is with a wet noodle," she countered.

What did *that* mean?

"That child creates nothing but trouble, Louisa."

I frowned, but that was a statement that I couldn't deny. In fact, I had an odd sense of waiting for trouble to find us.

Perhaps, I thought, hatching a plan, I could ward it off.

"William, how is your spy log coming along?" I asked him as I tucked him into bed that night. "Anything interesting?"

"No. This town is boring." That was another choice phrase he had adopted from Elisabeth. She said that everything and everyone in Copper Springs was boring.

I hated to ask him. I hated to stoop to this level. But...desperate times resorted to desperate measures. "Ever thought about spying on Elisabeth?"

He scrunched up his face as if he thought I had completely lost my mind. "Elisabeth?" There were moments, like this one, that William's expressions looked remarkably similar to his father's.

"Have you noticed that she doesn't come home after school? She shows up in time for dinner." I pulled the covers up to his chin. "Makes me wonder where she is in the afternoons."

I hooked him. He decided to follow her directly after school the next day. I was a little nervous about what facts he might unearth, but I knew we needed to put a stop to this organizing habit, and I was running out of ideas.

The next day, William zoomed off on his red bicycle to meet Elisabeth after school. I kept peering out the parlor window anxiously, waiting to see what he might have found out. But he didn't come home.

Finally, at six o'clock, without any explanation, they both blew into the kitchen. I gave William a suspicious gaze but he ignored me. Instead, he ran to get the dinner bowl for Dog before Aunt Martha started scolding him for being late. I followed him outside behind a hungry Dog. As he refilled the empty water bowl with the hose, I tapped him on the shoulder. "Well?"

He looked at me with a patronizing glance, another expression that was remarkably similar to his father's. "I'm not going to tell you, Mom. I promised Elisabeth that I wouldn't tell."

Now I was really worried. "Can you at least tell me if she's doing anything that she shouldn't be doing?"

He thought about that for a moment, then fixed a bright blue gaze on me. "Nope. She's doing something that she should be doing."

Why, oh why did I read *The Merry Adventures of Robin Hood* to him?

Robert took Elisabeth to her dentist appointment one afternoon, hoping to talk to Dr. Klein about the bill, to see if we could make payments on it. It made me sad that he had to take this step; Robert was a man who paid his bills on time and avoided debt. When he arrived home, I asked him how the conversation had gone.

"Just fine," he said. "Nothing to worry about. It's all taken care of."

He was lying. One of the first rules I had learned in Resistance work was when someone lied, his eyes involuntarily darted to the left...like Robert's just did. I sighed. I knew we had run out of options. I was going to have to teach piano to those atrocious Hobbs twins.

One evening at the dinner table, Elisabeth thrust a crinkled-up paper at me. "What is this?" I asked with a sinking heart, certain another teacher had sent a note home requesting a conference. The baby suddenly buckled a knee under my rib cage, making me sit up straight.

"Dat dumb school is having a dumb Christmas play."

I smoothed out the paper and read the invitation.

"So, all da dumb parents will be dere," she said.

I nodded.

"So, I guess dat you should be dere."

I nodded, trying to suppress a smile. She ran upstairs to her room. Dog raced up behind her; he seemed to be growing especially attached to Elisabeth. She and William even worked out a sleeping schedule with Dog to share him. I followed them up and made Dog get off her bed. "Off! If Aunt Martha saw you now, she would send you packing!" He jumped off with a hurt expression, and curled up next to the bed. I looked at Elisabeth. "Do you know what Christmas is all about?"

Elisabeth went back to the book she was reading, almost ignoring me but not uncomfortable with the fact that I was there. "Yust dat da Christ baby vas born."

"Do you know who the Christ child was?"

"Ja. He's da reason dat Hitler hates da Juden."

"Would you ever like to know more about Christ? I mean, more than what you know about Hitler?"

She looked up at me blankly. "Vhy?"

"Well, you live in a minister's home, and you attend church every Sunday. And because we believe that Jesus is God's Son." I sat down on her bed.

"I'll believe vhatever you tell me you vant me to believe. Yust tell me da rules."

"But Elisabeth, Jesus isn't a set of rules. He's a person who loves and guides us."

She rolled her eyes.

I looked back at her directly in the eyes. "And Jesus loves you."

"Vell, if He loves me, den he should not have made me Juden."

"You know, Jesus was Jewish. And he suffered, too, from evil people just like the Nazis."

She looked up at me sharply. From the surprised look on her face, I could tell she had never known that. I got up to leave, knowing I had said enough for now.

Later that afternoon, Robert and I were out in the garden. He had promised to turn a bed for me and finally had a free hour, but first insisted on throwing sticks for Dog. Dog would charge off after the stick, then come loping back up to him with the stick in his mouth, stopping off for a sniff here and there. Robert crouched down and scratched Dog's ears. William was riding his bicycle up and down the street. It was a peaceful moment.

Until Elisabeth flew through the front door with an angry look on her face.

Picking up the shovel to turn the dirt, Robert looked up at her and calmly asked, "Anything wrong, Elisabeth?"

"Dat Mr. Koops is making us do another dad-blasted essay. He vants us to describe vhich side of da house ve should plant a tree. It's da dumbest essay in da vorld."

Robert and I exchanged a look. "Well, in Arizona," he said, "it would be wise to plant a tree on the east side of the house, so that you can get shade when the sun is the hottest."

"But a southern exposure is always best for growing things," I added thoughtfully.

We debated the topic for a while as Elisabeth looked as if she was close to exploding. William rode his bicycle up to the house. "Vilhelm, vhat side of da house should you plant a tree in?" she asked, weary of our thoughtful dialogue.

He looked at her, cocked his head, and answered, "The outside." Then he zoomed off on his red bicycle, legs pedaling as fast as he could go, veering back and forth, as if darting around imaginary objects.

Elisabeth's face erupted into a gigantic smile. "See? Dat's vhy I ask Vilhelm dese tings. His answers are quick." And she ran inside the house to finish up her two-word essay.

A few days later, William and I attended Elisabeth's Christmas play, directed by Miss Howard. I scanned the bulletin to see if Elisabeth had a role in the play, but didn't find her name.

Just as I had thought.

Then, with a grin, William jabbed his elbow into my side and pointed to the piano. There, sitting on the bench, was my incorrigible but incredibly talented cousin, solemnly looking at the keyboard. Giant tears loomed in my eyes; soon they were splashing down my cheeks. Finally, as I started sniffing, William rolled his eyes and ran to the boys' bathroom to bring me a roll of toilet paper to mop up my face.

As the play was about to begin, William popped out of his chair and went to stand next to her as her page turner. He couldn't read music, nor could he hear it, but they had worked out an effective partnership. Whenever she was ready for the page to turn, she gave him a little bob of her head, and swiftly, obediently, he turned the page. She played the music score for the entire play.

I couldn't stop tearing up. I even let out a sob when the parents clapped enthusiastically for Elisabeth and William at the end. Elisabeth noticed my sloppy crying and glared at me, then completely avoided me afterwards. I went into the girls' pink tiled bathroom to compose myself.

I waited until the clump of parents left the room and then asked Miss Howard how she was able to get Elisabeth to play for her.

She laughed. "I told her I didn't know what to do without anyone to play the piano. She told me, 'Vell den, I vill play for you'. Didn't she tell you? I told her to ask you if it was all right that she stay after school. William said it was fine."

"William?"

"Well, yes. He's been here, too. He has stayed and helped me during practices." She spotted him filling his shirt pocket with cookies at the refreshment table. "He's quite a boy, isn't he?"

That only got me tearing up all over again. "I'm sorry," I sniffed. "It's this...it's my condition...I'm very emotional. I think you're the only person in the world whom she would have played for. Other than Robert. She adores you."

"Well, it's mutual. There's something about her..." Then an uncomfortable look crossed her face. "We had better sit down for a moment."

Oh no.

"I won't be Elisabeth's teacher after this quarter ends. The second grade teacher has to move. Her husband is returning from overseas duty and she's going to join him at Camp LeJeune in North Carolina. I've only been teaching part-time and I really need the work, so I'm going to teach the second grade class."

I was *so* disappointed. "Do you have any idea who will be taking your class?"

She hesitated, as if afraid to say.

I gasped. "No! Not... Mr. Koops?"

She nodded.

I sighed. Why was it that things always changed when you didn't want them to change? I gazed out the window at William and Elisabeth, now playing hopscotch. Suddenly I jerked my head back toward her. "Did you say second grade? Right here?"

"Why, yes," she answered.

I smiled. "Miss Howard, do you have a moment to discuss an interesting possibility?"

* * * *

Christmas was only a week away. Robert came in to the parlor one evening, frowning. "If *only* we had an organist. Just doesn't seem like Christmas without someone playing the organ. The carols just won't be the same." He sighed and sat down on the davenport. "Imagine 'O Holy Night' without the organ." He shook his head in despair.

I didn't say a word. I just continued my chess game with William.

"Or 'Hark the Herald Angels Sing' without the organ. A crime, really."

I shot him a dark look. "They will sound just fine accompanied by the new grand piano."

"Won't be the same without the organ," he sighed, glowering back at me. "And think of all of the weddings I've been doing lately. All of those servicemen coming home to their sweethearts, only to not have Mendolssohn's *Wedding March* on the organ! Hardly feels as if those poor young souls are really, truly married."

I rolled my eyes. "Robert. I can *not* play the organ."

"Yes, you can," he muttered. "You just *won't*."

"No. She really can't play," said Elisabeth, coming in from the kitchen with a peanut butter sandwich in her hands. "She's da vorst organist. I heard her vonce. She tried. She vas horrible." She shuddered, as if the thought of it was a terrible memory.

Interesting! Elisabeth had told me she didn't remember me from before the war.

Robert crossed his arms on the davenport, looking defeated.

"Oh fine, den," she said, as if she was giving in under great duress. "I vill play dat bloody organ."

Robert and I whipped our heads around to look at her. "You can play the organ?" he asked, incredulously. "You really can?"

"Ja."

"Elisabeth! Bless you! Why, the church will even pay you."

She looked at him suspiciously. "How much?"

"I don't know. I'll have to look at the records from last year. I'll go look it up right now, then we can go over to the church and practice." He looked triumphant. He finally had his organist. I heard him whistling as he went out of the house to cross into the office.

Elisabeth came over to sit next to William and me. "You never said you could play the organ," I said to her, one eyebrow raised.

"You never asked," she shot back. She rubbed her fingers over the tattoo on her forearm, as if she hoped to rub them off. "Vill it be enough money to have dis taken off?"

I stroked her thin, little shoulders. "Maybe. We're saving up for it, too. We'll need to talk to a doctor in Tucson to do it. I want you to have it done properly, so there will hardly be any scarring."

The next afternoon, Elisabeth was up in my room helping me sew a new skirt for her. I was trying to get as much done as I could before the baby arrived. I still wasn't prepared for the baby. Rosita had brought me diapers and pins, a few yellow receiving blankets and a long white baby gown. But, so far, that was all. This skirt pattern was so simple that I decided to use it to teach Elisabeth how to sew on the sewing machine, but her interest, as usual, was in short supply. "Vhy don't you yust make dis for me?" she asked, after I made her pull out a crooked seam and start over.

"You're the one who wanted a new skirt. I'd like to teach you how to make your own clothes. If you would just slow down, you wouldn't make as many mistakes."

She scowled at me, but carefully pulled the stitches out. I sat down besides her and smoothed some wisps from her foreheads. "Your hair is growing longer," I said. "Soon you'll be able to pull it into a ponytail."

"Like dat Trudy Bauer," she answered, head bent over the skirt. "She vears big bows in her hair."

I stroked her hair. "We could get you bows."

"And den I need saddle shoes. Dat's vhat Trudy vears."

I glanced down at her shoes. Hand-me-downs from Esmeralda. They *were* scuffed up. "Maybe someday."

"Trudy says dat American girls vear new clothes."

"Anything else?"

"She says dat I should change my name to Betsy. To be a real American."

"Is that what you want? To be called Betsy?"

She shrugged in that impossible-to-decipher-what-she's-thinking way of hers.

"Trudy has a lot of ideas for you, doesn't she?"

She looked carefully down at the crooked seam. "Trudy says dat you can only get to heaven if you believe in dat Jesus."

I sat there quietly.

"So is dat true?" she asked, putting the skirt in her lap and looking directly at me.

I stood up and went to stand by the window to think of how to answer that question.

Lord, help me not make a mess of this, I prayed.

I turned back to her. "When I was about your age, I wondered those same questions, so I decided to read the Bible for myself. And do you know what surprised me the most about Jesus? In the gospels, whenever Jesus met someone, He already knew all about them. He knew their name, what they did, what kind of trouble they might be in, what they might be hiding, the kind of person they were. Jesus knew people's hearts."

I sat back down on the bed next to her. "So, to answer your question, I think Jesus already knows all about each person, and we can trust Him to make the right decisions about who goes to Heaven."

"So how do I know about dat Yesus?"

"Well, the Bible can tell you. And listening to Robert's sermons can teach you."

She frowned at me. She played tic-tac-toe with William during Robert's sermons.

"The Old Testament describes the need for God's son. The New Testament has four gospels, which tell about Jesus' life on earth. The entire Bible shows how God is longing to know each one of us and have a relationship with us." I picked up my Bible and showed her the gospels.

"Da Yuden don't believe in da new part. Dat New Testament."

My hand went to my abdomen as I felt a sharp kick from the baby. "No. They are still looking for the Messiah to come."

"Danny says dat He has not come yet. Dat Elijah must come first."

I looked at her. Danny was still so important to her. She wrote to him nearly everyday, filling the envelopes with newspaper clippings about anything she thought would interest him.

"When I read the New Testament for myself, I found out answers to those very questions." I handed her my Bible, but she wouldn't take it. "If you change your mind and decide you would like to read it, you are welcome to borrow my Bible anytime."

She didn't answer, turning her attention back to the crooked seam.

* * * *

Christmas morning dawned cold and bright. After breakfast, we opened gifts in the parlor. Aunt Martha opened up her present from Ada. "What in the *world* is this?" It was a set of plastic tubs with lids. She looked at them curiously before reading the note:

"Darling Marty, This is the latest rage to hit Phoenix. It's called Tupperware. Invented by a man named Earl Tupper. It's to seal food and keep it from spoiling. I knew you'd love the concept. Yours, Ada."

Aunt Martha looked the plastic tubs over, raised an eyebrow at Elisabeth and murmured, "Maybe Elisabeth should have a set for under her bed."

I had made hair bows for Elisabeth, just like Trudy Bauer wore. There was another box under the tree for her from

Robert. She ripped open the wrapping, and there were saddle shoes. Brand new ones, sent from the Sears Roebuck catalog.

Elisabeth didn't react. She didn't even look up at Robert. But she did hold the shoes in her lap, running her fingers over the edges and the laces. She even smelled them, deeply inhaling the new leather aroma, which made Robert grin.

I looked at Robert fondly as he gazed at Elisabeth. "How did you ever guess her shoe size?" I asked him.

"William helped me. We traced her feet one day and said it was for a math assignment. Then I sent the paper to Sears, and they matched it." He turned to Elisabeth. "Try them on and see if they fit."

They did. Like a glove. No gift could have meant more to her. It wasn't just shoes. It was about belonging, fitting in to her peer group. For the first time in a long, long time, Elisabeth felt special. Robert had done that for her.

William couldn't wait to open the gift from Ada. She had bought it on a trip to Philadelphia. He shook the box and felt a thud; whatever was inside flew from side to side. In the box was an unusual sphere of coiled steel, in the shape of a tight cylinder. Curiously, he read the box and announced, "It's a Slinky!"

Then he ran to the top of the stairs, placed one end of the Slinky on the top stairs, and curled the top end on the next stair, and let go. Down it went, up and over, up and over, until it landed on the bottom stair, back in its original sphere. We watched it, stunned. Even Dog remained immobile, cocking his head, staring at this shiny metal thing.

Robert went over to pick it up, examining it, snapping it between his two hands like a deck of cards. "Fascinating!" he exclaimed, as if this piece of wire held the secrets of the universe. "It's like a tension spring!"

175

"Well, Professor," Aunt Martha said wryly to Robert, "help me get these wrappings cleaned up."

"Vait," Elisabeth ordered. "I have da present for you."

We looked at her, surprised. Besides the fact that Elisabeth had no money, she had never felt the need to reciprocate a kindness. She sat down at the piano, put her hands on the keys, took a deep breath, and played a beautiful score of music for us. It was the same piece I had heard her play when she didn't think anyone was home. Towards the end, she stopped and paused before turning shyly toward us. "I haven't finished it yet."

Slowly, like a cloud drifting past the sun, it dawned on me that she had *composed* it. Tears sprang to my eyes. I wanted to leap up from my chair and run to her, to hug and kiss her. I wanted to tell her how much I loved the music she created, and how touching it was to have her give us a gift. I wanted her to know that I felt it was one of the first signs that she was healing, from the inside. And the music was surprisingly soft, too, considering Elisabeth's personality was rather fierce.

But I held back. After the Christmas play, when I bawled openly, I knew better than to start gushing.

Robert and I exchanged a look, his eyes serious and shiny. He stood up and went over next to her, crouching down besides her. "Elisabeth? I hope you realize that when you give someone a gift, you can't take it back. Whenever I want to hear you play that piece, I hope you will oblige me and play it."

She nodded solemnly again.

"I think I might just have to hear it everyday."

And with that, she looked up at him and I saw a smile tug at the corners of her mouth. Another unexpected gift! Getting a smile out of Elisabeth was like panning for gold and finally finding a speck. He crouched down. "Thank you, Elisabeth."

Then came the most shocking words ever heard out of Elisabeth's mouth. "Tank you," she whispered.

Little by little, something was softening in Elisabeth's spirit.

Even Aunt Martha looked stunned. After Elisabeth had gone into the kitchen, she said, "So maybe there is balm in Gilead after all."

Late that evening, William and Elisabeth and Aunt Martha had gone to bed. Robert had made a small fire that crackled in the grate. I came down and curled up next to him on the couch, tucking my head under his chin. "Put your hand there," I placed his hand on my large tummy. "Feel the kicks?"

"I do. Maybe he'll be a football player."

"So you've decided this child will be a boy?" I said, smiling.

"Well, Ada said it was a boy and she's not one to be disagreed with." He handed me a small package.

"What's this?" I said, lifting my head and looking at him. "I thought we agreed not to give each other gifts this Christmas." On the day that we received Dr. Klein's enormous dental bill for Elisabeth, we made a promise to each other to forego presents. We were *that* low on cash.

"I didn't spend a penny, but I wanted you to have something."

I opened up the blue box. In it were two pearl earrings. I looked up at him, curiously.

"They were my mother's."

I held them in my palm and gazed at the tiny and perfect opalescent balls. I had never possessed any jewelry other than the thin gold wedding band Robert had given me.

"Don't you like them?" he asked gently. "You have a strange look on your face."

"I love them." I did, too. I was so touched. "I've always loved pearls. Do you ever think of the oysters that produced them, so long ago? To think a piece of grit in an oyster turns into a pearl. It's a miracle, really."

Now he looked at me strangely. "Sweetheart, trying to understand your mind is like trying to package fog."

I smiled, touched his face with my hands and kissed him tenderly. "Thank you. For the earrings. For Elisabeth's shoes. For everything."

* * * *

The next morning William and I were alone in the kitchen, washing breakfast dishes. "Why would anyone give a baby a shower?" he asked. "Seems like a baby would be too little for a shower."

"What would make you ask that?" I answered.

"I was spying on Mrs. Bauer and Mrs. Strang in Mr. Ibsen's grocery store and they said that the ladies at the church *should* give you a baby shower but no one *wanted* to."

I froze.

"So what's a baby shower, anyway?"

I looked at him. "It's a party for the baby. To give the baby gifts that he will need."

He looked at me curiously. "Why wouldn't they want to give our baby a party?"

"I'm sure it's because it's Christmas, and they know that the baby will get lots of gifts," I lied, covering up for those insufferable church ladies.

"That's not what *they* said. They said that the town klep...klepto..." he stopped and frowned, trying to remember the word.

"Kleptomaniac?" offered Robert, appearing from the parlor.

I turned my head slightly to look at Robert over my shoulder. Not hearing him, William didn't notice that he was there. "I can't remember the word," William continued, "but they said that the baby would be able to get everything he needs from that town person because that person lived with us." He looked at me intently. "So what did they mean?"

I shrugged, as if I didn't know. "Time to get dressed for the day, okay?" I said. I stayed at the kitchen sink after William left, staring out the window at Dog chasing birds in the yard.

Robert came up behind me and slid his arms around my waist. He tucked his chin on my shoulder and watched Dog out the window with me. "You can't let a few people bother you."

They did bother me, but it was more than slighted feelings. I was concerned that they were right. I was still worried about Elisabeth. "I'm just glad that I'm...that Elisabeth's...well, that she isn't causing an adverse affect at the church," was all that I said. The church was thriving, especially as servicemen were starting to arrive home to pick up their lives where they had left off. Robert was officiating at a wedding nearly every week, sometimes two. The Sunday church services were overflowing. "It's just that..."

"Just what?"

I folded the tea towel carefully. "Sometimes I feel as if all I ever hear from those ladies is a steady diet of criticism. They took me out to lunch last spring to inform me that the pastor's wife traditionally *ran* the Ladies Altar Guild. And then they even suggested that I might want to consider changing my clothing style. They felt I dress too youthfully."

He turned me around to face him. "Why didn't you ever tell me about that lunch?"

"Oh, I don't know. I suppose I do feel a little guilty that I don't do more. Especially with music. I want to do more...I want to help you...but..." The truth was that those church ladies made me uneasy and it had nothing to do with Elisabeth. The shift came when I stopped being a houseguest of the Gordon's, whom they generally ignored, and became Robert's wife.

The minister's wife.

Suddenly, there was a long list of invisible expectations that were placed on my shoulders. The ladies seemed to view the church with ownership rights, as if its purpose was to serve their needs, not the other way around. Mrs. Bauer had even complained to me that the children's Sunday school program was getting too crowded. She suggested that priority should be given to those children whose families tithed.

Did she mean, like paying country club fees? I asked her.

Her eyebrows furrowed together. She did *not* appreciate my question.

"I'm not a very good minister's wife," I said, defeated.

He stroked my hair back. "Louisa, you didn't marry my job. You married me. And I think you're a wonderful wife. You're the heart of this home. You hold our family together. And look at all of the responsibilities you have! You're teaching William, you're helping Elisabeth settle in. Not to mention that you're going to have a baby in a month or so."

Maybe. But those church ladies rankled me with their opinions. "I feel as if I could never do enough to please them," I said miserably.

"Not everyone feels that way," he said, reading my thoughts. "Not the judge. Not Rosita and Ramon. Not the people who matter to us."

I nodded.

"'As for me and my household, we will serve the Lord,'" he said, quoting from the book of Joshua. "Louisa, we live our life for God's pleasure and purpose. Not to please some gossips at the grocery store. If there's something we need to change, then let God do the telling to us."

"Even though we seem to be harboring the town organizer?" I asked him. "I can't really blame them. It is an *exasperating* habit."

He nodded in agreement. "Elisabeth is coming along, bit by bit. She'll give up organizing when she's ready, as she feels more secure. In the meantime, it gives the town something to talk about."

I put my arms around his waist and leaned into him, feeling protected by his close presence.

* * * *

True to his word, Robert asked Elisabeth to play the piano piece she composed each day. "When did you write it?" he asked.

"In da camp. During da night, I played. In here." She pointed to her head.

What a *wonder*. Even a camp like Dachau couldn't snuff out the wonderful spirit God had infused into her. I wondered how many other beautiful spirits were in those camps, silenced by the Nazis, but continuing to create music and books and ideas in their heads.

I was waiting for the right moment to tell Robert about having William enter Miss Howard's second grade class at the start of the new quarter. Finally, I couldn't postpone the task any longer. I went to his office one afternoon and sat down across from him.

"*What?*" he roared after I explained the idea. "You did this without discussing it with me? We had a *plan*. We were going to send him to the Southwestern School for the Deaf when he was ten-years-old. *That* was our plan. You *agreed* to that!"

"But he's not ten yet. Miss Howard is a wonderful teacher, and she's willing to accommodate him, and the principal will be willing to try." I hoped so, anyway. I hadn't *exactly* spoken to Mrs. Olasky yet.

He glared at me. "Why did you do this?

"Because he's getting too far ahead of me. I can't keep up with him, Robert. He's so hungry to learn. And he's hungry for friends, to play tag at recess, or throw a football around. Just to have a normal childhood."

He leaned back in his chair for a long moment. "Then maybe we should consider the Southwestern School for the Deaf now."

That was *exactly* the response from Robert that worried me. William would have to be a boarding student because the school was in Tucson, two hours away. "What have we got to lose by letting him try the local grammar school?"

"What if it doesn't *work*, Louisa? What if he is teased, or feels inadequate, or doesn't fit in...or doesn't make any friends...or what if he fails?"

I sat on the edge of my chair, leaning forward. "And what if he succeeds, Robert? What if he does make friends? What if he does do well in school?"

"Oh Louisa, don't be naïve. Look at Elisabeth! She's different...she's had a terrible time trying to fit in."

"But doing better, Robert. You can't deny that she's making some progress. And besides, William has a very different personality than Elisabeth. I think you're underestimating him. It's just so...providential...that the one teacher in this entire school district who might be willing to have a deaf child in her class is moving to his grade. It's a miracle, really."

"William's miracle is Elisabeth's loss."

That was true. I was concerned about the affect of more school periods with Mr. Koops. Elisabeth's stomach aches were still severe and frequent. "Would you at least *talk* to William and see what he thinks about it?"

He scowled at me but finally agreed.

Later that night, I was reading in bed when Robert came into the room, walked over to the window, staring outside into the dark night, his arms folded against his chest. "So...did you have a talk with William?" I guessed.

He took a deep breath and exhaled. "He said, 'Dad, you *have* to let me go.'" He turned to look at me. "My seven-year-old son told me that I have to let him go. And we both know he meant more than attending second grade." He turned back to the window, sighing deeply.

Robert felt so protective of William, a quality I found endearing. "Parenting is hard," he finally said, more to himself than to me.

I went over to him and tucked my arm in his, looking out the window. An owl hooted once, then twice. "Hear that?" I asked. "An owl has talons to cling on to a branch. It can even walk. But it has wings to fly. It's *meant* to fly."

He stared out the window for a long moment. "Why do things have to change?"

"You sound just like Elisabeth," I said, smiling. "She thinks that change always means things get worse. Sometimes, change can be for the good."

"Sometimes," he said, "change can mean disaster."

Chapter Eleven

Over the next few days, Robert grew distant and distracted. I would catch him deep in thought at odd moments, staring off into the distance. During dinner one night, he didn't say a single word. Afterwards, he went back to his office. As soon as I could, I went over to join him. I closed the door and leaned against it. "What's bothering you?"

He gave me a sideways glance. "Nothing."

"Nothing? Nothing at all?"

He leaned back in his chair but kept his eyes on his desk. "I received a letter in the mail the other day from my editor. The...uh...the publisher changed his mind about my book. About publishing it."

I wanted terribly to ask him questions, but I pressed my lips shut. I knew him well enough by now to wait for him to elaborate, rather than pepper him with questions. After a period of silence, he lifted his head and said without emotion, "Apparently, they learned that I have been...divorced. And they felt they couldn't publish a book from a minister...who was...divorced."

"They didn't even care about the circumstances?"

"Apparently not."

Amazing. It was *amazing* to me to see the damage Ruth caused continue on and on, even beyond her death. "They said nothing about the content of the book?"

"They liked the book. They're paying me a kill-fee."

I tilted my head. "What's a kill-fee?"

He gave a short laugh. "Kind of a consolation prize. They're paying me *not* to publish it."

"If you accept the kill-fee, then it won't be published?"

"That's right."

I crouched down beside him. "Send it back."

He looked at me, puzzled.

"We need to find another publisher."

"Don't you think another publisher will come to the same conclusion?"

"Then we'll just keep looking until we find one who will publish it. This book *needs* to be published."

He cleared his throat, unable to speak.

"I'll help, Robert."

"You always do," he answered, reaching an arm around me and brushing his lips against my temple.

"Good. Then help me up," I said. "I think I'm stuck."

That evening I had the house to myself, a rare occurrence that didn't happen nearly often enough. Elisabeth was at Esmeralda's; Robert had taken William and Aunt Martha on an errand to Bisbee. William insisted Dog should come along, despite Aunt Martha's objections.

I decided to take a bubble bath and read through Aunt Martha's latest *Good Housekeeping* magazine. I found her magazine in the kitchen and started to absentmindedly thumb through it when one of my pearl earrings fell off. I picked it up and put both earrings on the kitchen window sill, a reminder to ask Robert to fix the backing. Then I went upstairs to settle into a lovely, luxurious time of pure indulgence.

At least it *was* an indulgence until I heard the kitchen door slam shut. I jumped out of the tub and hurried to dress, eager to avoid Aunt Martha's disapproval. I flew downstairs, expecting to find them home from Bisbee. No one was there. I peered out the kitchen window to see if the car was there but the driveway was empty. And it was then that I noticed my pearl earrings were gone. My heart sank.

Later that night, I asked Elisabeth if she had taken my earrings but she denied it. "I won't be angry if you tell me the truth, Elisabeth. I have seen you try them on once or twice."

"I did not steal noting," she snapped, fixing a defiant gaze at me.

I wanted to believe her. I *really* did. But I felt a growing alarm.

When I told Robert, he said it was time we started locking up the house. When I asked if he thought he would be locking someone out, or locking Elisabeth in, he only shrugged. "We've got to do something, Louisa. Things are getting out of hand." He was right. I couldn't shake the feeling that something dreadful was brewing.

* * * *

The next afternoon, Aunt Martha marched into the house, her lips tightened, after a meeting with the mission committee at church. She started dicing an onion for dinner, chopping with such vehemence that the onion looked pulverized.

"Did something upsetting happen at the meeting?" I asked.

She slammed the refrigerator door shut. "Every single year I have been asked to chair the annual mission supper. Every single year for as long as I can remember. And now, they've asked someone else. Someone who couldn't cook a decent meal if her life depended on it."

The annual mission supper was a matter of grave importance to Aunt Martha. She planned for it all throughout the year.

"Whom *did* they ask?" I asked, not really wanting to hear the answer.

"Evelyn Bauer." She slammed her pocketbook on the table. "That woman has more airs than a duchess. I never dreamed I'd see the day when...well...it's all because..." Her eyes darted upstairs.

"Because of Elisabeth?" I finished for her.

Aunt Martha pressed her lips together as if she just swallowed a teaspoonful of vinegar. Then she looked straight at me and said, "I want to borrow those pictures you showed me. And those news clippings. I think those church ladies need a little education at the Ladies' Altar Guild meeting on Friday. They need a dose of Christian charity in their withered old bones."

My eyebrows shot up. "They're on Robert's desk," I replied.

She gave a brief nod, as if she had just mapped out a war game, and started up the stairs.

"Aunt Martha?"

She stopped half-way up and turned around.

I looked up the stairs at her. "I'd like to go with you."

On Friday, we went to the Ladies' Altar Guild meeting and sat through a very tedious discussion of whether the children in Sunday school should be served apple juice or water because of the spills on the carpet. Finally, just as the meeting was about to be adjourned, Aunt Martha rose to her feet. In a bold voice she announced, "I have something to say."

Mrs. Bauer, who led the meeting, looked annoyed.

Aunt Martha plowed ahead. "You are all aware that my nephew, the *Reverend*..." she pronounced that word with great pride... "and his wife, Louisa..." she tilted her head slightly toward me... "have taken in a child from Germany. Louisa's cousin, Elisabeth."

With the mention of Elisabeth's name, whispers started hissing. "I believe our family owes you all an apology," Aunt Martha continued.

Feathered hats bobbed toward each other, in complete agreement.

Aunt Martha carried on. "I think we have been remiss in not giving the church an understanding of what that girl has been through."

She explained how Elisabeth and her mother had been in hiding for over a year, until they were turned in by the farmer's wife. She described the train ride to Dachau, how people were crammed so tightly into cattle cars that many were crushed, and bodies were tossed outside like dead carcasses when the train made stops to collect more prisoners—forced labor—on the way to the camp. She spoke of Dachau, of lines of prisoners led to their senseless executions.

Aunt Martha must have read every word of those newspaper accounts I had gathered. And today, she held nothing back. She was far more explicit than I would have been. At the climactic point of her speech, she pulled out the pictures I had taken and passed them around.

As the pictures made their way through the ladies, row by row, gasps could be heard. Several ladies reached for hankies. Then Aunt Martha delivered her closing argument. "It just seems to me if we are going to call ourselves Christians, we need to earn that title and show that child some compassion." Then she sat down, chin jutting forward, head held proud.

Even Mrs. Bauer was at a rare loss of words. "Um...is there...anything else before we ...um...adjourn?" she asked timidly, breaking the awkward silence.

"Yes!" I said, standing up cheerfully, invigorated by Aunt Martha's bravado. "I have an idea about showing Elisabeth how we share the love of God with others. In fact, for those of you who have German heritage, such as you, Mrs. Bauer, and you, Mrs. Klein...," I noticed they both looked nervous when I singled them out, "...this winter has been particularly hard for Germans. There are many shortages in Germany; people need basic supplies to stay alive." I told them about the man who offered me his oriental rug last summer, in exchange for a loaf of bread.

"What if," I continued, "Elisabeth and I held a piano concert and raised money to send to Germany? Think of all of the people around here who have relatives in Germany! They would come. We could charge admission and play music from German composers."

That wouldn't be hard. The only music Elisabeth and I had been allowed to learn, while in Germany, was music from the German composers. Hitler had banned any other composers, except for Mozart.

"That's a very sweet idea," said Mrs. Bauer in a patronizing tone, "but it seems as if no one would come to hear a local piano teacher and a young girl play a few melodies."

To my astonishment, Aunt Martha leapt to her feet. "Evelyn Bauer!" she said with loud authority, "Louisa Gordon is the finest pianist in the state of Arizona, with one exception. Elisabeth is an even better one. And I happen to know that's true because my cousin Ada is on the Board of the Phoenix Symphony and she told me so herself!"

And she sat down crossly, gripping her shiny black purse as if someone might snatch it. I gazed at her with great admiration. Aunt Martha was outdoing herself today with indignant support of Elisabeth and me.

"It's true," agreed Mrs. Hobbs. "Martha is right. They're both remarkable pianists."

I turned to Mrs. Hobbs with a newly acquired fondness, deciding immediately that I wouldn't postpone teaching her twins any longer.

Suddenly, a group of church ladies turned into enthusiastic patrons of the arts. "What a marvelous idea, Mrs. Gordon," said Mrs. Bauer, in an abrupt shift. "Let's plan the concert to coincide with our mission supper! It could be the kick-off! Oh, this will be wonderful! The most successful mission supper ever!" she gushed, as Aunt Martha frowned at her.

Oh no. That soon? I looked down at my gigantic middle, wondering how I could manage to prepare for a concert with a newborn? I thought weakly about the last time I had really practiced the piano—it was during Thanksgiving, when Ada was visiting. And, somehow, I had to convince Elisabeth to play with me. If I could talk her into it, I knew *this* would be the way to endear her to the town of Copper Springs.

On the lazy afternoon of New Year's Day, our dentist, Dr. Klein, knocked on the door. Elisabeth answered it and came in to the kitchen with an ashen look on her face. "Dat dentist is at da door. I hate dat dentist. Vhy is he here?" She looked panicked, worried he was making a house call to fill her cavities.

Robert and I left the kitchen to go see why he had come, on a holiday of all days. "My wife told me," started Dr. Klein, "she told me...about Elisabeth...in that awful place. Well...I just didn't know. I had no idea. Here's something from me to your family," he said gruffly. He handed Robert an envelope and abruptly left. Robert closed the door behind him and opened the envelope. In it was the bill from his office, stamped 'paid-in-full' in red ink. Robert handed it to me, eyes shining. "1946 has been ushered in with a miracle."

"Does dat mean I don't have to go back to dat dentist?" asked Elisabeth, coming downstairs after she was certain Dr. Klein had left.

"No," Robert said. "It just means your smile is priceless."

* * * *

The next day, I put on my sweater to go outside to garden. In the pocket was the undeveloped film William had taken over a month or so ago. I handed it to Aunt Martha to take to Bisbee on the next trip and went out front to my beloved little Eden. I was tilling egg shells and coffee grounds into the soil when a woman drove by and slowed her car in front of the parsonage. She stopped but didn't turn off her engine. Just as I was getting up off the ground, which took some time at this advanced stage of pregnancy, she drove away.

Later that afternoon, she drove up again. This time, I spotted her from the parlor window. *Why was she staring at the house?* I hurried outside to ask if I could help her.

"Does Robert Gordon still live here?" she asked, talking to me through her car window.

"Why, yes. Shall I get him for you?"

She looked at my round middle, curiously, hesitantly. "No, but thank you." And she drove away again.

I watched the car disappear down the road until I heard Aunt Martha call everyone to the evening meal.

"Vhat is dis dinner?" Elisabeth asked in an overloud voice as Aunt Martha placed a plate in front of her.

"Spaghetti and meatballs," said Aunt Martha. "It's a new recipe I found in the newspaper."

"It does not look good." Elisabeth inspected it with her fork.

"Try it before you give your opinion," I responded with finality. Accustomed to Elisabeth's critical assessments, we all let the moment pass.

"How's the spy log coming along, William?" Robert asked, pulling a pitcher of milk from the fridge and filling a glass. "Anybody?" He held up the pitcher.

"Not so good," William answered, holding up his glass to be refilled. "People keep getting mad at me for spying on them. Mr. Ibsen said the Gordon family has gone to the bow wows."

Gone to the bow wows? What was *that* supposed to mean? I cast a worried look at Elisabeth. What *else* could she be up to? I wondered if we might need to do our grocery shopping in Bisbee. I avoided Robert's and Aunt Martha's eyes and looked down at the long strands of noodles on my plate.

Just then, the doorbell rang. Elisabeth ran to answer it and brought in the woman who had driven by the parsonage earlier today.

When Robert saw her, his face drained of color. Aunt Martha froze, her fork suspended in mid-air.

I stood up, a little confused. "I believe we met earlier. I'm Louisa." I put out my hand.

"Hello, Louisa," she answered. Her eyes were on Robert's face. "Robert. Aunt Martha," she said, giving them a nod.

Of course! Tall, slender, thick dark hair, grey eyes. *How* could I have missed the family resemblance? Even the guarded expression on her face. This woman was Alice! Robert's missing sister.

Slowly, Robert stood up and said, "So, Louisa worked her magic and found you."

Alice glanced at me sharply.

"Robert, I told you I sent a letter to the O'Casey's," I said defensively. At least I thought I told him. I *meant* to.

"And they forwarded it to me," she answered. All of a sudden, it became clear to her that Robert was not the one who wanted to find her.

I gave Robert a pleading glance and quickly said, "Please, Alice, sit down and join us."

After introducing Alice to William and Elisabeth, I made a place for her at the table. Like Robert, Aunt Martha did nothing. She seemed paralyzed, unsure of what to do, not wanting to upset Robert. "Alice, I'm so glad you're here," I said with great sincerity. "I've wanted to meet you for such a long time, ever since Robert told me about you."

She looked at me gratefully, but sat awkwardly, not even touching the dinner I placed in front of her. I kept trying to break the ice without asking her any questions. She seemed to subscribe to the Gordon Way—growing silent under investigation. So, as I often found myself doing with Robert, I just kept talking.

At last, Elisabeth stepped in. "So," she said, with her usual candor, "vhy are you here?"

"Just passing through." Alice also had the Gordon Economy of Words.

"From vhere?" persisted Elisabeth.

"I had been working for the military at a camp in Colorado, but the camp has closed. I'm going to retire from active duty, and hopefully, soon, my husband will join me."

"Vhere is he?" asked Elisabeth, her mouth full of a meatball.

"He's stationed overseas at a military hospital. We're both in the medical field. That's how we met," she said, casting a glance at Robert, as if she expected him to say something, or ask something. She seemed painfully uncomfortable. And still,

Robert said nothing. If I had been sitting closer to him, I would have kicked him under the table. *Hard.*

"So, you are a nurse?" asked Elisabeth.

"No, I'm a doctor."

Elisabeth's eyes grew as large as saucers.

What an *interesting* woman! "What kind of medicine do you practice, Alice?" I asked.

"I'm a dermatologist."

"Vhat's dat?" Elisabeth asked.

"She fixes skin rashes," Robert answered curtly.

I glared at him. He glared back at me.

Alice kept her eyes on Elisabeth. "I had been a nurse in the navy, then went to medical school. Not long after Pearl Harbor, I was sent to run the internment camp in Colorado until the last few months, when it closed."

"You *ran* it?" I asked, impressed.

She nodded. "They needed me, with so many doctors sent overseas."

"After I am da Miss America, denn I tink I vill be a doctor, too," announced Elisabeth.

"I'm going to be a doctor, too," added William, gulping down a half glass of milk.

As soon as William spoke, Alice realized that he was deaf. Her eyes scanned his amplifier.

"You yust said dat because I said I vanted to be a doctor," Elisabeth said defiantly.

"No, I didn't," William said.

"Yes, you did," asserted Elisabeth. Suddenly, her face tightened up as her hand pressed against her abdomen, a sign that her stomach was cramping.

"You said you want to be Miss America and I sure as heck don't want to be that!"

Now Aunt Martha stepped in. "William, don't *say* that word."

"What word?" he asked innocently.

"Heck," Robert supplied.

"Ernest says it all of the time," William said.

"Ernest is the telegraph operator," I explained to Alice.

"Ernest Houghton?" asked Alice. "I remember him. Small head, big, thick glasses?"

I nodded, trying to suppress a smile. Just then, we heard an odd sound coming from Elisabeth, as she made the connection. We looked curiously at her. She was laughing. It wasn't downright merriment, it sounded a little rusty, but it was an actual laugh.

William didn't hear it. "So you and Dad had the same father?"

"Yes," Alice answered, turning towards him so he could see her lips.

"Ernest said Grandfather Gordon only had two sermon topics. One was fire and the other was brimstone," William said, concentrating on trying to cut up his meatball, which kept scooting off of his plate when he jabbed it with a knife.

"Robert, I told you that boy spent far too much time at the telegraph office last summer," scolded Aunt Martha.

"Ernest was teaching me Morse code! For my spy work!" objected William.

I had to look down at my plate and bite my lip to keep from grinning.

"William, you speak very clearly. How did you learn to lip read and talk?" Alice asked him.

"Mom taught me," he answered. He took a biteful of spaghetti and sucked a noodle into his mouth with gusto.

Alice looked a little puzzled.

"He means Louisa," Robert interjected flatly.

I frowned at him, then turned to Alice. "I'm so glad you're here, Alice. I hope you can stay with us."

"No, thank you. I have a room at the Copper Queen hotel in Bisbee."

Silence covered us like a blanket. I shot a pleading glance at Aunt Martha.

"You look well, Alice," said Aunt Martha.

Finally! I looked at Aunt Martha gratefully, expecting her to say something else. But nothing else came forth. So my mouth started up again. I started chattering about William, about Elisabeth, about the baby coming, about anything. I was afraid that if I stopped, she might jump up and leave; I knew Robert wouldn't stop her.

There came a moment when it was clear what needed to happen next. I took a deep breath and said, "Well, it seems as if it might be wise to let you and Robert have some time alone."

Aunt Martha darted up the stairs, always eager to avoid an emotional encounter. I motioned to William and Elisabeth to go upstairs. "Robert, won't you make your sister a cup of coffee?" I shot him an aggrieved look to let him know I was furious with him. He shot it right back at me.

I supervised William as he brushed his teeth, tucked him into bed and had him read a chapter of *The Adventures of Robin Hood* to me. Then I went in to see Elisabeth. She was rolled up like a ball on her bed.

"I like your idea of being a doctor one day. You'd be a good doctor."

She nodded, one hand tightly pressed against her stomach.

I sat down on her bed. "Is your stomach hurting tonight?"

"It started when I ate dinner."

I rubbed her back to try to distract her from the cramps. "Have you ever thought about pursuing your piano? Going to University to study music?"

"No! No piano!" she said loudly and decisively. She still didn't trust the piano. It was too painful for her. It held too many memories of her childhood. I understood that, but I hoped she would realize that music could heal her, too. I hoped it might become the one good thing she could take with her from her past into her future. With a jolt, I realized that I still hadn't brought up the subject of the church concert.

Unexpectedly, she asked, "Vhat University?"

"There's one in New York called Julliard."

"Is dat Yu-lliard any good?"

"Yes, Julliard is the best." I kissed her, and enveloped her hands in mine for a prayer. "Lord God, bless Elisabeth's future, and make plain your path for her. We know that You are able to do immeasurably more than all we ask or imagine. Amen."

Elisabeth never joined in with my prayers, but she didn't seem to mind them, either. Tonight, she looked at me, earnest and unwavering. "Vhy don't you tell dat Lord God to do someting for Danny?"

Suddenly, I felt impaled by a huge stab of guilt. I had never thought to teach her to pray for Danny even though she had never stopped talking about him or worrying about him. Humbled, I prayed for Danny aloud, for his safety, for his well-being, for finding his relatives. I promised Elisabeth that I would pray every day for Danny with her. "What did Danny's letter have to say?" I asked her, knowing she had received a letter from him today. In it was another unsettling letter from Karl Schneider, asking more questions about Herr Mueller. I wasn't sure if I would respond.

"Dey can not find anyone for him. But he says it is okay. He says he vill be yust fine. He says vhen he turns eighteen, he vill go to Palestine."

I went to my bedroom and tried to read. After a long period of quiet, angry voices exploded in the kitchen. I didn't even need my radiator pipe to hear Robert and Alice arguing. Thankfully, William and Elisabeth were sound asleep. Aunt Martha came to my door, an anxious look on her face. She wanted me to go downstairs, but I told her that I shouldn't. "No, Aunt Martha, they need to get this worked out."

"What happened to your dream of being an engineer?" Alice loudly challenged Robert. "You went to college to major in engineering! You were going to run your own mines. You let Father steal your dreams!"

"Stole? You want to talk about stealing things?" we heard Robert roar. And Robert never roared. "You stole from us, Alice. You stole the reputation of our family! Mother was never the same after you left. She could never hold her head up. When you ran off, it broke her heart."

"You sound just like him! Blaming me for everything that went wrong!"

"Do you have any idea how it felt to have a sister who ran off, pregnant with some kid's baby? And then to hear you *divorced* him? In this small town, do you have any idea how that hurt us? All of us, Alice. A minister's family?!"

"How dare you lecture me about making a mistake! You of all people! The O'Casey's told me about Ruth. I know she left you for another man."

Oh no, Alice! Don't hurt him like that.

Even Aunt Martha shuddered. "She fought like that as a child. Whenever Alice took off her boxing gloves, things would turn ugly. She's still the same," she said sadly. Then she turned back to me with a scowl. "You just couldn't leave well enough alone, could you?" And she left to go to her room.

No, I never could. It was one of my worst faults. And tonight, in particular, my good intentions had blown up. I took the cap off the radiator pipe to hear the rest of their conversation.

"Look, Robert," I heard Alice say in a surprisingly conciliatory tone, as if she realized she had gone too far. "I wanted my own life. I wanted to go to college. That's all. And Father would never have let me. So I had to find my own way. I had to get out of Copper Springs. I'm sorry if that hurt you. I admit I wanted to hurt Father. But I never meant to hurt Mother. Or *you*."

I heard her walk a few steps, then stop to turn back to him. "It was a mistake to come back. I'm sorry." So she left.

And he let her go.

I wasn't sure if I should go downstairs, or wait until he came upstairs. Hours passed. Finally, he came up to bed, stretched out and turned away from me.

"Robert?" I asked gently.

"Don't... even...start," he said coldly, in slow measures.

I turned away from him. I could not understand how he could offer peaceful solutions to so many in his congregation, yet not seek peace with his own family member. And it was so *long* ago. So much had happened to them since, so much had happened to the world since then. Why couldn't they get past it now?

At least Alice was willing to try. She *came* to Copper Springs. That took so much courage. It took her three attempts before she could even knock on our front door today. She must have guessed what a cold reaction might be waiting for her. I felt such admiration for her. But for this man sleeping next to me, for the first time ever, I felt a great disappointment.

I listened to his breathing. I could tell he wasn't asleep yet. Should I say it? Probably not. Never good at heeding my own advice, I said, "Forgiveness is...well, it's everything." As soon as I spoke, I regretted it.

He erupted. "Well, you would know, wouldn't you?" he said sarcastically. "You've forgiven Nazis for murdering your father. You've forgiven the guards at Dachau for mistreating Elisabeth. And you keep trying to fix everybody else's life. Sometimes I feel as if I'm married to a saint!" He spat the word out. "Isn't there anyone in your life whom you can't forgive?" And he stormed out of the room, not waiting for an answer. Down to the lumpy davenport.

Yes, Robert, I thought gloomily. There *is* someone in my life whom I haven't been able to forgive.

I switched on the light and re-read Karl's letter, thinking back to the afternoon of that awful discovery.

Two weeks had passed since my father had been killed. Karl and I were having coffee in a coffee shop. He had been urging me to return to classes and get on with my life. I had no interest in school any longer, nor the piano. "I still don't understand why he was singled out," I said, chin resting on my elbows. "We were so careful."

Karl put his coffee cup down. "Annika, you have to stop thinking about it. It's over. It's done with."

"It's not that simple," I said sharply.

"Your father wouldn't want you to just...languish. He would have wanted you to get back to class and remain in school."

Karl couldn't understand how I felt. He just wanted me to feel good again, especially to share in his happiness over the opportunities he was facing. His face softened. "So what do you think about getting married next month?" He was leaving soon to travel to Hitler's summer home and wanted me by his side.

I tilted my head at him. "Karl, I could not be in the same room as Hitler."

He glanced around the coffee shop. "I wish you would stop making those remarks in public." He reached out and covered my hand with his. "You don't have to be in the same room. That could be dangerous." He grinned. "For Hitler," he whispered. He wove his fingers through mine. "Couldn't you just put aside your political views for your husband's career?" He pressed my hand to his lips.

"Should you not be putting aside your career for your political views?"

Karl's body tensed up. "I should get to class." He squeezed my hand. "You will think about it? About getting married?"

I nodded.

He bent down to kiss me on the top of my head. "I love you," he whispered. He crouched down beside me. "You know that, don't you?"

"I love you, too," I said, meaning it.

After he left, I swirled the cold coffee in my cup, not really sure what to do next. If only I knew what to do, which way to turn. I had never felt so lost. There had always been a goal ahead, but my father's death changed my future. I could no longer tolerate the injustices that plagued Germany, the injustice of my father's murder. I felt so helpless. Next to grief, helplessness was the heaviest feeling in the world.

Last night, Diedre had encouraged me to marry Karl. She thought it would give me needed security and distance me from my Jewish heritage. "You love each other, Annika. That's plain to see. What's to stop you now?"

What was stopping me?

Maybe Diedre was right. Karl and I did love each other. And now, he was all I had left.

Lord God, I prayed silently, throw light on my path. Show me where to go or what to do.

As I swiveled in the chair, my foot knocked over Karl's forgotten book satchel. I picked it up and hurried to catch up with him. A few blocks down, I found him waiting at the bus stop, talking to two young men. Karl's back was to me. Just as I was about to interrupt him, I stopped short, realizing his voice was raised in anger.

"Why did you kill him?" Karl asked them.

One shrugged. "You said he was a Jew."

"I said to rough him up. That's all." Karl spoke in an icy staccato. I didn't recognize his voice, he sounded like a stranger. "You pinned a star on his chest? You fools!"

In the back of my mind, a hammer tripped. Slowly, like a fog lifting, my mind grasped the meaning of his words. My heart slammed in my chest, sharp enough to hurt. The bus arrived; Karl pushed himself roughly between the two men and climbed up the steps. The men moved along, ambling down the street as I stood planted, too stunned to move. Just as the bus pulled away, Karl spotted me. The stark look in his eyes told me everything.

I spent the rest of the afternoon wandering the streets of Berlin. By nightfall, still trembling, I knocked on Dietrich Bonhoeffer's door. He opened the door cautiously, as expected. I blurted out, "I'm sorry to bother you at home, Reverend Bonhoeffer, but I am here to join the Resistance Movement."

He smiled and threw open the door for me to enter, allowing the light to chase away the shadows.

Chapter Twelve

The next day, Robert and Aunt Martha took William and Elisabeth to Bisbee to see a movie. I passed; I had other things I needed to do and I was still frustrated with Robert about how he had treated Alice. I hadn't slept well last night; my back felt stiff after a restless night.

As the Chrysler pulled out of the driveway, I almost cheered, eager for a quiet day at the house. There were still a few things that I needed to finish sewing for the baby's layette. I was down to my last month and knew it would fly by. After bending over the sewing machine for an hour or two, the mild ache from last night turned into radiating back pain. By mid-afternoon, I could hardly take a step or two without needing to lean against the wall.

I glanced at the clock. Robert said the matinee started at two o'clock. At the latest, they would get home by six. I groaned. I wasn't sure what was wrong, but now it felt as if my lower back muscles were in spasms.

I hated my helplessness. At this moment, I hated Robert, too.

Carefully, I lay down on the bed, hoping to relieve the spasms as hot pain shot down my legs. Dog stayed close by, as if he sensed something wasn't right. Grateful for his company, I even let him climb up on the bed with me. He stared at me with worried eyes.

Around four o'clock, I heard a car drive up, but I couldn't get up fast enough to see who it was. As soon as I heard high heels clicking up the path, I shouted for help. Dog ran downstairs, barking relentlessly at the door. I was worried that Dog's loud bark might drown out my shouts. "Wait!" I called, in between Dog's barks. "Please don't go! I'm upstairs!"

I heard someone's steps fly up the stairs. Alice poked her head in the bedroom door, saw me lying like a beached whale, and burst through the door. "Louisa? What's wrong? Have you fallen?"

"No, no. I'm just having terrible back pain. I must have twisted it. I'm so relieved you're here!"

Alice transformed into an efficient doctor, assessing my condition. She put her hands on my swollen belly, just as my back seized up again. "Oh Louisa, you're in labor!"

I turned wide, horrified eyes on her.

She grabbed my hand and put it on my stomach. "Look what a rock your abdomen turns into during a contraction."

"No! No! This can't be labor. Rosita said labor feels like cramps." This felt like knives running down my back. "And it's too early."

"Everything will be all right. I'll get you to a hospital." She stopped herself. "There is a hospital in Copper Springs by now, isn't there?"

"No."

She swore under her breath. "What about an obstetrician?"

"There's just Dr. Singleton."

"No! *Really?* Is that old goat still alive?"

I nodded, gritting my teeth through another contraction.

"You're having another contraction so soon? How long have you been in this much pain?"

"An hour or so," I said between panting. This wasn't going the way I had expected. Not at all. I wasn't prepared for this. And where was Robert? At the movies, I thought sourly. "You could try calling Dr. Singleton from Robert's office. The phone number is by the phone."

She ran downstairs, out through the kitchen door, into his office. When she returned, she had a worried look on her face. "There was no answer."

I locked my eyes on her. "Alice, you can help me. I don't need anyone else. God sent you." A new worry barged into my mind. "We have to get extra towels and sheets. I can't make a mess for Aunt Martha."

Alice shook her head, puzzled at the thought of that. "You've *got* to be kidding. You're having a baby and you're worried about getting a scolding from Aunt Martha about housekeeping?"

I bit my lip in pain and nodded. "Yes."

Alice went to the closet and pulled out all kinds of bedding to place over the bed. Carefully, I stood up, held on to the bed post and tried to breathe slowly during what felt like a python squeezing my spine before swallowing me whole. Alice quickly prepared the bed, and then helped me climb back in.

"I'm so glad you're here. What made you come?"

"I was coming to say goodbye," she said as she patted the covers over me. "I appreciate what you were trying to do, Louisa, bringing Robert and me together; but, it just isn't going to work."

"You have to...give him more...time, Alice..." I puffed during a contraction. "He can change. He can soften. He just...needs time to get to know you."

"Don't talk anymore. I'm going out to my car to get my medical bag. And I'm going to try to call the doctor one more time. I'll be right back."

I didn't know Alice well, but I was a little concerned by the anxious look on her face. "Wait. Alice, what's wrong? Is something wrong with the baby?" I asked, grabbing on to her arm.

She sat down on the bed. "No. It's just that...the back pain you're feeling could mean that the baby is...positioned a little funny." She smiled. "This baby just doesn't want to come out and face the music. Everything will be fine, Louisa." She patted my leg. "You let me do the worrying."

Face the music? "Oh Alice, what a good idea! Would you mind turning on my radio? Over on my bureau?" I had it tuned to a classical radio station. Music, always music, could help settle my mind. It established order in the midst of chaos, and today, my body and emotions felt chaotic. As the room filled with symphonic sounds, my mind calmed and my anxiety lessened, de-intensifying the hold of pain. I wondered if I would always associate labor pains with Mozart's *Horn Concerto #2 in E flat*. I hoped not. It had been one of my favorite pieces.

"Quite a difference," Alice noted when she came back into my room. "I'll have to remember that."

Still, the next few hours dragged by. She tried to distract me by getting me to talk. It worked for a while. I told her about coming to Copper Springs, about adjusting to the Gordon home, the breakthroughs we had with William and his language development, my discoveries about Ruth, and even about Herr Mueller. Then I asked her a question I had wondered about for over a year. "At the internment camps, did the government really use people for hostage exchanges?"

"Where were they going to send you?"

"Crystal City, Texas."

Her eyebrows shot up. "And you said you had information about a prisoner in Germany that the Nazis wanted to indict?"

Now I nodded. "So...would I have been sent back? Had I not married Robert?"

She glanced down at the floor. "Most assuredly."

A contraction interrupted this conversation, but I hadn't quite finished. "Alice? Please don't tell Robert that I asked you that." Another contraction hit me like a wave. "I don't regret marrying Robert." Well, right this minute I did. "I just always...wondered."

"I won't, Louisa. I understand. He's just like Father."

"No, Alice. He's not. He's...very tender-hearted, and he's a wonderful minister. His congregation adores him. He can be open-minded and willing to change, and he doesn't have the prejudice that Aunt Martha does. Look at me—I'm half-Jewish! Can you imagine how your father would have felt about me?"

She raised her eyebrows at that thought. "Well, Robert inherited the cautious and law biding genes in the family. I'll grant you that."

The contractions started rolling in, yet I never seemed to get closer to the end. I could tell Alice was concerned by my lack of progress. I wasn't able to carry on a conversation anymore. She started to tell me stories about growing up in the Gordon home—something I would've loved under ordinary circumstances—but I couldn't concentrate.

Finally, close to midnight, Robert's car pulled up in the driveway. A minute later, Elisabeth burst into my room. "Dat d--- car broke again." Then she stopped and stared at me. "Vhat is da matter vit you?" She took one long look at me, and then at Alice. Robert flew up the stairs carrying a sleeping William, alarmed by the tone in Elisabeth's voice. Aunt Martha followed. All of them stood by the door, peering at me.

"Louisa! What's happened? Are you hurt?" Robert asked, his face full of worry.

Alice answered for me. "She's in labor, Robert. She's been laboring all day. It's just slow going."

"Oh, dear," was all Aunt Martha had to offer before quickly disappearing into her room.

"Have you called Dr. Singleton?" Robert asked Alice.

"Yes. No answer."

"We've got to get you to Bisbee to a real doctor," said Robert, looking at me with a frantic look.

I saw the hurt flicker past Alice's eyes. "Alice is a real doctor, Robert."

"She's a *dermatologist!*" He had that look again, as if I had lost my mind.

"I don't know what might have happened to me if she hadn't come by when she did. She's been a godsend. And I'm sure she's delivered plenty of babies." At least I hoped so. "Isn't that right, Alice?"

She nodded with reassurance, but darted her eyes to the left.

Oh, no.

Robert still looked worried. "I just meant...we should get you to a hospital."

"I know *exactly* what you meant," Alice said, the coldness back in her eyes. "She can't travel now, Robert. It's way past that. Maybe if you had a phone in the house, she would've been able to call someone for help," she snapped, shooting him a look of daggers.

The contractions started piggybacking on top of each other; I could hardly get some relief. I was squeezing Robert's hands so tightly they became mottled, white and purple.

Suddenly, Alice's face lit up. "Louisa, the Japanese women in the camp sat up when they were in labor, so gravity could help the process. Would you be willing to try?"

I was desperately uncomfortable, with contractions rolling over me like waves. "I would be willing to try anything to get this baby *out*," I said, through clenched teeth.

"Robert, I need your help. Get behind her and support her back."

Robert looked tentative. "Maybe I should go get Aunt Martha. I really don't think a man should be—"

The hesitant look on his face made my temper flare. I grabbed his narrow tie and pulled him toward me, snarling, "You got me into this. You are going to stay and see it through."

"That a girl," Alice whispered.

"And why can't you put a telephone in this house?" I growled.

Robert looked stricken, as if I had just slapped him, but then he rallied into action. Finally, finally! Movement seemed to unspool the chains on my body and it was willing to release this baby into the world.

"My goodness," Alice said breathlessly, "it's working!" She sounded surprised.

I was feeling a new kind of pain now, a good pain. By dawn, a cry went through the house, but this time it wasn't from me. Our daughter arrived in howling perfection. Alice quickly wiped her down and handed her to me. She had a thatch of black hair, just like Robert's, dark blue eyes that stared at me, as if she was just as curious about me as I was about her. She had a tiny nose and a rosebud mouth, and she was perfect.

Alice couldn't stop smiling at the sight of her niece. "I think that old doctor had your dates wrong. She looks full term to me. In fact, she's a big gal."

Tenderly, I passed the baby to her father's waiting arms. "Can you believe it, Robert? We have a daughter." He sat down on the bed next to me, his baby in his arms. I leaned against him, my head pillowed on his shoulder. For now, I had everything I wanted.

Alice quietly slipped out the door to tell Aunt Martha the news. When the door shut, I said to Robert, "I don't know what I would have done without Alice. She arrived mid-afternoon; I was already in great pain. And to think you didn't get home until midnight."

He groaned. "I know. The car broke down just outside of Bisbee. It took me hours to fix it. I'm so sorry, sweetheart. What rotten timing." He pointed to a fat envelope on the top of the bureau. "But I did remember to pick up William's pictures at the film store."

I passed the baby to him. He held her as if he was afraid she might break. "Alice is an excellent doctor, Robert."

"It's a wonder she stopped by when she did."

"She said she was leaving." I looked directly at him. "She said that it just wasn't going to work between the two of you. That you could never forgive her."

Robert continued to gaze at his daughter.

I stifled a yawn. "Are you going to let her go like that?"

He looked back at me. "No, I'm not." He stood up. "Try to sleep. When you wake up, if you're up to it, I'll let William and Elisabeth come in." He tucked the baby in the bassinet we had borrowed from Rosita. "Call if you need me."

I smiled sleepily at him as he bent over to kiss me. The first hit of exhaustion swelled over me; I didn't even remember him leaving the room.

A few hours later, Robert knocked quietly on the door, waking me up, to bring me some hot tea and toast. He peeked at the baby. "She's still sleeping. Alice said you should eat before she wakes up for a feeding."

I yawned. "Oh, good. I'm starving."

"I figured as much. Aunt Martha is making you a real breakfast. This is just to get your strength up." He set the tea and toast on my nightstand. "You know, you're a little crabby when you're in labor."

I raised an eyebrow at him. "Don't...even...start. Is Alice still here?"

"Yes. She's downstairs."

I took his hand in mine.

"Robert, I've been thinking. I'd like to name this baby Marta Elisabeth. After Aunt Martha and after Elisabeth."

He looked at me for a long moment. "No."

I looked up at him in surprise. "*What*? Why not? I thought you would be pleased to name her after your aunt."

"I want her to be her own person. That's why I didn't want William to be named after me, the way I was named after my father."

I tilted my head, suddenly understanding more about him. His father had been determined to have Robert carry on after him. Robert never really felt he had the chance to live his own life. So that was why Robert hadn't named his son 'Robert Joseph Gordon the IV.' "Do you still wish you had become an engineer instead of a minister?"

He was gazing at his daughter's tiny starfish hand. "No. I'm happy to be doing what I do. You helped me with that." He leaned over and kissed me.

"What kind of name were *you* thinking of?" I asked him, suspiciously.

"I don't really have one in mind. I just don't want her named after anyone."

"Then I always liked the name Isabel."

He gave me that well-practiced you-*can't*-be-serious look.

I scrunched up my face. "What about Katherine? In German it's Katrina. We could call her Katie or Kat."

"No. No nicknames. I abhor nicknames. Besides, Dog would object to that name." Then he thought for a moment. "I want to pick a name that is easy for William to pronounce."

On that point we agreed, but that was the only point we agreed on.

"Well no doubt about whom the father is," Aunt Martha remarked when she came upstairs with scrambled eggs and bacon, eager to inspect her grandniece. "What's her name?"

Robert and I exchanged an exasperated look. He explained that we were having a little difficulty making a decision.

Aunt Martha rolled her eyes. "Are the two of you waiting for the creek to rise?"

I looked at her, confused. There seemed to be an endless supply of bromides tucked into her mind.

"Are you just going to call her 'Baby' for the next few years until you finally stumble on something you both like? It's going to be just like calling a dog 'Dog'."

That very thought had already crossed my mind. "When are Elisabeth and William coming in to meet her?"

"As soon as they wake up," Robert said. "I let them sleep in."

After Robert and Aunt Martha left, Alice came upstairs to check on us both before she went back to the hotel. "I can't thank you enough for being here, right when I needed you," I told her, meaning every word.

"My pleasure. It really was." She pulled up a chair next to my bed. "Louisa, when I was out at Robert's study to call the doctor, I found newspaper clippings and photographs on his desk."

"Yes, he's writing a book."

"Where would he have gotten this picture?" She handed me a picture of a young naval private standing next to a jeep.

"I took that. Last summer, I returned to Germany to get Elisabeth." I pointed to the picture in her hand. "That private was assigned to drive me down to Munich and back."

"Do you remember his name?"

"Oh yes. He was wonderful to me. Private Ryan Wheeler." Suddenly, a small light flickered in my mind. I leaned back in my bed, recalling his conversation about his parents coming from a backwater Arizona town. Both of his parents were doctors in the military. "Alice Wheeler. Could...Ryan...belong to you?"

Slowly, she nodded, her face registering that strange happenstance. "I'm...speechless. I can't believe...the chance of that kind of...coincidence...the fact that you met—"

"Providential," I interrupted. "There's no such thing as a coincidence in God's world."

She smiled. "I would have disagreed with you yesterday, but not today, Louisa. Not after this," she said, lifting up Ryan's picture.

Alice told me about Ryan's growing up years, that his father had deserted them soon after his birth. She explained that she ended up getting nurses' training in the military, to support Ryan and her, and how she met her second husband, Charles Wheeler, when she was assigned as his nurse on surgical rotation. "He was the one who encouraged me to finish my degree, then to go to medical school. And he has been a devoted father to Ryan. Ryan even chose to take his name."

Her face lit up when she talked about her husband.

"I hope we'll all be together again soon. Charles is in the Pacific, managing a military hospital. Ryan is still in Germany."

I wondered how it would feel to have those you love scattered around the world in active military duty. How lonely Alice must be. She needed us.

Then I told her about my day with Ryan, about how kind he was to me, so patient with Elisabeth, that he helped me get through Dachau. "He said he wants to be a minister."

She laughed. "Can you believe it? The last thing I *ever* wanted for him. I didn't even raise him with any religion. I wanted him to be able to choose for himself. And here he is following in his grandfather's footsteps!"

"And his uncle's."

She gave a short laugh. "So he is."

"Robert needs to meet him."

"Maybe someday." She got up to leave.

"Alice, would you mind telling Robert and Aunt Martha about this? Show them this picture? I doubt they would believe me."

"Oh Louisa, I hope Robert knows how lucky he is to have you."

Appearing suddenly at the open door, William peeking in around his waist, Robert said, "Trust me, he knows."

"I'm the lucky one, Alice. I got the package." I waved to William to come in and meet his new sister. He held his arms out in the air like a surgeon, still wet to the elbow from Aunt Martha's scrubbing. "There's your new sister, William." I pointed to the waddled bundle in the bassinet.

He peered at her as if he'd never seen anything so small in his life. "She's like a pink doll," he said. The baby let out a cry and fell back asleep. "Mom? Do you think she can hear?"

Touched by the worried look on his face, I tried to reassure him. "I think so. I know she can yell." In her few short hours of life, this baby had already surprised me with a few bone splintering howls.

He looked relieved.

I patted the bed to have him hop up. "William? It doesn't matter, does it? We'll love her just the same." He smiled and nodded his head, scrambling up on the bed. "Is Aunt Martha making Elisabeth scrub her hands before she comes in?"

William shook his head and quickly turned his head away.

Something seemed odd. "Robert, is Elisabeth coming in to meet the baby?"

He looked uncomfortable as he answered. "Not yet, sweetheart. She says she's not interested. She says babies are da vorst."

That sounded like Elisabeth.

Then Alice surprised me. "Louisa, what has Dr. Singleton said about Elisabeth?"

I glanced at her. "What do you mean?"

"Those stomach cramps she had at dinner. Has he given you any diagnosis?"

I was surprised she had noticed Elisabeth rubbing her stomach, especially with everything else going on at dinner. "A diagnosis?"

She rubbed her chin. "Hasn't he talked about her condition?"

"What condition, Alice?" Robert asked, just as puzzled as I was.

Alice sat back down on the chair. "Well, her size, for one. She seems quite short for her age."

"Her growth has been stunted from being in the camp. She nearly starved."

"Yes, of course. I understand that. But..." she hesitated.

"Alice, what exactly are you trying to say?" asked Robert.

"Well, do you have any idea what she ate while she was in the camp?"

"I think some stale bread, twice a day. I think she was lucky to get a bowl of watery soup now and then. Or something that resembled it."

"So she has eaten mostly grains? No vegetables?"

"There was a boy who gave her his potato."

"No protein?"

"There were worms in the broth; she said they ate them for the protein."

Alice shuddered. "What has Dr. Singleton recommended?"

"That she eat as much as she can."

"Breads?"

"A lot of bread. He said she needed carbohydrates."

Alice nodded, a detective gathering information.

"Alice, *what* are you thinking?" Robert asked, growing impatient.

"I can't be sure...but it's possible that Elisabeth's body has a reaction to grains. And that could be why she hasn't gained much weight in the last few months, and why her hair isn't growing in very quickly. Even why she's so irritable and cranky."

Robert looked at her, stunned. "A reaction to grains...like an allergy?"

"It's more than an allergy. Her body might have an inability to digest gluten, which is a protein found in grain. The lining of the intestine becomes irritated from undigested gluten, and that leads to malabsorption of other nutrients."

"Is there a way to find out if she has this...this...?" Robert asked.

"It doesn't really even have a name, other than celiac disease. It's genetic. Can you remember if anyone in your family might have had this, Louisa?"

I shook my head. "I do remember that my father had a sensitive stomach." I tilted my head. "But I always thought it was my cooking. Could that be why Elisabeth complains about stomach aches so often?"

Alice nodded again, biting her lip in deep thought.

I leaned back on the pillow. A puzzle started to fit together. I looked at Robert. "How did she ever survive that camp? The only nourishment might have made her sick."

Quietly, Alice said, "That boy who gave her potatoes might have kept her alive."

"Can anything be done about it?" Robert asked her.

"Well, that could be the good news. The cure for this is to stop eating any grains—oats, rye, wheat, barley— permanently."

I looked at Robert hopefully. "Wouldn't it be wonderful if she wasn't so irritable?"

He gave a short laugh. "It's certainly worth a try."

Alice stood up to leave. "I'll go downstairs and write down a list of foods to avoid for a while, to see if there is a difference. Glutens are in all kinds of food—cereal, for example. If we're on the right track, you should see an immediate improvement. She should start gaining weight soon."

William climbed up on the bed to keep me company after Alice and Robert went downstairs. "Aunt Alice told me funny stories about Dad."

"Really?" Gingerly, I sat up, placing a pillow behind me.

"Once Dad took apart Grandfather Gordon's car engine and put it back together, but he had extra pieces leftover. He hid the pieces in the basement so Grandfather Gordon wouldn't get mad at him."

I laughed, but had to stop quickly because it hurt my stomach. "I wonder if the pieces are still hidden. Might be something to track down with your spy work."

He stood up on the bed to look into the bassinet. "What is the baby's name?"

I sighed. "Dad and I can't agree on a name yet."

"How about Maid Marian?"

"From Robin Hood?"

He sat back down on the bed, cross-legged. "She tried to be a good person."

"I like Marian, too." In fact, I liked it quite a bit. "Do you want to ask Dad if he likes that name?"

And Robert did. So our baby was named Marian Marta-Elisabeth Gordon, which William immediately shortened to Meg when he realized what her initials would be. It was even easier for William to say than Marian, I explained to Robert when he complained it was a nickname.

After everyone left me to rest again, I tried to sleep but kept hearing low voices rumble in the kitchen. Slowly, oh so slowly, I got out of bed and went over to my radiator, leaning against the window for support.

I heard Alice ask, "Did Ruth ever tell you I stopped by?"

"No," Robert answered. "When?"

"With my boy, Ryan, years ago. I hoped to see you, but you were away at a conference. She wasn't very interested in seeing me."

There was a long silence. I leaned my forehead against the window. I knew this was painful news for Robert. To think that Alice had made some effort to see him, and he didn't even know about it. Had he only known, they might have reconciled years ago.

I was too tired to listen any longer. I stayed in bed for the rest of the day, dozing off and on. Alice woke me once to say she was leaving. She took my hand. "Good-bye, Louisa. I need to return to Colorado tomorrow."

"God bless you, Alice," I said with feeling. I hoped we would see her again.

By evening, Elisabeth still hadn't come in to see me or meet the baby. I heard her familiar stomp upstairs to get ready for bed. Slowly, I got out of bed and picked up the baby. It wasn't easy to bend down and reach in the bassinet to pick baby Meg up, but I was determined.

I knocked on Elisabeth's door and went inside. She was sprawled out on her bed, reading, and looked up at me, surprised. "You wouldn't come to see us, so we came to see you," I said. Ever so carefully, I went over to her bed and sat down on it, ever so gingerly. "Don't you want to meet your cousin?" I asked, gently setting the baby between us on the bed.

Elisabeth gave her a brief sideways glance. "She looks like dat Reverend. She has his hair." Baby Meg had a thick patch of black hair that looked like the top of a thistle. "She has more hair den me," she added. She went back to her book, ignoring me but not objecting to my presence.

"Your hair is growing in fast," I lied, stroking it gently. "Did Robert tell you her name?" She shook her head. "Marian Marta-Elisabeth. I wanted to give her your name and Aunt Martha's name. We're going to call her Meg."

She stared up at me. "Yust because she has my name, I not going to help take care of dat baby. I don't like babies. And dis one is noisy. She has da vorst cry."

Meg *was* loud. Aunt Martha already complained that she sounded like a cat with its tail stuck in a door. "I didn't give her your name so that you would feel you have to help. I gave her your name because you're so important to me."

She looked down at Meg, who was staring solemnly back at her. "I thot you were going to die. Yust like da ladies in da camp. Dey died when dey had da babies. You yelled yust like da ladies."

My heart melted towards her. So that was why she wasn't interested in Meg. "I was pretty noisy, wasn't I?" I said. She nodded vigorously. "But I wasn't dying, Elisabeth."

She looked down at my saggy stomach. "Your tummy looks like Tante Marta's yello."

It did! It looked and felt like Jell-O.

"I am not ever going to have dat babies. Too hard."

Today, I shared those sentiments exactly. I put my arms around her and squeezed, and if I wasn't mistaken, I felt a light squeeze back.

Chapter Thirteen

The next few weeks were a roller coaster of highs and lows in our home. Elisabeth started her gluten-free diet with immediate, astonishing results. She complained less frequently of stomach aches, started gaining weight, her concentration for schoolwork improved, and we received less frequent requests for conferences from the school.

Insults were starting to drop off, as well. Mostly, though, she was looking more like a girl than someone who had grown old before her time. Again and again, I thanked God for Alice's intervention. I found myself peering into Elisabeth's face, searching it out. Was something different? Softer? Less hostile? A wound was starting to heal.

William began second grade with Miss Howard. It had taken quite a bit of persuasion with Mrs. Olasky, but finally, she acquiesced, worn down by the Gordon family. Miss Howard's enthusiasm won her over. "William's desk will be up front where there will be fewer distractions," she explained to reassure Mrs. Olasky, "and so that he can read my lips more easily. We'll take things step by step, to see what works and what needs to change."

Actually, it was Robert who needed the reassurance. He still had reservations about this experiment. I had none. I knew I had done all I could for William. William needed to be a normal little boy, to make friends, to toss a football or swing a bat during recess. There was no doubt about his capable mind; he would keep up easily. And even Robert couldn't disagree Miss Howard was a perfect match for him.

I spent another restless day watching the clock when he headed off to school with Elisabeth that first day. Miss Howard prepared her class to understand William's disability, that he sounded different, and would need them to look right at him, so he could read their lips. But, still, I worried; children could be cruel.

My worry was for naught. William came home acting as if he'd been attending school all of his life. "Mom, I'm going to need a desk in my room to do my homework," he said importantly, tossing his empty lunchbox on the kitchen counter. "Miss Howard piles a *ton* of homework on us kids."

"Can't you do your homework at the kitchen table like Elisabeth does?"

"Nope. She only sits there because she wants us to do her homework for her. I need a real desk."

I asked him if the kids said anything about the amplifier that hung around his neck. "One boy thought it was a radio and asked me to tell him the baseball scores." He guffawed loudly. "Baseball teams haven't even started spring training yet!"

I half-expected to hear from the school principal this afternoon, with complaints about William or Elisabeth or both. But there was nothing. No news meant good news, I reasoned hopefully. Day one was a success. At least for William.

Elisabeth's school day lasted an hour longer than William's. She stormed into the house after school, slammed the kitchen door and came looking for me. I was up in my bedroom, nursing the baby. She stomped up the stairs and burst into my bedroom, full of shaky fury. "You told! You told everyone!"

"About what?" I asked, baffled. "What did I do?"

"About dis!" She pointed to her tattoo. "Mrs. Graham vants me to give a class lecture on dat camp! And she said you have pictures of it! And you didn't yust tell the teachers. You told da church ladies, too. Trudy told me!"

Oh no. *Lord, help me.* From the look on my face, Elisabeth knew that her information was correct. "You hypocrite! Vhen I told da Reverend dat you vere going to have a baby, you said dat vas your story to tell. Dachau vas my story to tell!" she cried out in frustration. "I vish you had left me dere. I vant to go back. I vant to be vid Danny. I'd rather be dere dan here vid you!" She spun on her heels to leave, then turned back to me, narrowed her eyes, and added as punctuation, "I *hate* you!" She slammed the door behind her.

I felt as if a piano just landed on me. Elisabeth opened her bedroom door and shouted something in German, then slammed her door again.

"What was that?" Aunt Martha asked, rushing to my room.

I looked at her. "It was a very uncomplimentary curse upon my mother." I went down to the kitchen with her to explain why Elisabeth was so angry with me.

Aunt Martha looked mortified. "I'm the one who told the church ladies. Maybe I should try to explain it to her."

I gave her a half-smile. "It's best if she's only mad at me, not you and Robert. She has *every* right to be mad. That *was* her story to tell."

The day following the incident in my bedroom, Elisabeth refused to speak to me. She pretended I was invisible. I tried to apologize, but she would hear none of it. I wondered how long her unresponsiveness would last. It was the first time I realized that silence has a sound. I wasn't too concerned until I happened upon the library to drop off a book one morning.

223

Miss Bentley, the librarian, confided to me that Elisabeth asked for help to plan a one-way trip to Germany.

A few nights later, I was changing the baby's diaper up in my bedroom, when I heard Robert's voice in the kitchen. I knew Aunt Martha was at choir practice and that William was splashing in the bathtub. I went over to the radiator pipe to investigate.

"Louisa didn't share that information without giving it a lot of thought, Elisabeth," I heard Robert say. "She felt she needed to let the teachers know why you were behind in school."

And why she looked half-starved, why she was so small, why her head had been shaved, and why she had a tattoo on her arm.

"I *hate* her," Elisabeth spat out.

I heard Robert pull out a chair and sit down. "I know you're angry with her. Maybe you're right about being angry. But I don't ever want to hear you say you hate her again. Louisa loves you; she went all the way to Germany to get you, you're the only blood relative she has left. You might be mad at her, but you *don't* hate her. And in this house, we never, ever speak to each other like that."

Elisabeth didn't respond to him. I could just imagine her scowling, head bowed, kicking her legs back and forth under the table. "I'm going back to Germany. I'm going back to vhere Danny lives. As soon as I have money."

"Are you that angry with Louisa?" he asked gently.

"I do not belong here. I vill never belong. My name is not Gordon."

I heard Robert walk over to the counter and bring something back to the kitchen table. "Look at this berry pie Aunt Martha made for the judge."

Silence.

"Our family is like this pie." I heard him scrape a plate on the table as he cut into the pie. "Look at it now, with one piece missing. That's what it would be like if you were to leave. Like a piece of the pie is missing. It would always be missing for us. You do belong to us. It doesn't matter what your name is."

Silence.

"If you were to leave, do you know who would miss you even more than William, and Dog and Aunt Martha? Maybe even more than Louisa?"

"Who?" she asked.

"Me. It would break my heart if you were to leave, Elisabeth. I love you as much as I could ever love a daughter. I just couldn't bear it if you were to go."

Silence. Then I heard her quietly say, "You have your own girl now."

"There's no one who could ever take your place in my heart. My life would always feel like this pie, with a big piece missing."

Silence.

"Elisabeth, I think school is going to be better for you. Soon. I think there will be some wonderful surprises ahead for you."

Nice thought, Robert, but I wasn't sure that I agreed, especially with Mr. Koops as her teacher. All day long.

I heard the kitchen chair scrape along the floor as she pushed it back.

"Any chance you'll change your mind and stay with us?" he asked.

"I'll tink about it," I heard her finally grumble, in a tone somewhere between sulky and sour.

My heart swelled with gratitude for Robert. I wish I could have told him I heard the conversation, but I was too ashamed to confess about my habit of eavesdropping. But tonight, I didn't feel guilty. I needed to hear him say those words, too.

Just as Elisabeth began to thaw out, baby Meg started to cause her own set of problems. She slept during the day, but in the quiet of the evening, just as everyone was settling to sleep, she would start to whimper. As her cry finally brought forth noise, it nearly blew the roof off. Doctor Singleton diagnosed it as a case of colic that she would grow out of, sooner or later. Even he had to admit he'd never heard such a piercing cry on such a little girl.

The parsonage was so small that I resorted to taking baby Meg over to Robert's office during the wee hours. I would walk her around and around and around, hoping to coax her back to sleep. "You should stop spoiling that child," advised Aunt Martha. "Let her cry it out a few nights."

If I weren't so tired, I would have laughed. No sane person would *dare* to wake up Aunt Martha in the night.

"I just don't know why that baby has such a loud cry. No Gordon baby ever had such a wail," Aunt Martha complained. I rolled my eyes, growing accustomed to the fact that any positive aspect to this baby seemed to be directly related to the Gordon lineage, and anything negative seemed to be the result of my own dubious pedigree.

A good night's sleep seemed like a distant memory to me. I was exhausted, short on patience, and hadn't yet gained my energy back after the delivery. Robert tried to help as often as he could, but I tried not to ask him for help unless I really needed it; he was often interrupted in the night for minister's duties as it was.

Once, he mentioned that William had cried a great deal as a baby, too. Neither of us said it aloud, but in the back of our minds was the worry that baby Meg might be deaf, too. It was too early to tell. At times she startled easily by noise, but other times, such as when Elisabeth stormed my bedroom, she slept or nursed right through.

One night, I took baby Meg to Robert's study, to settle her down. I rested her small head against my shoulder and swayed, back and forth, rocking her gently in front of the window. It was a moonless night and the stars were luminescent.

Suddenly, a shiver crawled down my spine.

Out on the street, a man stood, hands on hips, watching me. I blinked a number of times, expecting him to disappear, like a mirage. The man didn't budge. His eyes were locked on me. My heart started pounding. Oh, why didn't I bring Dog with me? I couldn't see his face distinctly, but there was something eerily familiar about him. Not just his stature, but the way he stared at me, not caring that I saw him.

It was Friedrich Mueller. I was *sure* of it. Blood pounded in my temples. It felt like as if ice water coursed through my veins. Even the baby seemed to quiet suddenly, as if she sensed my fear. I glanced down at her, and when I looked back up, he was gone. I ran back to the house, locking the kitchen door behind me, still trembling as I reached our bedroom.

"Robert? Robert? Wake up!" I shook him on the shoulder.

"Ummhmm," he mumbled.

"I think I just saw someone outside."

"What? What are you talking about?" he said sleepily.

"When I was walking in your office with the baby. A man was outside."

"At this hour?" he asked through a yawn. "On a Monday night?"

I shook him again. "I think it was Friedrich Mueller."

Now his eyes popped wide open. He sat up. "Louisa, you're so tired you're starting to imagine things. Probably because of that news report tonight."

I had been closely following the Nuremburg Trials, an international war tribunal to bring to justice the war criminals of Germany. Tonight, a French journalist had given heart-wrenching eyewitness testimonies of the atrocities at the death camp Auschwitz. The news report added that many of the defendants looked bored during the testimony. *Bored!*

When we heard that, Robert flipped off the radio. He knew how those accounts stirred up my memories of Germany, but I still felt it was important to stay informed about the trials. I prayed over them, begging God to bring justice in the verdicts over the next few months.

Maybe Robert was right. Maybe Friedrich Mueller was a figment of my active imagination. "But Robert—"

"Louisa. Enough! Mueller is over and done with," he said sharply. More gently, he added, "The baby is asleep now. You need to sleep when she is sleeping. I'll get up with her when she wakes up again. You really, *really* need to get some rest."

I lay down and tried to sleep, nestled in his arms. It was true. I was beyond exhaustion. Could I be seeing things? *Was* it my imagination? I still hadn't responded to Karl Schneider's most recent letter. Could that be why Herr Mueller was on my mind?

Or did I actually see Herr Mueller?

* * * *

I had completely forgotten about William's photographs until I noticed them on the dresser where Robert had left them. After dinner, William laid them out on the kitchen table to compare them. It was fascinating to see the exact same scenery colored by changing black and white light.

"Who's that?" asked William, studying the pictures carefully.

"Where?" Robert asked.

William pointed to a few pictures of the church that he had snapped, the last on his roll. There was someone coming out of the church side door. The next picture showed the person running down the street. Still dawn, it was just a shadow of a dark figure, clearly a man, judging by his size. Robert glanced at me, a look of alarm in his eyes.

Later, in our bedroom, out of earshot of the family, I said, "I told you! I told you I saw someone last night and you wouldn't believe me!"

"You said it was Friedrich Mueller, and Louisa, that is *ludicrous*. Do you honestly think Mueller would be stealing carrots from your little garden?" He rolled his eyes. "And I don't want you telling anyone else your theory. You'll get everyone all riled up again. He's probably just a drifter, looking for some free eats. He'll head out of town soon enough." He looked worried, but then he brightened. "Maybe Elisabeth isn't the town organizer, after all. Maybe someone else is."

* * * *

I was starting to think having a baby was harder than being in the Resistance. On Friday morning, I went over to Rosita's and burst into tears when she asked me how I was doing. "I think I must be a terrible mother, Rosita," I sobbed. The more anxious I felt, the more the baby cried.

Even Rosita looked worried. "What does the doctor say?"

"He thinks it's colic and that she'll grow out of it."

That night, baby Meg woke up yelping around one a.m. I plucked her out of her crib and walked down to the kitchen, surprised to find Elisabeth following me.

"You go back to bed," Elisabath said. "I vill take care of dat noisy baby tonight."

I looked at her large brown eyes and nearly fought back tears of joy. It was the first time Elisabeth had shown empathy for someone else. "Why are you doing this, Elisabeth?" I asked.

"Because it hurts my eyes to look at you. You got da raccoon eyes. You look schrechlich." *Awful.*

Well, I did ask.

"Yust tell dat Tante Marta to let me sleep in tomorrow. She always tells me she wants me up wid da roosters and we don't even have roosters."

I handed the baby to her. "Please don't go outside. Even if Meg is loud. Just stay downstairs. In the house." I was still uneasy about that sighting—apparition, Robert called it—of Herr Mueller the week before.

I went up to bed and tried to sleep, but worries kept bouncing in my head about the rapidly approaching concert date. What made me think I could perform a concert so soon after having a newborn? What was I *thinking*? I could barely find time to practice, and when I did, I had trouble concentrating on the sheet music in front of me. It often became blurry, forcing me to stop and blink a few times. Today, I found myself nodding off, right on the piano bench.

I punched the pillow and rolled over. *Lord, help me.* I was so discouraged. And even more intimidating was the conversation I had yet to have with Elisabeth about performing with me in the concert. Soon, I thought wearily. Soon, I should talk to her.

I must have finally fallen into a deep sleep, because suddenly Robert was shaking me, telling me to wake up. A blood curdling scream rose up from the parlor.

We hurried downstairs, Aunt Martha rushing behind us. We found Elisabeth hysterical, her face was white as death. I grabbed the baby from her, thinking something had happened to Meg. The baby was screaming, too, but seemed to be more upset by Elisabeth's frantic screams than by anything else. Robert turned on the light and tried to calm Elisabeth down as I tried to settle the baby. "What's wrong? What happened?" he asked her, his hands on her shoulders.

She was shaking with fear. She pointed to the parlor window. "Ein mann! Ein mann! In der garten!" *A man! A man. In the garten!* She could hardly speak. Robert went over to the window to look, but turned back to her with a puzzled expression. "He vas taking Louisa's food, in da garten. Den, vhen I saw him, he came up to da porch and looked at me through the window. He just stared at me. Vhen I started to scream, he ran off."

Robert's eyes spoke for him. We were thinking the same thought. It was the same man whom I had seen, the same man who was in William's pictures. But only I was convinced it was Friedrich Mueller.

"What's happening to this town?" murmured Aunt Martha, more to herself than to us.

Elisabeth finally calmed down long enough to go upstairs. She got Dog out of William's room to come sleep with her. She had fewer nightmares when Dog kept her company. Robert checked the locks on the doors. "Whoever it is, I don't think he'll be coming back."

"Whoever it is, he is getting bolder. Maybe out of desperation. Especially after you started locking the church up," I pointed out.

"Who could it be, Robert?" asked a nervous Aunt Martha.

"Just a drifter. A hobo. I'm sure he'll be moving along soon, now that he knows he's been spotted," he reassured her.

I tried to go back to sleep, but it was a restless night for each of us, except for William who slept peacefully through the drama.

Surprisingly, Robert started the day especially cheerful despite missing sleep due to our strange nocturnal visitor. After lunch, his eyes distant and a little mysterious, he said he had an errand to run. Only Elisabeth could go with him, not even William and Dog. Elisabeth scrambled into the car, happy to be singled out though she had no idea where they were headed.

They were gone for hours. Finally, right before dinner, Robert's Chrysler pulled into the driveway. I hurried to meet them at the kitchen door, curious about this mysterious errand. "Where have you been?" I asked him.

I looked behind Robert at someone getting out of the car beside Elisabeth. Elisabeth's face was transformed. Her eyes sparkled. Her eyes had never sparkled! She had a broad grin on her face and took the hand of the boy, pulling him towards me. "Louisa! Here is my Danny! Da Reverend brought me my Danny!"

My eyes widened, and my expression changed from confusion to surprise to delight. I was stunned. Robert had never said a *word* to me about trying to bring Danny here! I looked at this boy standing in front of me, brown eyes large like Elisabeth's, but soft whereas hers had been so hard. He was nearly as paper thin as she was, hair cut in a crew cut, thick horn-rimmed glasses that were held together on one side with a bent paperclip. A boy on the verge of becoming a man. He looked at me shyly, politely waiting for a reaction, hoping for acceptance.

Elisabeth burst in between us. "Look, Danny. Here is dat noisy baby dat I told you about."

I handed baby Meg to Elisabeth, and took Danny's face in my hands. "Welcome to our home, Danny. To your new home." I reached over and pulled him into my arms and held him for a long time.

"See, Danny? I told you she vould vant you." Elisabeth dragged Danny inside to find William and Dog and Aunt Martha. Right before she closed the door behind him, she hurried back to my side and whispered, "Now Danny knows dat he is not alone."

Robert closed the car door and walked up to me, a sheepish grin on his face. "You don't mind, do you? I didn't think you'd mind. She talked about him so much, and when I found out that he didn't have any relatives...well...after Alice. Well, do you remember when you told me that everyone wants to be found?"

I nodded, dizzy with the surprise of it all.

"I realized you were right." He grinned. "Like *always*. So that very day I sent the Red Cross Tracing Service a telegram, and next thing I knew...they sent me back a telegram. Danny was going to be transferred to the Displaced Persons Bureau in Germany that week because they had given up on locating any of his relatives. That very week! Talk about providence. And then the Red Cross expedited some paperwork...and the judge's nephew helped with the red tape...and suddenly I received news that they were on their way. I didn't have much notice. But you don't mind, do you? The more, the merrier, isn't that right?" He searched my eyes for the answer.

I smiled. "Of course I don't mind." Then I saw the "they" that Robert referred to. In the car was another man, waiting. Slowly, cautiously, he stepped out of the car. He smiled a little and tipped his head toward me.

When I saw his face, dread rose in my throat like bile. My heart started racing.

Robert noticed that I noticed him. He turned to the man and said, "Forgive my manners. Louisa, this is Karl. Karl Schneider. He's the gentleman from the Red Cross who was kind enough to escort Danny to America."

"Hello, Mrs. Gordon," Karl Schneider said politely, as if we'd never met before.

Robert glanced nervously at the kitchen. "I'd better get in and check on Aunt Martha. This will be a bit of a shock for her. Excuse me for a moment." He gave a nod to Karl and went into the kitchen.

Karl walked up to me. "Hello, Annika." His voice was gentle.

I felt my cheeks grow warm. Hot, actually. "Karl, what are you *doing* here?" I stammered.

"I volunteered to be the Red Cross escort to bring Danny to Copper Springs."

"But...why?" I asked, nervously glancing behind me through the kitchen window to see where Robert was. I turned back to Karl, narrowing my eyes suspiciously. "Why did you come? Why are you here?"

"I had some news for you. Good news. And when Reverend Gordon's telegram arrived, well, it seemed like a wonderful opportunity to deliver the news in person."

He stepped closer to me, eyes dancing with delight. "Annika, I made you a promise and I intend to keep it. I have a lead on Friedrich Mueller. He's here, I'm sure of it, somewhere in Copper Springs."

Chapter Fourteen

Karl Schneider seemed in no hurry to leave. After dinner, Robert politely offered to let him stay at our home. Thankfully, as if on cue, just after Robert extended the invitation to Karl, baby Meg started to wind up like a siren. Elisabeth showed Danny how to put cotton in his ears. Aunt Martha scooted upstairs to listen to her radio show. Dog scratched at the door to go outside. Only William seemed unaffected.

"Does she do that often?" Karl asked, looking horrified.

"Oh yes!" I answered, hoping that would convince him to decline Robert's invitation.

Karl quickly insisted that he planned to stay at the Copper Queen Hotel in Bisbee. The louder Baby Meg got, the more eager Karl looked to leave. Robert volunteered to drive him over to Bisbee but Karl insisted that he would find his own means.

Robert started to tell him that there *were* no such means in Copper Springs but I interrupted him. "Karl found his way to Copper Springs, Robert. He can certainly find his way to Bisbee. Even back to Germany." From the way Robert's eyebrows shot up, my words must have come out harsher than I intended. I tried to smooth the look on my face.

"Nonsense," Robert said, frowning at me. "Borrow my car, Karl. I won't need it for a few days."

"Thank you, Reverend. I'll take good care of it and return it soon. I plan to stay in the area for a while and take a much needed holiday."

I glared at Karl but he avoided my eyes.

As we settled Danny into William's room, Elisabeth actually volunteered to help change sheets, show Danny where to keep his toothbrush in the bathroom, and even helped him to unpack, which didn't take long.

As I studied her face, I realized that I had never seen her look happy, truly happy, before this evening. Robert gave her that by bringing Danny here. He gave her happiness.

William, too, was beaming. He had the older brother he never knew he wanted.

We found some old pajamas of Robert's for Danny to wear, though the pants legs folded in puddles around his ankles. I took Danny's tattered clothes downstairs so Aunt Martha could wash them for school in the morning. She looked the clothes over and shook her head.

"The next time we go to Bisbee, we'll have to get Danny some new clothes," I said.

Aunt Martha picked up the clothes with two fingers. "Well, that Danny has done something no one else could do."

"What is that?"

"Elisabeth finally stopped talking. Not a word during dinner. She just stares at him as if she was seeing Lazarus back from the dead."

She was right. Elisabeth's eyes followed Danny's every move as if she thought she was dreaming and might wake up.

Later, in my bedroom, after baby Meg gave up her last howl for the night and fell into a sleep so deep that an explosion couldn't wake her, the time had come to tell Robert about the past Karl and I shared, but I...I just couldn't make myself do it. Not now.

Soon, though.

Maybe, I reasoned, Karl might just return to Germany.

Or maybe, just maybe, it could be true that Karl was close on the trail of Friedrich Mueller.

In my mind, Karl's only redeeming feature was that he was willing to pursue Herr Mueller. The judge's nephew, on whom rested my greatest hope for justice, showed no interest despite my repeated pleas. Repeated badgering, Robert would call it, if he knew, which was exactly why he *didn't* know I was still trying to locate Herr Mueller. Last month, the judge's nephew sent me one terse, typed reply: "Find proof, Mrs. Gordon. Then, we'll talk."

Perhaps Karl *had* discovered irrefutable evidence. As I brushed out my hair, I decided to write to the judge's nephew tomorrow, imploring him to come to Copper Springs at once.

In the morning, Elisabeth and I walked Danny to the high school to register him for tenth grade. Mrs. Olasky's eyebrows were raised in alarm as we entered her office. "Another one?" she asked, looking distressed, as she pulled out registration forms to fill out.

I steeled myself for a three o'clock phone call from the school, expecting a litany of complaints about Danny just as there were for Elisabeth. But the call never came. I went outside with baby Meg to watch for their homecoming. After a while, I saw Danny turn the corner, reading a book as he walked, with Elisabeth hurrying behind to keep up with his long stride. In the kitchen, Danny ate a snack, then two more, went straight up to his room to do his schoolwork, finished, came downstairs and asked if he could help.

Aunt Martha raised an eyebrow at Elisabeth, sitting at the kitchen table with her school books spread open. She still hadn't even started her homework. Before Aunt Martha could think up a chore, William offered to show Danny around town. Elisabeth slammed her math book shut and hopped out of her chair to join them but Aunt Martha pointed at her empty chair. "Sit. Do your spelling."

Elisabeth glared at her but plopped back down in her chair. She had found a worthy opponent in Aunt Martha. When it came to mule-headed stubbornness, I'd say they were evenly matched.

After dinner, Robert flipped on the radio to hear the evening news while we were all in the parlor. The announcer said a team of five hundred German scientists, led by Wernher von Braun, had been scooped up by the Americans after surrendering. The U.S. Army had installed the team in Texas to help develop rockets.

"Have you heard of Wernher von Braun, Danny?" Robert asked, noticing the thoughtful look on Danny's face.

"Ja," Danny replied, a serious look on his face. "Wernher von Braun created the first self-contained rocket."

"That's right! The V-2," Robert said, looking pleased.

The 'V' was for 'Vergeltungswaffen,' meaning weapons of reprisal. Revenge. Robert had recently shown me an article about the V-2. One had recently been confiscated and brought to the United States to dissect; it was discovered to have been based on the design of American scientist Robert Goddard.

"Danny, how did you ever learn so much about rockets?" Robert asked, turning the volume down on the radio.

Danny cast a sideways glance at Elisabeth. "There vas a man in the camp who vas sent to Dachau from Mittelwerk."

My eyes went wide. "Mittelwerk? The plant where they made the V-2's?"

"Ja." Danny nodded.

"Then he worked with von Braun?"

Danny looked uncomfortable. "For him. Not vit him."

"He worked for von Braun?" Robert asked, practically jumping out of his chair.

"Ja," Danny answered solemnly. Danny didn't look quite as excited as Robert did.

Neither did I. To be fair to Robert, he didn't know what Danny and I knew about Wernher von Braun or about Mittelwerk. Von Braun had joined the Nazi party in 1933 and later became an SS guard. Next to Mittelwerk was a concentration camp; Von Braun's team used slave labor to help build the V-2's.

"Where is your friend now?" I asked Danny, hoping the man was still alive.

Danny pushed his glasses up on his nose. "The Nazis used him for a while, to help create the rockets, then after he taught them all he knew, they sent him to Dachau. He vas a Jude." He lowered his head, then lifted it up, symbolically.

I noticed he didn't answer my question.

Danny looked at Robert. "I think that God sent me to the camp to meet that man. I vant to go to University and become a rocket scientist. But I vant to use them to go to outer space. Not to kill people, like the V-2."

I glanced protectively over at Elisabeth. Her face looked tight, her lips in a thin, white line. Her fingernails dug into her palms. I could see her anger building; she looked as if she was just about to explode. In my mind popped a countdown: Five, four, three, two, one.

"Stop!" she shouted, just as I expected. "Stop talking about it!"

Danny calmly turned to her. "I don't vant to ever forget, Elisheva," he softly answered, calling her by the Hebrew version of her name. "Do you vant to forget the villager who threw apples at us over the fence every so often? Or the day vhen a voman threw a loaf of bread at us, sliced vit butter, vhen ve vent outside the barracks to collect lumber from the train? There vere good people, too, Elisheva."

She jumped up and faced him, eyes blazing. "And do you vant to forget the day vhen you voke up in the barracks and found dat man dat you talk about—dat rocket man—vas dead? Do you vant to forget dat you took his clothes off and vore them yourself? Do you vant to forget how hungry ve vere? So hungry dat ve ate vood one day! No! I do not vant to remember dos tings."

Unfazed by her outburst, Danny said quietly, "Elisheva, ve do not have to be chained to our memories. But ve must not forget."

"Steig ab! Sprich nicht davon!" *Stop talking!*

"Elisheva, if ve do not remember, it could happen again to our people."

She stared at him for a long moment, before she flew upstairs to her bedroom. I exchanged a sorrowful glance with Robert and followed her up, finding her face down on her bed.

"Go avay. I vant to be alone," she sputtered as I rubbed her back.

I knew she wanted me there, but I also knew to stay silent. What could I say, anyway? What words could heal that hurt?

Soon, she rolled over and sagged onto me, sobs racking through her tiny body. She began to weep, great heartbreaking cries. A healing cry, I hoped.

Later that night, Robert turned toward me in bed, head propped up on his elbow. "Louisa, were you ever as hungry as Danny and Elisabeth? So hungry you would eat wood?"

I switched off my bedside lamp and lay facing the ceiling. "No, not like that."

"But you were hungry?"

"Yes. Often."

"I remember how thin you were when you arrived here. The bones of your wrist were as light and delicate as my mother's china."

"No longer," I said, holding my hand up in the air. I had gained plenty of weight since moving to America. And, as Aunt Martha frequently pointed out, I still hadn't lost extra weight from my pregnancy.

"I'm so sorry."

I glanced at him in the dark. "It was in the past, Robert. And it's in the past for Elisabeth and Danny."

He took my hand and kissed its palm, then held it close to his heart as he laid his head on his pillow.

Now, Louisa, I told myself. *Now* would be the time to tell him about Karl. *Say it, Louisa.*

But then I heard Robert's steady breathing deepen into sleep.

Not tonight, then, but soon.

The next morning, before breakfast, Danny picked up William's Slinky on the counter. "Interessant," he murmured under his breath, looking at it with the same fascination that Robert had. He pulled it apart. "It must be based on Hooke's law of physics."

"Hooke?" Robert asked, putting down his coffee cup. "Robert Hooke?"

"Ja," Danny answered knowledgably, eyes glued to the Slinky. "A scientist of the seventeenth century. His law explains these coil springs." He glanced over at Robert. "The change in dimension is proportional to stress." Danny continued to play with the Slinky, putting it on the top of the kitchen table, letting it roll down and continue on its path, undeterred by Dog's persistent barking.

Robert watched Danny with an unmistakable gleam of admiration shining in his eyes.

Even Aunt Martha seemed pleased Danny had joined our family. Well, pleased would be a strong adjective to describe Aunt Martha. *Not unpleased* might be more accurate. Somehow, though, I think her sweetening temperament had more to do with the judge's frequent visits to the kitchen than with Danny's arrival.

Later that day, the judge found me at the clothesline hanging up diapers. "Louisa, any chance that you know of something Martha is particularly fond of?"

"Pardon? Something she is fond of?" Aunt Martha wasn't fond of anything. She disapproved of most everything. And everyone.

"Well, yes. Something to do."

Oh! Now understanding, I looked at that kind, courtly man. "She enjoys going to the picture shows in Bisbee," I said, trying not to smile. I handed him a clean wet diaper and two clothespins to hang it with but he looked at them as if he had never before seen such things.

"What's that smell?" he asked, sniffing the diaper.

"Clorox bleach. It kills germs. Aunt Martha likes to use it for laundry. And just about anything else she can bleach." Not that a germ could stand a chance around Martha Gordon. "Judge, have you heard any word from your nephew? Do you think that he will be coming to visit Copper Springs soon?"

The judge peered at me with twinkling blue eyes. "Still convinced you can nail ol' Mueller, eh Louisa? Well, I admire your tenacity." He handed me the diaper and clothespins and walked away, whistling.

The judge didn't take my intent to find Herr Mueller seriously. No one did.

Except for Karl.

* * * *

"Dad? Did you know that we're kike lovers?" asked William during lunch on Sunday.

Everyone stopped eating, forks suspended in mid-air. Unaware, William pounded the bottom of the ketchup bottle to get the ketchup moving. Finally, he stopped hitting the bottle and looked at Robert.

Robert was scowling. "William, please don't use that word."

"What word?" William asked.

"You know what word," Robert said.

Williams tilted his head. "But what does it mean?"

Robert's eyes darted between Elisabeth, Danny and me. "It is a rude word to describe a Jewish person."

"Oh," William said, sticking a knife down the ketchup bottle to get it moving. "Then what's a Jewish person?"

Robert sighed. "A Jewish person is one born to the Hebrews. From the tribe of Judah."

William opened his mouth to ask another question as a car backfired in the driveway. It sounded like our Chrysler.

Elisabeth ran to the kitchen door. "It's Karl!" She opened the door and waved him in.

Karl tousled her hair as he passed by her, causing an uncontrollable grin to spread across her face. He returned the keys to Robert without volunteering how or where he had spent the last week. "I filled up the tank with gas, but there is an odd noise in the engine," was all he said.

"Vhat kind of noise?" Danny asked. "A rattle or a pop?"

"I don't know," Karl answered. "Maybe both."

Danny jumped up from the table. "Reverend, if you don't mind, I vould like to take a look at it."

"Mind?" Robert jumped up. "I don't mind at all! Let's go see."

Robert, William and Danny ran outside to check the engine in that useless car. Even Robert admitted recently that it drove so slowly he wondered if the engine came from a sewing machine. Aunt Martha started to clear the table. I stood to help her, but she told me to go keep our guest company. She shooed Karl and me out of her kitchen as Elisabeth slipped out the door to join the boys.

Karl and I went into the parlor. Awkwardness settled over us like a blanket. I sat down and looked out the window.

"Annika—," he started.

"Louisa," I corrected, giving him a sharp look. I quickly looked away again. Karl had dangerous eyes—mysterious and distant. Even after all of this time, it was hard to look at them for very long without feeling swept away.

"I hear you are planning a concert to benefit Germany. I'd like to join you."

"Where did you hear that?" I bit my lip. "Elisabeth is supposed to be playing, too, but I haven't even talked to her about it. She doesn't like to play." I looked down at my hands and said, more to myself than to Karl, "She needs to do this, though. The people in this town need to hear her play the piano."

"She is quite good, as I remember."

Still looking out the window, I answered, "It's...too painful for her to play." I turned to him. "She doesn't want to remember." Nor did I.

"Perhaps I could convince her to play." He tilted in his head. "It would be good for her to come to terms with her past."

We both knew he was talking about more than piano playing.

I frowned at him. "But the concert isn't scheduled for a few more weeks. You won't be here that long."

He shrugged. "I'll stay on."

I looked at him skeptically. "Just how long do you intend to remain in Copper Springs?"

He leveled his eyes at me. "As long as it takes to find Mueller. I made you a promise and I intend to keep it."

I glanced into the kitchen, worried Aunt Martha could hear us. "So what exactly have you learned about Herr Mueller?" I whispered, almost combatively.

He sat down next to me and lowered his voice. "I think he is close by."

I stood. "Yes, you already told me."

He stood, too. "I have spent the last few days trying to track down his latest steps."

"And have you learned anything?"

He went over to the window to watch Danny lean into the car engine. "I bought a motorcycle. Used."

"Why?"

Patiently, as if he was talking to a child, he explained, "How else could I pursue leads on Mueller?"

"*What* leads, Karl?"

Just then, William burst into the parlor from the front door. "Mom! Danny found the problem. It was the carber-thing. He fixed it!"

"Carburetor," Karl supplied, smiling at William. Then he looked straight at me. "I should go. Annika, I want to help with this concert. Anything to help our country. Anything to help Elisabeth."

"Louisa," I answered flatly.

Karl shook his head, as if trying to etch that name in his mind. "Forgive me." He opened the door to leave. "I won't make that mistake again. You can count on me."

Could I?

William watched him go and turned to face me. "Why did he call you Annika?"

Little slips, little slips.

I looked at his earnest little face. His cobalt blue eyes missed nothing. "I must remind him of someone he once knew."

* * * *

"Mom!" William burst into my room on Saturday morning while I was changing the baby. "Danny is going to teach me how to build a rocket with stuff in the garage. Okay?"

"What stuff? William, what stuff?"

Too late. He had already rushed back down the stairs and disappeared into the garage.

I shook my head. Why was I worried? How many things could be in our garage that could actually create a rocket?

Danny and William spent the day clanking around the garage. I kept peeking nervously through the kitchen window, but all I could see was Elisabeth, sitting on the workbench, swinging her legs back and forth, looking bored.

Later that day, Robert received an irate call from the priest at the Catholic church to come down to collect William, Danny and Elisabeth. Dog, too.

It wasn't long before they all returned. Looking pale, Danny, William and Elisabeth quietly marched through the kitchen to head straight to their rooms, silently passing Aunt Martha and me as if on their way to walk the gang plank.

Robert, though, had a different take on the situation. "Apparently," he explained, eyes twinkling as he filled a glass of milk from the icebox, "the boys rigged a toy wagon with some leftover fireworks they found in the garage. Danny knew they needed a wide street to set it off so he picked a spot near the Catholic church. Unfortunately, he fired it up just as a wedding had finished and people were pouring out of the church doors."

Robert started laughing and had to put his glass on the counter to keep it from spilling. "It was just bad timing. Danny had no idea there was a wedding going on. But the bride's mother was furious." Still grinning, he turned to head out the kitchen door to his office, shaking his head in wonder. "Sorry I missed it. Sounds like that toy wagon took off down the street!"

* * * *

"Milk is here, Martha!" called out the milkman early one morning, stomping his legs on the kitchen stoop. She waved him in and hurried to fill up a cup of hot coffee. "It's cold out there this morning."

"Don't complain. Summer will be here soon enough," she answered, handing him the steaming cup.

He leaned against the counter and sipped, watching the steam curl out of his coffee.

"So what's new in Copper Springs today?" I asked him as I put the baby in the bouncy chair Barb Bunker had loaned me.

"Actually," he started thoughtfully, "it's what *isn't* new. Nothing missing for over a week now."

I exchanged an uneasy look with Aunt Martha. I hadn't given a thought to the town scrounging since, well, since

Danny arrived. The coincidence of the timing was hard to ignore. Elisabeth had barely left the house since Danny had arrived, preferring to follow him around like a devoted puppy.

* * * *

The concert date was right around the corner. Karl had found time—from whatever it was he was doing to track down Herr Mueller—to have a talk with Elisabeth about the concert. She readily agreed to participate, he told me, which only irked me.

This afternoon, Karl arrived to practice for the concert. He came early to supposedly help Elisabeth with her spelling words. The two of them sat at the kitchen table, going over words again and again, until she felt confident. It was the very first time Elisabeth showed interest in homework. Somehow, that thought didn't cheer me.

As conflicted as I felt about having Karl participate in the concert, it definitely felt more professional with his involvement. We ran through the entire program, twice.

"Stay for dinner," Elisabeth ordered Karl when we finished for the day.

"Not tonight," I interrupted. "Robert performed two weddings today for Reverend Hubbell over in Douglas and he will be tired."

Karl fixed a bright blue gaze on me. "Another time," he said smoothly. He turned to Elisabeth. "When people get older, they tire more easily."

I shot a suspicious look at him but he avoided my eyes.

Robert was exhausted when he arrived home just before dinner. He did look older tonight, I thought, annoyed with Karl for pointing that out. I thought I even noticed a feather of gray at his temples. He went upstairs to wash up as I called to the boys to come inside.

Suddenly, a thunderous explosion came from the direction of the garage.

Aunt Martha dropped the milk bottle, splattering milk and broken glass all over the kitchen. I ran outside as both Danny and William tumbled out of the garage, eyes wide but laughing. Danny's glasses were nearly sideways on his face.

"We did it!" they shouted. "We made a rocket!" William did a little dance of joy.

Robert burst out the kitchen door. "What just happened?!"

I thought he would be angry, angry in the way Aunt Martha got when children were out of control, but Robert was delighted with the boys' ingenuity. His eyes twinkled with possibilities as he listened to their recounting. "Tell you what," he said. "You've got the right idea. All that we need to do is put fuel in a tube and a hole at the bottom of it."

"Vhat kind of fuel?" asked Danny.

Robert grinned. "Probably something besides old powder from cherry bombs." He turned over the remains of their flashlight-turned-rocket held together by splayed electrical tape. "I think there might be a way to improve this model. You did a great job considering you had crude equipment."

He glanced up at the hole in the roof of the garage and then over at the kitchen, watching Aunt Martha wipe milk off the inside of the window. "But from now on, I think we'll set off the rockets in the desert."

* * * *

After lunch on Saturday, Karl stopped by to practice for the recital. He had chosen a duet for the two of us to perform, a piece we had played together years ago. I wasn't comfortable with his choice but at least I was familiar with the music. At this late date, I couldn't afford to be choosy. "First, though, I brought a book for Danny. Is he here?" he asked, when I answered the door.

Danny heard Karl's voice and bolted downstairs.

"Look, Danny! I found a book on physics. It has a chapter on Newton's third law," Karl said when he saw him.

"Vhat's dat?" asked Elisabeth, trailing behind Danny.

Danny lunged for the book, flipping it open to its table of contents. "For every action, there is an equal and opposite reaction," he said, pushing his glasses up on his nose.

Robert came to the door, interested by the discussion. "I was just about to help Danny and William mix up a new fuel. Want to help us?" he asked Karl.

The hopeful look on Danny and Elisabeth's face made me snap. "Karl has some practicing to do," I answered for him, sounding ruder than I intended. "For the concert." The last thing I wanted was for my family to become attached to Karl Schneider. I already knew he had stolen Elisabeth's and Danny's heart. Even Aunt Martha seemed to be less cranky when he was around.

"She's right," Karl said, laughing. "We'd better get to the church. I need the practice."

But he really didn't. Karl was a remarkably gifted pianist. He had such sensitivity to the music, a oneness with the composer's intention. The music was powerful, achingly beautiful.

Today, when we finished the duet, at just the right notes, at just the right moment, as if we had rehearsed it for weeks, I remained silent, looking down at the keyboard, watching our hands.

For one fleeting, dangerous moment, time reversed. It felt as if we were back in Berlin University practice rooms, before the war had started, with my father at home waiting for me.

Everything was so familiar. Even Karl's smell. His aftershave took me right back. I squeezed my eyes shut, remembering.

He gently traced my chin with his finger before resting it on my lips.

So familiar.

So wrong.

With a jolt, I opened my eyes and was back in Copper Springs.

Leaning closer, he whispered in my ear, "Do you remember our dream to travel the world and give concerts?"

"You ended that, Karl." I scooped up the music sheets, preparing to leave.

His face dimmed with regret. "And look what I have done to you now."

I narrowed my eyes. "What does that mean?"

"You were destined for greater things than the life of an ordinary hausfrau in a provincial town, raising somebody else's children."

"There's nothing ordinary about my life," I said, sounding peeved. I *was* peeved. His words cut me to the quick. "And I love my family."

"Loving them is different than being in love." Then he quietly added, "He is old enough to be your father."

"Robert and I are only eight years apart, Karl." Nearly nine, but eight sounded closer. I stood up to leave.

He grabbed my arm and turned me to face him. "I know, I know. I'm not trying...I don't mean to interfere..." His eyes started to glisten.

I shook his hand off of my arm. "Karl, *why* are you really here?"

"I need to make it up to you. Somehow, I must make amends. I will find Heinrich Mueller for you and bring him to justice."

I tilted my head curiously. Heinrich Mueller was the head of the Gestapo. He disappeared after Hitler committed suicide and had yet to be found. "Friedrich," I corrected. "Friedrich Mueller."

Karl shook his head as if it was a minor verbal error. "Of course, I meant Friedrich Mueller."

"Karl, find proof that Mueller is here. Soon." My arms crossed over my chest, determined. "Or, after the concert, you must leave Copper Springs."

He looked as if I had slapped him. I turned to leave.

"Mom!" William burst into the church and ran up to me. "Baby!" he shouted, gasping for air. "Crying hard!" He pulled on my hand, wanting me to hurry. "Aunt Martha's mad!"

He ran ahead, holding open the church door for me. As I joined him, he peered at me, still panting heavily. "What's wrong?"

"What do you mean?" I asked.

"Your face looks upset." He pulled his face with both hands, making it tight and tense, to show me what he meant. "You always look that way around Karl."

Alarmed at his perceptivity, I tried to smooth that particular look off of my face. No doubt my face looked just the way I felt: unsettled and uncertain.

As soon as I got back to the parsonage, I rescued the baby from Aunt Martha and took her upstairs to calm her down, holding her fuzzy down head close to me. Karl's remarks nettled me, stirring up discontent. Even back in University, he told me my dreams were too small.

What frightened me was that everything Karl said was true. Ever since Meg had been born, I felt as if I could see my life stretched out ahead of me: changing yet another diaper, facing down another day of Elisabeth's defiant attitude, acting as a buffer for the on-going battle of territory between Aunt Martha and Dog, teaching piano lessons to those incorrigible Hobbs boys to help pay for basic bills.

I fought a sinking feeling that my days of significance were over.

I tucked the baby, now asleep, in her bassinet and caught a glimpse of myself in the mirror hanging on the closet door. I put my face right up to it. Was that really me? Dark circles under my eyes from a wakeful baby. Extra pounds from my pregnancy that I couldn't quite get rid of. I put a hand up to my hair. I used to love my hair. Thick dark waves that cascaded down my back. It was my favorite feature. Now, I threw it into a ponytail just to keep it out of my way.

Karl was right. I had become a dull hausfrau. I lay down on my bed, fighting tears, feeling sad. Feeling guilty. I was horrified with myself for letting down my guard with Karl. I had nearly let him kiss me. What was happening to me? I almost didn't recognize myself.

I must have drifted off, just long enough to fall deeply asleep and wake up disoriented, in a thick haze. I heard the telltale backfiring of Robert's Chrysler as it pulled up into the driveway. The kitchen door banged open. Sounding like cavemen back from a successful hunt, Robert, William and Danny's cheerful voices floated upstairs as they described the rocket launch to Aunt Martha. Dog barked once, then twice, to be let in the door, as Aunt Martha grumbled loudly about his dirty paws. Elisabeth sat down at the piano bench and began to play her song.

I heard their voices, a happy chaos, and my heart melted. From somewhere deep inside of me, joy bubbled up, dispelling doubts Karl had planted. We weren't a perfect family, but we loved each other. We belonged to each other.

Later that night, just after switching off my bedside light, I peeked over Robert's shoulder to see if he was still awake. "Robert?"

"Hmm?" he mumbled.

I put my chin on his shoulder. "I know I've told you I love you, but have I ever told you that I'm in love with you?"

He yawned. "Is there a difference?"

"I don't know. Maybe not. I just wanted you to know."

He rolled over, looked at me curiously for a moment, then pulled me close to kiss me.

* * * *

After that upsetting conversation with Karl on the piano bench, I decided not to be alone with him any more. I made certain Elisabeth was included for the remaining practice sessions.

When the night of the concert finally came, we waited in Robert's office for the church to fill. As I finished putting a large bow in Elisabeth's hair, suddenly she looked unsure. "Do you really tink I can do dis, Louisa?" she whispered.

I smiled at her solemn, hungry eyes. "I know you can, Elisabeth."

Karl stood up, cucumber cool. "Ready, ladies?" He opened the door for us. I took Elisabeth's hand and we walked into the church, as ready as we were going to be.

Afterwards, when the concert was over, the three of us stood in front of the audience and took a bow, one by one. I bowed first, cheeks blushing as I caught the look on Robert's proud face with baby Meg in his arms. Next to him, standing on his chair, William clapped wildly. Even Aunt Martha couldn't hide her pleasure, but it might have been because the judge was seated next to her. Cousin Ada was seated on the other side of the judge. She looked as if she might faint from an overdose of happiness, though that was not an uncommon look for her.

Next came Karl's turn to bow. The audience's applause grew even louder, just as I would have expected. I played well, Elisabeth played even better, but Karl played brilliantly. *As if his life had never been interrupted by a world war.*

How foolish it was for him to think that he needed to bump me out of the competition years ago. Karl's talent far exceeded mine or anyone else's. He was *always* the best.

But then Elisabeth took her bow, and the entire audience rose to their feet. She looked puzzled at first, not understanding. Then her face erupted into joy.

Smiling, I glanced at Karl. As he realized that Elisabeth was receiving a standing ovation, I saw a dark shadow flit across his face.

Suddenly, what had been a blur for me came into sharp focus.

The Ladies Altar Guild held a reception for us in the church basement. As we headed down the stairs, Ada swooped toward us. "Louisa, I insist that you let me have Elisabeth for the summer. I know a music teacher in Phoenix who can prepare her for Julliard. That talent must be developed! Surely you agree! It won't happen here in Copper Springs."

Aunt Martha interrupted. "She's not your show pony, Ada."

Robert and I exchanged a look of surprise. Aunt Martha seemed bolder with Ada now that the judge seemed to be courting her openly.

Uncharacteristically, Ada raised an eyebrow but let that comment pass by.

"You should go this summer, Elisheva," Danny volunteered.

Elisabeth turned to look at Danny, chin quivering, her face filled with a painful awareness. "You vant me to go avay?"

He nodded. "You have a chance to develop God's gift. You should go."

She looked as if she was about to cry. "Fine, denn. I vill go," she spat out, before turning and running back up the stairs.

Danny watched her go, undisturbed, and turned to me. "Vhat is Julliard?"

"It's a university for musicians."

"She should go." He spotted William, already down at the cookie table, stuffing cookies into his coat pocket, and hurried to join him.

I followed Robert to the punch table and asked him why men were so oblivious to women's feelings.

"How so?" he asked, pouring a glass of punch.

"How could Danny not even realize that Elisabeth is in love with him?"

"What?!" He roared, spilling the punch down his trousers. He grabbed some napkins and started to pat his pants down. "Don't tell me I brought two teenagers in love into our home? Please tell me I didn't do that."

"I don't think Danny feels that way about Elisabeth, if that makes you feel any better."

"Somehow, it doesn't," Robert said, looking pale. "It makes me feel worse."

As we got ready for bed that night, Robert asked me if I really thought Elisabeth loved Danny. The thought was bothering him. It bothered me, too, but it was hardly a new thought for me.

"Haven't you noticed how she looks at him? Even Aunt Martha has noticed." And Aunt Martha was not a woman known for noticing.

He frowned. "But how could I have missed that?"

How indeed! "Well, anyway, first love is sweet."

Still distracted, he buttoned the top button of his pajama shirt and climbed into bed.

Say it, Louisa. It's time to tell him. "Robert, do you ever wish we had been first for each other?"

"Hmm?" he mumbled, pulling the blanket up over him.

"Do you ever wish we had met each other first? If my father had emigrated before the war, like I had wanted him to, and if we had moved to the United States. Maybe you and I would have met and loved each other first."

He gave me a patronizing look. "Louisa, I'm nine years older than you."

"Eight."

"Nearly nine," he corrected. "We met when we were meant to meet." He switched off his light.

I sighed. This wasn't easy.

He rolled over to face me. "What do you mean about loving each other first?"

"You know." I meant Ruth. And Karl.

"I know what you mean for me, but what did you mean for you?"

I took a deep breath, steeling myself. I should have told him months ago, when I first returned from Germany. "When I first attended University, I met a young man."

He propped up his head on his elbow, now giving me his full attention.

"He became an important person to me."

"Just how important?" he asked.

I looked down at my hands. "We had planned to marry."

Robert raised his eyebrows, interested. "So what happened?"

"He made a terrible decision one night, and it could never be the same between us." I told him how this man had betrayed my father. Robert listened carefully but I could tell he hadn't made the connection of Karl yet.

Lord, please help him to understand.

"Why haven't you told me this before?" was all he asked as he leaned back on his pillow.

I took a deep breath. "Because that man was Karl Schneider."

He jerked his chin up and accidentally hit the back of his head on the headboard. "Ouch!" Rubbing the back of his head, he sat up and switched the light on. It looked as if this was going to be a long night.

There were a number of reasons that I dreaded telling Robert about Karl. Mainly, Robert's first wife, Ruth, had an affair with Herr Mueller. I thought Robert would immediately assume that he would be betrayed again. I expected him to withdraw, cold and distant.

Tonight, he shocked me. He calmly questioned me about Karl. I explained how Karl had found Elisabeth. "I had no idea Karl was the one who tracked me to Copper Springs until I saw him at the shelter."

I still hadn't found out how he was able to locate me. Karl gave me vague answers whenever I asked him. That was one more thing that bothered me about Karl. His story wasn't adding up.

Robert stood up and went to gaze out the window, crossing his arms against his chest. "What does he want from you now?"

"He said he wants me to forgive him."

He turned and looked directly at me. "So that's why he hasn't left yet?"

"Yes. No. Well...you see..." This was the other reason I had avoided telling Robert about Karl. I took a deep breath. "I told Karl the only way that I could forgive him would be if he found Friedrich Mueller."

Robert groaned, covering his face with his hands. "Louisa, what do you think you will gain by catching Mueller? Do you think you will make right all the wrongs Germany committed?"

"No, of course not." But it *would* be a start.

"Mueller is long gone, Louisa. How many times do we have to go over this?"

"But what about the man in William's photographs?"

"A drifter." He sat down on the bed. "The scrounging has stopped, too. If...and I mean this very hypothetically...if Mueller were still here... things would continue to disappear. Mueller still has to eat."

"What if he knew Karl was closing in on him? Maybe he is going to Douglas or Bisbee for supplies."

Again, Robert rolled his eyes. "Louisa, Mueller is a very rich man. Why would he be hiding in Copper Springs, stealing food out of your little garden? It's preposterous. Mueller is in some remote part of the world, having a heydey with all of the other Nazis." He leaned over to switch off the light. "It's time to put an end to this, Louisa. As long as you think you can find him, you are still letting him control our lives."

He stretched out on the bed. Suddenly, he bolted up and switched the light back on. "What did you just say? What did you mean when you said Karl was closing in on him?"

Oh that. I explained that Karl thought he had found some evidence Herr Mueller had never left the area after killing Ruth, Robert's wife. He had disappeared without a trace.

Robert hung his head, as if he couldn't believe what he had just heard. I braced myself for a stern lecture about Herr Mueller. Again, I was wrong. Instead, he said, "Look at the lengths Karl has to go to, in order to earn your forgiveness. I never imagined you as a hypocrite."

My eyes grew wide.

He reminded me of the many times I had admonished him to forgive others. "Most recently," he pointed out, "my sister, Alice. You invited her to our home and practically demanded that I forgive her! But you were right, Louisa. It was wrong of me to hang on to old bitterness."

I shifted uncomfortably on the bed. I hadn't expected this line of reasoning and wasn't prepared for it. "You can't compare a runaway sister with a man who was responsible for the death of my father."

"What about Ruth, then? You told me I needed to forgive her, too."

He had me there.

"So there's a limit to forgiving someone?"

I glared at him. "That's not what I meant."

"Louisa, you told me if someone asks for your forgiveness, it would be a sin to withhold it. *You* said that."

"Yes, but—"

"Why are you always so sure about others and so blind about yourself?" Now he was starting to use his pulpit voice.

I tried to jump in to cut off his sermon, but he held up a hand to stop me from interrupting.

He listed all of Karl's sincere efforts to seek forgiveness: finding Elisabeth and tracking me down to reunite us, delivering Danny to Copper Springs.

My excuses faded. I never dreamed I'd be listening to Robert defend Karl Schneider.

"And he has *asked* you for forgiveness, Louisa. How can you refuse someone who asks for forgiveness? It isn't true forgiveness if it comes with conditions."

Maybe not, but if Karl could find Herr Mueller, it would be easier.

Chapter Fifteen

At church the next morning, everyone flocked around Elisabeth, like birds at a feeder, to tell her how well she had played at the concert. I loved seeing her shy pleasure. I even enjoyed watching Trudy Bauer bestow temporary favored status on Elisabeth, insisting they sit together for the service.

On Monday morning, Ada displaced Robert from his office. She said she needed to make emergency phone calls to the Phoenix Symphony to arrange details for Elisabeth's summer.

At lunchtime, Robert drove Ada back to Tucson to catch the train.

The boys had finished making another rocket and were eager to set it off, so I borrowed Rosita's Ford truck and took Danny and William out to the desert where Robert had taken them for launches.

"We can't stay too long," I told the boys. "I have to be back before the baby's nap is over. Aunt Martha said she would only babysit if Meg slept."

"Last time, Mom, the rocket shot up thirty feet!" explained William solemnly.

Danny corrected him. "Only four feet, Vilhelm. Scientists do not exaggerate."

Today, though, the rocket didn't go straight up but tipped over and streaked toward an abandoned cave. William volunteered to retrieve it and ran off to the cave.

Danny face was crestfallen. "I don't understand vhat I did wrong," he murmured to himself.

I looked at the launch pad. "Maybe the platform wasn't sturdy enough."

Danny frowned as he examined the pad. "Vhen vill the Reverend get home?"

"By dinnertime. He'll know what went wrong with it," I reassured.

It took William a long time to retrieve the rocket. Danny and I had already packed up the platform and climbed into the Ford to wait for him. When William finally returned, he had something tucked under his shirt. I was just about to ask him what it was when Danny distracted me by shouting, "Look!" He pointed out a motorcyclist passing by on the highway. It was Karl. "Vhere is he going?" Danny waved but Karl didn't notice. No wonder; we weren't in the Chrysler.

"I don't know," I answered. "Bisbee, I guess."

"Isn't Bisbee the other way?" William asked.

I glanced at Karl's figure, receding down the highway. On the back of the motorcycle was a crate filled with grocery bags. Where *was* he going?

William pointed to the odometer. "How far are we from town?"

"Only three or four miles," I answered, turning the truck onto the highway. "Why?"

He shrugged, but seemed preoccupied for the rest of the trip.

The Chrysler was parked in the driveway when we arrived home. I could hear baby Meg howling for dinner. I hurried inside to rescue Aunt Martha, but it was Robert walking the baby around, trying to settle her. Aunt Martha was in the kitchen, making dinner, with ear muffs on as if she lived in Alaska. Looking panicked, Robert held the baby out to me, eager to pass her off. I rushed upstairs to nurse her.

Just as I was shifting the baby to the other side, Elisabeth burst into my room. She crossed her arms and stuck her chin out. "I wish dat Reverend had never brought Danny here."

Baby Meg heard Elisabeth's voice and jerked her head to look at her, smiling.

"You don't mean that," I said.

"Ja, I do." She plopped on my bed and stroked the baby's foot with her finger.

The baby started kicking her, giggling. Dinner was over, I decided, lifting the baby up onto my shoulder. I looked over at Elisabeth as she watched the baby. "Don't you think Danny is happy here?"

She scowled. "I don't tink it matters vhere he is."

In an odd way, she was correct. Danny was completely content, serene in his circumstances. That remarkable quality was probably why he not only survived the camp, but helped others survive it, too.

But that was not what Elisabeth wanted from him.

"Elisabeth, Robert brought Danny here so he would have a family."

Her frown deepened.

"Everybody needs a family."

She stood up to leave.

"Danny does care about you. He just isn't thinking about you the way you think about him. That's the way boys often are."

She didn't want to hear that. She put one hand on the door handle. "I tink dat stupid Trudy Bauer vants him for a boyfriend. She vaits to valk home vit him every day."

"I think Danny probably has his mind on rockets and not on Trudy."

She brightened. "Really?"

I nodded. "You can count on it."

When I tucked William into bed that night, I noticed today's newspaper rolled up and stuffed in his jacket pocket. When I asked him about it, he pretended to fall asleep.

Early Saturday morning, Aunt Martha banged on our bedroom door. "William is gone!"

Robert jumped out of bed and opened the door. Aunt Martha held out a note to him. I went on a bike ride. Back by lunch. Dad, do not worry. William

In the kitchen was evidence William had made his own breakfast. Sticky jam was all over the counter, a loaf of bread was out, and Dog was settled in the corner, licking clean an empty peanut butter jar. Hearing the commotion, Danny wandered into the kitchen, rubbing sleep from his eyes. "Danny, do you have any idea where William went?" I asked.

He shook his head, yawning. "Nein."

I looked at Robert. "Should we go looking for him?"

Robert scratched his head. "Maybe we should."

We spent the morning searching the streets for any sign of William. Finally, around lunchtime, as promised, he peddled up to the house as if he had just gone around the block. Angry and upset, Robert ran outside to meet him. "Where did you go?"

William hopped off his bike. "On a bike ride." He kept his chin tucked down.

Robert stepped in front of the bicycle. He crouched down so William would have to face him. "Seven-year-olds do not just disappear on a bike ride at the crack of dawn. You gave us a scare."

William gave him a sheepish look. "But I left a note. I told you not to worry."

I opened the kitchen door as they came in. William hurried past me, avoiding my eyes. Robert held up his hands, exasperated.

William was definitely up to something.

The next afternoon, Karl found me in the library, hunting for a book on Palestine for Danny. "What do you want?" I asked, flustered. I craned my neck to see if Miss Bentley had spied him. She noticed everything.

Karl looked victorious. He reached into his pocket and pulled something out. Dramatically, he slapped the object in the palm of my hand. "I found it. I found proof!"

He explained he had discovered the ring in a pawn shop in Bisbee. Working on his assumption that Herr Mueller was nearby, Karl had the idea he might be trying to sell off assets to stay alive. Karl went into local pawn shops to ask if the shopkeepers had seen a man that fit Herr Mueller's description. And one had, quite recently.

I clenched my fist around the ring. "I need to show this to Robert."

His face became subtly guarded. "Of course," he said.

I went directly to Robert's office and entered without knocking. He smiled when he saw me, but it quickly faded as he listened to me. "Robert, Karl found proof that Herr Mueller is nearby."

Robert covered his face with his hands and groaned.

I went to him, took one of his hands and held it out, palm up. In it, I placed a gold wedding band, inscribed with the words: "To Ruth, with love, Robert." The very ring Ruth had placed on his pillow when she left him. He looked at the ring, stunned.

Afterwards, Robert and I walked over to the kitchen together, surprised to find Karl seated at the table, helping Elisabeth with her arithmetic homework.

"Elisabeth?" Robert started. "Would you mind if I spoke to Karl privately?"

"Vhy?" Elisabeth asked.

I grabbed her hand and pulled her upstairs.

"Dat Reverend doesn't look happy," Elisabeth said loudly. "Did Karl do something to make him mad?"

"No. And it's time you got started on your homework. Danny and William are in their room studying."

"No, dey are not. Dey are in da garage building da world's biggest rocket. Tante Marta is taking a nap. She has a...kopfweh." She pointed to her head.

I was starting to have a headache, too.

Elisabeth leaned over to kiss the baby, asleep in her bassinet, then left to go to her room. I closed the door behind her, trying, oh so hard, not to do what I knew I was going to do. But I couldn't help myself. I went over to the radiator pipe and unscrewed the cap.

I heard Robert pull out a chair, scraping the leg on the kitchen floor. "Karl, my wife has told me that you shared a past with her."

"Then she told you about her father? About what I did?" I heard Karl ask.

"Yes," Robert answered.

"I owe a great debt to her, as I'm sure she told you." Karl's voice cracked, as if caught by emotion. "I made a grave error, Reverend. A foolish mistake that caused her great pain. I am only trying to make amends."

In his pulpit voice, Robert said, "There are times when we have to live with the consequences of our actions. Karl, sometimes the only answer is to ask God for forgiveness."

"Perhaps, but in this situation, I hope to rectify what I have done, Reverend."

"Yes, but—"

"Have you ever wished you could have a chance to make something right?"

There was a pause. Then I heard Robert quietly answer, "Yes."

I wondered what or who Robert was thinking about right now.

"This is my chance to make things right for Louisa. Surely you can understand that."

"Not if it means a wild goose chase to find Mueller."

"Wild goose chase?" Karl sounded confused.

In that patronizing, end-of-discussion tone that I knew quite well, Robert said, "Mueller is long gone."

"But I have proof he is near!"

"Louisa showed me the ring. Chances are that Mueller tried to pawn the ring off years ago. Or even that my...Ruth...might have tried to sell it."

"That's not so, Reverend," Karl politely corrected. "The pawn shopkeeper purchased it just weeks ago." Karl's chair scraped against the kitchen floor. I heard him pace a few steps. "I am sure Mueller is near. Maybe even in Copper Springs." His voice grew with excitement, as if he was holding an excited dog on a leash. "I think—"

"That's enough!" Robert's voice had a brittle edge to it. I heard his chair scrape on the floor, too. "It's over and done with. I don't even want to think about him anymore." He pounded his fists on the tabletop, angry.

269

Then there was an eerie silence, until Karl spoke, in a tone of icy staccato I had overheard once before, when he argued with those two youths at the bus stop. "You sound just like Louisa after she killed the SS officer."

My eyes went wide with shock.

"Surely she's told you that story. It's quite a tale. It put a bounty on her head."

Robert must have been stunned. He didn't respond to Karl.

"Pardon me, Reverend. I thought your wife had told you everything about her past. Please forgive me." Karl stood up and walked to the door. "Again, my apologies." And he left, having detonated a verbal grenade in our kitchen.

I went into Elisabeth's room and told her to watch baby Meg for me for a while. She looked alarmed. "Vhat if she starts dat crying?"

"Just do what I ask!" I said sharply.

Her eyes looked hurt, but I didn't have time to worry.

I hurried down the stairs, not sure what to say or do next.

Carefully, I turned the corner into the kitchen and saw Robert leaning against the kitchen table as if he might fall over if something didn't hold him up.

Trying to sound calmer than I felt, I said, "Is there somewhere we can go to be alone?"

He stared at me as if I was a stranger.

We drove up to the Mesa, where we'd gone before to have important conversations. On the way up, Robert concentrated on his driving. I remained silent.

Please Lord, give me the right words, I silently begged.

The truth, I sensed the Lord's guidance. *Just the truth.*

After he parked, I turned to him and told him the story of how I had killed a SS officer. Robert's eyes remained fixed ahead.

"One evening, two Resistance workers were supposed to meet with someone who worked for Hitler's personal staff. Someone who was willing to give information about Hitler's daily schedule." I paused. "Do you remember that Dietrich wouldn't let me talk to anyone on an assignment?"

Robert gave a short nod, his eyes still on the windshield.

"But, that night, Dietrich asked me to accompany the two as a lookout. The meeting place was in a remote part, outside of city limits, far in the country. I had kept myself completely hidden, but I could see my two colleagues and the man they were meeting far below me, in a ravine. I was positioned so I could throw a rock down by them if there was any cause for alarm. Suddenly, a military jeep drove up. He cut the engine and coasted in the last few hundred feet. Then the guard got out of the jeep. He seemed to know exactly what, or whom, he was looking for. I was positioned behind him. There was no way I could let my colleagues know they were being watched. The guard pulled out a Schmeisser and aimed at them. I realized we had walked right into a trap."

"What's a Schmeisser?" Robert interrupted, turning his body toward mine.

A good sign, I hoped. He was still talking to me.

"It's a submachine gun. With the Schmeisser, the guard could fire as fast as his trigger finger could squeeze a round. He kneeled down at the edge of the ravine, preparing to shoot. I did the only thing I could think to do. I released the emergency brake of the jeep, and it...silently...rolled straight into the guard. He lost his balance and fell off the ledge, far below. The jeep went over, too."

Suzanne Woods Fisher

"What happened to the Resistance workers?" Robert asked, peering at me intently.

"They heard the guard scream as the jeep hit him. They watched the whole thing happen. We left as fast as we could."

Robert turned and faced forward again.

I watched the moon for a long while. Finally, I broke the silence. "Had I not released the brake, the two would have been killed. I would do it all over again."

Robert didn't say anything for a long while. Then he turned his head slightly to look at me, lifting one dark brow. "How many more surprises are there?"

"None." I glanced up at him. "Well, not exactly like that one, anyway. That guard...that man, he was the only one whom I think I killed."

"Louisa, why didn't you ever tell me about this?"

"I didn't mean to keep it from you. I just wasn't interested in remembering it. And...I thought you'd never let me drive."

Robert bowed his head. A slight smile tugged at the corners of his lips. He exhaled, as if relieved, then wrapped his arms around me and held me close.

Despite sharing this dark secret, I felt closer to Robert than I would have ever expected to feel. Karl's slip could have put a permanent wedge between us. Instead, it drew us together.

But was it a slip?

That thought sent a shot of panic through me, rising up like a flock of frightened birds. I pulled back to face Robert. "I don't know how Karl could have ever known about that night. Unless..."

Robert looked at me curiously. "What do you mean?"

"I know for a fact that there were only five people who knew about that meeting. Dietrich, the two Resistance workers, me—"

Robert's eyes widened. "What are you saying?"

"—and the man who met with them in the ravine."

"But that would mean—"

"Karl was that man. He was the one who set up the trap."

* * * *

Finally, finally! Robert was willing to discuss Herr Mueller's whereabouts. Robert quizzed me carefully about every comment Karl had made to me recently about Herr Mueller. He looked for Karl the next day, but he was nowhere to be found. Robert called over to the Copper Queen Hotel but they said Karl Schneider had checked out the night before. We drove around town, asking people if they had seen him or his motorcycle, but Karl seemed to have vanished.

Robert spoke to Judge Pryor. The judge called the International Red Cross to see if they knew where Karl was. It turned out the IRC had been looking for Karl, expecting him to have returned to Germany a month ago, after escorting Danny to us.

Armed with that information, the judge agreed to call his nephew and ask him to come to Copper Springs. His nephew said that he would take the next train to Copper Springs.

Finally, finally! People were taking me seriously about Friedrich Mueller.

As distracted as we were by the hunt to find Karl, William had another agenda. He and Danny had plans to launch their most recently built rocket that weekend. The biggest, most improved rocket to date. They named it Copper Fire. William decided to invite everyone in town to see the rocket launch. He put posters up around the town, inviting

273

people to come out to the desert at 8 o'clock Saturday night, when the moon would be at its fullest, to witness Danny's latest rocket invention.

Why at night? Everyone asked.

Because this rocket will reach the moon, William earnestly promised.

On the ride out to the desert, William was strangely quiet as Danny reviewed details for the blast-off with Robert.

I nudged William with my elbow. "Are you feeling all right?" I asked.

He nodded and turned back to look out the window. He didn't look all right. He looked preoccupied, somber, almost.

William had already scouted out a new launch site for Danny to set off the rocket—right in front of an old, abandoned copper mine. Danny objected. "Ve vill see the rocket better if it's out in the open."

William shook his head. On this point, the launch site, he was adamant.

"Danny is right, William," Robert said. "It's possible that the explosion might cause the mine to collapse."

"I've checked out the mine, Dad. It's okay." William insisted.

"*When* did you check out the mine, William?" I asked, suspicion starting to mount, but he had turned away from me to look at the site and didn't hear me. Either that or he was ignoring me. Probably the latter.

Robert turned to me. "Louisa, the rocket will only fly a few feet. I think it's okay."

Something didn't seem quite right, though.

As the boys set up the rocket, a small crowd arrived to see the rocket launch. Rosita and Ramona, along with Esmeralda and Juan, watched from the safety of their Ford truck. A little braver, Mr. Ibsen, Ernest, and the Catholic priest stood at a cautious distance, curious about the bold claims of Copper Fire. At the very last minute, the judge zoomed in with his nephew, freshly snatched from the Tucson railroad station. The two men hurried to join us.

Danny looked at the crowd and turned to William. "Ready?"

William nodded. "Go ahead, Danny. Light it."

Danny tossed a flaming gasoline-soaked rag to light the fuse that ran through the large metal pipe, packed with gun powder. Danny ran back and ducked for cover, but William hesitated. He kicked one platform leg out so the rocket was now tilted, then he hurried to join Danny, hiding behind a steel garbage can lid. "Vhy did you do that?" Danny asked.

William shook his head, eyes focused on Copper Fire.

Watching the light on the ignition fizz, everyone quieted. As the fire slid up the fuse, the rocket sputtered. "Uh oh. It is a dud," Elisabeth whispered loudly to me.

Just then, sparkles of fire dribbled out of the rocket's base. The rocket roared to life, leaping off the platform. A tail of fire lifted up into the darkness, spinning and spewing bright sparks. But its angle from the tilted platform caused it to soar sideways, arcing toward the opening of the old copper mine. The crowd watched, wide-eyed and silent.

As the rocket hit the mine, it exploded. A burst of fire illuminated the opening of the mine. Smoke from the gun powder billowed forward.

Suddenly, silhouetted against the smoke, two dark figures emerged, running, coughing, gasping for air.

For an eternity, we remained frozen, stunned, until the smoke cleared. One of the men, clearly, was Karl Schneider. The other, looking as if he had been an outlaw for quite some time and badly in need of a shower and shave, was Friedrich Mueller.

William seemed to be expecting him.

He set off in a gallop toward Herr Mueller and began to kick him. Mueller grabbed William's neck, pulling him toward him. With the other hand, Mueller pulled a knife from his pocket.

Robert gasped and took a step forward, but the judge pulled him back.

"Don't hurt him, Herr Mueller. Please!" I begged. Panicking, I turned to the judge's nephew. "He will kill him. He would kill anyone."

Herr Mueller started backing toward the cars with a tight grip around William's neck.

I practically threw baby Meg into Aunt Martha's arms. Then I started walking slowly toward Herr Mueller. In a voice so steady it could not have been my own, I said, "Herr Mueller! Nehmen sie mich. Lassen Sie meinen Sohn frei." *Take me. Let my son go.*

Karl's face lit up with undisguised delight. "Ja! Ja, Friedrich, sie koennte uns von Nutzen sein. Der Junge wird uns im Weg sein." *Yes! Yes, Friedrich, she could be useful! The boy will get in our way.*

Encouraged, I cautiously took a few more steps closer to Herr Mueller.

"Louisa, do...not... move," I heard Robert say.

Herr Mueller stared at me for a moment, with that same hungry glint in his eyes that had unnerved me from the first moment I had met him. Then, his eyes narrowed, as reason took hold. He spat at Karl. "Du Idiot! Wir haetten schon vor Wochen weggehen sollen, so wie ich es vorhatte. Aber Du wolltest sie nicht verlassen! Du musstest in dem

Klavierkonzert spielen! Sieh, was Du angerichtet hast!"You stupid fool! *We should have left weeks ago, just as I wanted. You wouldn't leave her. You had to play in that concert. Look what you've done now!* He tightened his hold on William. "Throw me your keys," he shouted to the judge.

"Take mine!" yelled Robert, throwing the keys at Mueller's feet. "It's the car closest to you."

I looked sharply at him, horrified, but his eyes were locked on Herr Mueller. Why would he *offer* his car?

Karl reached down and picked up the keys. They started to move toward the car. William's eyes were bulging by the firm grasp Mueller had around his neck. No one moved.

In the stillness, Robert whistled.

Dog, that glorious beast who received so many deserved and undeserved scoldings from Aunt Martha, heard Robert's familiar whistle, leapt out of the back window of Robert's car and lunged at Herr Mueller. William wiggled out of Herr Mueller's grasp and ran to Robert. It seemed like time stood still as Herr Mueller and Dog were locked in a wrestling match.

Then Dog dropped.

While our eyes had been on the battle, Karl had reached for the car keys and jumped into Robert's car. "Friedrich! Das Auto!" he shouted.

Herr Mueller jumped into the car as Karl veered around and peeled off.

The judge and his nephew jumped into their car to follow them.

William threw himself on Dog, sobbing. Robert pulled William off of Dog, tossing me a handkerchief as I quickly tried to create a tourniquet. Blood was pouring out of Dog's abdominal cavity.

Behind me, I heard a wail that broke my heart. It was Elisabeth. Danny turned her away from Dog and held her close to him as she wept. Robert and William crouched next to Dog's big head, softly stroking him. Dog's tail thumped a few times, like the needle on a metronome, before it went silent.

William turned and flung his arms around me, crying loudly. Slowly, Robert stood up. He reached into his pocket and pulled out Ruth's wedding ring. He squeezed his eyes shut as he tightly gripped that ring. Then he opened his eyes, lifted his arm and hurled that ring with all of his might, far out into the desert.

Chapter Sixteen

In the middle of the night came a persistent rapping on the kitchen door. Robert bolted out of bed to open the door, hopeful for news of a capture. I threw on my bathrobe and hurried behind him.

"We nailed them, Robert," the judge said, grinning ear-to-ear. "The Chrysler broke down on Mueller and Schneider near the border. We nabbed them without a fight."

"How involved was Karl?" I asked. I had to know.

"You and Louisa had better sit down for this," the judge answered.

Robert and I exchanged a look as we sat down at the kitchen table.

The judge leaned forward, chin on his elbows. "Guess what piece of information my nephew found out?"

We shrugged.

"Take a guess at the maiden name of Karl Schneider's mother."

Robert looked at me as if I should know. I had met Karl's parents a number of times, but I had no knowledge of his mother's maiden name.

Triumphantly, the judge leaned forward to enunciate the word: "Mueller."

My eyes went wide; I was too stunned to speak.

"Yes! Friedrich Mueller is her brother! Karl Schneider is Mueller's nephew!" He pounded his fist on the table as if it were a gavel.

Mind whirring, Robert leaned back in his chair. "That means that Karl is also related to Heinrich Mueller. The head of the Gestapo."

"Yes!" shouted the judge. "There's more!" He looked ecstatic. "Mueller wouldn't talk, and Karl didn't say a word, either. But as soon as we separated them, Karl started singing like a canary. He wants to cut a deal." He clapped his hands together. "Karl told us they had plans to re-connect with Heinrich after the war—win or lose—and share their booty." The judge couldn't hold back a grin. "So my nephew is pretty sure they're going to lead them to Heinrich Mueller. The Number One Wanted Nazi Criminal!" He shook his head as if he couldn't believe such good luck.

I was still speechless.

"So Karl had never lost touch with Friedrich Mueller?" Robert asked.

"Apparently, he did. For a short time after all that happened here." The judge paused, referring to when Herr Mueller had kidnapped William and me and whisked us off to his hideaway in Mexico. We had escaped, interrupting Herr Mueller's getaway plans, forcing him to flee. "But Karl said when he saw Louisa in Germany, when she came to get Elisabeth, she provided enough information that he was able to pick up his uncle's trail again. Karl located Mueller in Mexico, and they agreed to rendezvous in Copper Springs as soon as they could, because this was where Mueller had hidden his loot."

Robert looked at me, horrified. "You *gave* him information about Mueller? While you were in Germany? You *gave* him information?"

Oh no. Another sizeable topic I had neglected to tell him. I avoided his glare.

"Sit tight, Robert, there's even more!" The judge was nearly jumping out of his chair. "It was Karl Schneider who traced Louisa to Copper Springs in the first place! Years ago! He was the one who told Mueller she had information about Bonhoeffer. He was the reason the German government wanted her back, to help indict Bonhoeffer!"

"But...how?" I asked, my mouth finally catching up with my racing mind. "How could he have known where I was living?"

"Schneider had infiltrated the Resistance Movement. He worked in Hitler's office and fed information to Resistance workers." The judge paused for a moment. "He volunteered that tidbit to us! He's hoping to avoid extradition."

"Then he *was* the one who met the others in the ravine that night you killed the SS guard," Robert said quietly.

The judge's bushy eyebrows shot up. "What?"

Robert nodded and scrunched up his face. "Long story."

Before the judge could ask about it, I changed the subject. "Did Karl look for Elisabeth after the war ended? Is that why he joined the Red Cross?"

"Nope. Purely accidental. He just happened to recognize her at the children's facility. Strange coincidence."

It was no coincidence, of that I was sure. It was part of Elisabeth's miracle. Evidence that God loved her.

The judge shook his head in disbelief. "Bold move, that Mueller. Who would have ever thought to look for him right here? Under our very noses?"

"Who, indeed?" I asked, smugly, still avoiding Robert's eyes. And, I realized, the timing of Herr Mueller's return coincided neatly with Elisabeth's arrival in Copper Springs. No wonder the scrounging began when it did. And ended when it did. Herr Mueller had no reason to scrounge for food after Karl arrived. Karl provided it.

"After you left tonight, a few of us ventured into the cave and found Mueller's hideout. We started to bring out bags and bags of town treasures. It'll take a few days to get everything sorted out." The judge scratched his head. "We thought all of those things were in Germany, but they were less than a few miles from town."

Exhausted of information, the judge yawned and stood to leave. "One more thing. Louisa, Karl Schneider asked me to relay a message to you. He's staying in the jail over in Bisbee. My nephew is going to escort him and Mueller to Washington D.C. to be formally indicted in a few days. Then they'll probably be sent back to Germany." He paused, correcting himself. "Actually, Mueller is a U.S. citizen, so I'm not sure what will happen to him, other than being convicted of treason."

And murder, I thought, thinking of Ruth.

The judge's eyes darted uncomfortably to Robert, then back to me. "Anyway, Schneider asked to see you. He wants to explain. He told me to tell you, well, uh, that he will always love you."

Robert's hands slowly clenched into fists.

The judge looked down at his feet. "So I'll be heading over there tomorrow, if you're interested in going."

I looked at my husband and placed my hand on top of his. "No, thank you. Please tell Karl he has no idea what love is."

Robert squeezed my hand.

"Ask him, Robert," I whispered, as the judge reached for the kitchen doorknob. "Ask him what his nephew's job is."

"If he wanted us to know, he would tell us," Robert whispered back.

The judge overheard us and whispered, "No one knows. Not even me. Probably better that way." He winked at us and quietly closed the door.

* * * *

As tired as he was, Robert preached the finest sermon at church that next morning I have ever heard him deliver. He threw out his prepared sermon and spoke from his heart.

One moment, in particular, would forever be etched in my mind. "There is nothing God can not use for His purposes," Robert said, looking down from his pulpit at Danny and Elisabeth. "Absolutely nothing God can not use and redeem for good."

That afternoon, we held a funeral service for our beloved Dog in the backyard and buried him in my rose garden, a place he had loved to dig up on a regular basis. Robert conducted the ceremony, even wearing his ministerial robes in tribute to Dog. He cleared his throat, unable to speak. "Dog helped us become a family," Robert finally began. "He came into our life when we needed him the most. He gave his life when William needed him the most."

That got us all crying. Even Aunt Martha wiped away a tear or two.

After the service, Robert left on an errand with William and returned with two new puppies, sired by Dog, courtesy of Mitzi, Mrs. Bauer's prize poodle. "I was only going to get one but...well... they were so attached to each other, and Mrs. Bauer seemed eager to get rid of them," Robert explained, sounding surprised.

"Dey belong together," Elisabeth announced. "Dey need each other. Everybody needs a family."

I went over to Elisabeth and hugged her. If I wasn't mistaken, I felt a hint of a squeeze in return.

"I think Dog would be pleased," I said, but that only got all of us tearing up again, sorely missing that big yellow hound. It helped, though, to watch his little offspring tear around the kitchen.

"What are you going to name them?" Aunt Martha asked.

"Big Dog and Little Dog," said William, hugging the puppies.

"You can't deny they are amusing, Aunt Martha," I said, watching them pull at William's shoestrings like a robin pulls at a worm.

Rolling her eyes, Aunt Martha muttered, "And who doesn't need a little more amusement around here?"

The next day, we were quietly eating breakfast as if it were any other morning. The judge stopped in for his usual cup of coffee, but something was on his mind. He couldn't stop grinning at Aunt Martha. Finally, he asked for everyone's attention. "So, Martha, shall we spill the beans?"

"Now? At breakfast?" Aunt Martha asked.

"Why not?" he asked, eyes twinkling.

Then she blushed furiously. *Blushed!* "You tell them, Edward."

Robert exchanged a look with me. He waved to William. "William, put the puppy down and come listen to the judge."

Now everyone was still, eyes on the judge. "I've asked Martha to be my wife."

All eyes turned to Aunt Martha.

"And I said yes," she said bravely.

Robert was the first to react, as if he wasn't at all surprised. "That's wonderful news!" He hopped up to congratulate her.

She held up a hand in warning. "That means that I'm going to move to his house. I'll have to leave all of you."

"Oh Aunt Martha, it's just down the street," Robert said.

"And Louisa will have to cook."

Robert's eyebrows shot up. Elisabeth gasped. William grabbed his throat as if he was being poisoned. Even Danny looked alarmed.

I frowned.

"Perhaps the judge would enjoy moving in with us," Robert said, hopefully.

Aunt Martha looked at him as if he were daft. "Why would any man in his right mind chose to live in a household of four children with rockets blasting off through the roof? And now, two wild, undisciplined puppies?"

"I always wanted a houseful," Robert answered, putting his arm around her.

"Well, you've got it," she said tartly. Slowly, carefully, she looked around the kitchen as if seeing it for the last time. William had returned to the floor to wrestle his sock out of one puppy's mouth while the other puppy had squatted, making a puddle where the linoleum was worn away to all black near the sink. Elisabeth rested her chin on her elbows, watching Danny, moonstruck. Danny had returned to his book, unaware of Elisabeth's devoted gaze, absentmindedly pushing his glasses back up on his nose. Baby Meg bounced in her bouncing chair, happy for a brief moment. The judge leaned back in his chair, sipping coffee, looking pleased.

Then her eyes rested on me, locking for a moment. And they filled with tears.

Topics for Questions and Discussions

In what ways are Louisa and Elisabeth alike?

Is there a hero in this story?

What motivated Karl Schneider? Was it a single motivation?

Was Danny's arrival the turning point for Elisabeth's healing? Or had it begun before that?

Danny did not struggle with the anger that Elisabeth did, though they both were victims of gross injustices. What made Danny able to forgive his enemies so readily? Have you ever met a person like Danny?

Near the end of the novel, Robert admonishes Louisa to forgive Karl Schneider. "And he has *asked* you for forgiveness, Louisa. How can you refuse someone who asks for forgiveness? It isn't true forgiveness if it comes with conditions." How did you feel about Robert's comment?

Is this story about love, or loyalty? Or are they the same thing?

Discuss the final moments of the novel. In what ways have the characters changed?

Copper Fire

Acknowledgements

To Steve, Lindsey and Josh, Gary, Meredith and Tad—whom I love.

A special thank you to my invaluable, eagle-eyed first draft readers—the How girls, Deb Coty, Barbara Woods, and Linda Danis. Also, a thank you to Rita McGaughy, my German language consultant.

Grateful thanks to my editor, Dawn Carrington, for her commitment to excellence.

Copper Fire

About the Author

Suzanne Woods Fisher writes books and publishes articles from her home in the San Francisco Bay Area. She shares a busy home with her husband, four kids, and a steady stream of puppies she raises for Guide Dogs for the Blind.

Her first novel with Vintage Romance Publishing was released in 2007, has garnered three awards, and has consistently maintained the number one spot on the bestseller list.

Find her on-line at: www.suzannewoodsfisher.com

Copper Fire

Coming August 30, 2008
Vintage Spirit
www.vrpublishing.com

<u>Grit for the Oyster: 250 Pearls of Wisdom for Aspiring Writers</u>
Written by *Suzanne Woods Fisher, Debora M. Coty, Faith Tibbetts McDonald, Joanna Bloss*
Writing/Non-fiction/Inspirational

A powerful motivator for aspiring writers, *Grit for the Oyster* offers wit, wisdom, and inspiration to take that first step and persevere through the writing journey. More than a how-to, this confidence-building book is designed to draw readers to a closer relationship with God, to affirm their calling to write, and to offer pithy practical guidance from successful writers like Terri Blackstock, Martha Bolton, James Scott Bell, Liz Curtis Higgs, Dr. Gary Chapman, and David Kopp.

<u>What others are saying about *Grit for the Oyster*</u>:

"In these pages, you'll find a helpful and soul strengthening community." -David Kopp, best-selling co-author of *The Prayer of Jabez*

"This is definitely a book you want to keep within close reach as you work. It's like having your own personal writer's group and cheering squad right in your own home!" -Linda Danis, best-selling author of *365 Things Every New Mom Should Know*

"To those who feel called to write for the glory of God, *Grit for the Oyster* is like the 'Writer's Bible.'" -Ruth Carmichael Ellinger, award-winning author of *The Wild Rose of Lancaster*

CPSIA information can be obtained at www.ICGtesting.com
Printed in the USA
LVOW100224260112

265643LV00001B/4/P